D1823079

The Fool's House

The Fool's House

The *Fool's House*

Ata Burchardt

SEPTIMA

The Fool's House

Published in 2015 by FeedARead.com Publishing programmed with Arts Council funding.

Cover design: Lucia de Monto. Photography: Titus Szekelius

A CIP catalogue record for this title is available from the British Library.

To Michael,
for the surprises

The Fool's House

Let the doors be shut upon him,
that he may play the fool, but in's own house,
Farewell

Chateau de Noirlac, May 25th

The chair stood at the bottom of the lake, wrapped in algae. A coat of arms crowning its high back had become blurred by green slime. It seemed more like a throne, vacated by some illustrious nobleman. The edge of the diver's flipper scooped the soft sediment; sand swirled, exposing the chair's legs. He was about to turn away when he saw what was weighing it down. Wound around its claw feet lay a heavy chain, keeping it upright in the shifting waters. Tiny creatures, light as snowflakes, darted in and out of the curls of its armrests. The police diver circled the chair. Hunting down old furniture, thrown into the lake long ago, had not been part of his brief.

The Inspector had summoned the Englishman and his French wife to come to the lake, but the couple seemed unable or unwilling to divulge more than what was mentioned in the letter they had found. After a while the diver had discovered a body as described in the note. One man alone could not extricate it, so now they waited for reinforcements.

'While you're down there,' the Inspector had said, 'have a nose around at the bottom of the lake. You never know....'

Using his knife, the diver gently scraped the top of the chair's crest to remove a patch of algae. A sudden shaft of sunlight cut through the green water and hit the spot he had exposed - a flash of mellow gold and the light faded. He had a sudden impulse to glide his hand along the armrest, stroking it, as one might console a lonely child. His fingers hit a number of small ridges. Strands of loosened algae floated. A thin chain had been wound tight around the armrest; a rusted lock that secured it was still in place. Something was trapped under the chain; a number of thin, parallel sticks, four in total, packed close together. They were white with a break in the middle. As the last of the algae unfurled he uncovered a fifth, shorter than the others. It was neatly tucked underneath. Bones; chained fast to the armrest the diver saw the slender bones of a hand.

*

Stand dumb and do not speak to him

1

Chateau de Noirlac, one month earlier, April 24th

The bleached barn doors stood wide open. Inside hay, stacked over the winter, released a sweet dusty scent as the sun began to warm the morning air. The wings of insects in random flight flickered in a cloud of gold against the blinding light.

Romain lay among the bales of hay, humming. He spread his arms wide and pressed his feet together. His head tilted to one side. 'Little Jesus on the cross,' he whispered. In another, distant life he had come up here with his brother and the farm boys to tumble in the straw. Chickens ventured into the barn to scratch for grains and the boys chased them until they fluttered to the top of the stacked hay in terror, shrieking hysterically.

Today Romain waited. There was a delicate rustling. He froze. From a gap between two bales a set of twitching

3

whiskers appeared. Two black eyes, shiny as glass beads, assessed if it was safe to come out. A sand-coloured harvest mouse emerged, its long tail coiled around an overhanging stalk. Perfect little fingers nimbly worked themselves forward. Romain watched without blinking, eyes still like a dead man's stare.

He listened. There was no noise of children's play. His brother Alain was gone. How easy it had been to clamber up onto the hay today. Back then it had felt as though he was climbing a mountain, always the last to make it to the top. His father's horses were no longer being led across the farm yard by the stable boys; the cows had gone; their stubborn legs no longer sent the milk buckets flying with a great clatter in the early evenings; there was no clucking of the chickens, no triumphant crow of a cockerel. There was silence. Did his mother still stand by the window, arms crossed, frowning, looking down to the lake? Where was everyone?

Romain slowly closed his eyes so as not to frighten the mouse. High above the wind sucked through the rafters, soft as silk.

When he had squeezed through the gap in the wall and passed by the greenhouse, it had all looked strange. Instead of tomatoes, melons and vegetables, there were just flowers, flowers everywhere. A fence, in a criss-cross weave of willow branches, surrounded a mass of waist-high, white flowers. He felt the star-shaped heads watching him, red slit-eyes trembling on thin stalks. He had kicked down the enclosure, torn the blooms from the sap-laden stems until their perfume had made him feel quite drunk. Soon his hands were full so he had laid them down in a circle in the barn

4

entrance, gone back to pick some more, and then some more, until he was all done and none were left standing.

There was a sudden crunch of footsteps on the path to the barn.

'No… no..., oh, no,' a woman's voice cried.

He turned. 'Maman?'

A woman stood in the barn entrance, her outline shining against the light, the face in shadow like the statue of the Virgin Mary in the chapel of that place full of echoes where he had lived before coming back to his father's house. He didn't remember his mother looking like this.

'What have you done with my lilies?' the woman gasped.

'There, flowers,' Romain indicated the white blossoms lying in the dust, their heads drooping like dead swans, 'for Maman.'

'Who are you?' the woman cried. 'Get out, get out …!'

He slid to the ground to crouch with one knee in the dust, moving sideways, edging towards the open barn door.

'Maman angry? Don't go.' Tears ran down his cheeks. 'Romain good boy… Romain good boy.' He buried his face in his hands; the viscous sap from the flowers stuck on his lips.

'I'm not your mother.' The woman grabbed his arm and shook him. 'Who are you?'

They locked eyes, each expecting an explanation from the other.

'Maman, stay. Romain good boy.' Still on his knees he swung around, lurched forward and threw his arms around her legs.

'I'm not your maman. I'm Ophelia.' She freed herself from his embrace and pulled him up, suddenly horrified by the violence of her reaction. Now that he stood up he was taller than her, probably also stronger. She grabbed hold of his shoulders and braced herself.

'You are Vilmorin's son, aren't you?'
Romain gazed at her mouth which was moving very fast, but he didn't hear. Yes, she looked like his mother, he was sure. She had left him; that's why his father had sent him away. But now she had come back.

'Get out,' the woman shouted and now he heard her clearly. She let go of him abruptly and pointed to the bottom of the garden. 'You … don't… live… here… anymore.'

Still crying, Romain began to run, turning now and then to check that she was still there. 'I'll come back, ' he called to her, 'Maman ... don't go,' and he disappeared in the undergrowth by the perimeter wall.

*

.

But when they ask what it means, say this

2

Carcassonne, South West France, same day, April 24th

Léa stepped into the shadows of the timber framed houses. Their overhanging upper floors let no sunlight onto the broad pavements. She tripped over something and nearly fell. At her feet something moved. As her eyes adjusted to the gloom she saw an emaciated figure propped up against a pillar with a monkey on a chain. The dark-skinned man wore a red waistcoat with cheap gold braiding and pantaloons of turquoise satin. One of his feet was bandaged with a dirt-encrusted rag. His pillbox cap had slid to one side. He appeared to be dozing, unaware that the monkey was fixing him with an anxious stare. The animal turned and made a sudden movement towards Léa. It pulled on the short chain, jolting the man awake; he blinked up at Léa, lifting his upper lip as if to speak. She saw his tobacco-stained teeth, long like

7

those of an old donkey. The man mumbled something to the monkey about it not being time yet. The ragged creature gave Léa a furtive look, hopped onto the man's chest, nestled down with a backward glance, slung his arms around his captor's neck and both man and animal lay back as if sleeping.

Léa shivered. Her bare ankles were turning to ice. The massive paving stones beneath her feet pumped out cold air; they had not seen the sun in centuries. She turned and quickly crossed the sunny square to catch up with Sam.

'I've just seen the strangest thing, look, over there.' She turned to indicate the man in the shadows. The spot where she had seen him was empty, man and monkey had vanished.

Earlier that morning, they had set out at the foot of the rocky outcrop that dominated the lower town with its chequer-board layout left over from Roman times. Street sweepers, clearing gutters and hosing down the cobble stones over which thousands of feet had trodden the previous afternoon, swept past them, nodding a friendly greeting. Once across the bridge and through the archway of the gates, a myriad hole-in-the-wall shops shouted out their wares - plastic helmets, swords, breast plates and crude imitations of Provençal cloth in garish colours, which had nothing to do with the Roussillon traditions. In the boutiques artefacts, advertised as the creations of Occitan artists, only too clearly showed the signs of 'made in China'. But seduced by guide book images of the castellated walls of the fortress high above the town, most visitors had no time for close inspection.

The tangle of narrow alleys snaked its way up and met at the medieval square of the basilica St. Nazaire. The timber framed buildings lined three sides of the square. Their protruding upper floors, no longer level, had the heft of broad-hipped old women as they rested on rough carved pillars. In the cavernous shade pavements cafés offered inviting tables and chairs. Traders, grateful for the cool spaces, sold fresh fruit, vegetables and goats' cheese from their stalls all summer long. At this time of year the tourist buses from Toulouse did not arrive until the afternoons and few stallholders found it worthwhile to set out their produce until after lunch.

'This is how it looked when people travelled by donkey,' Sam said as he turned to take in the deserted square.

'Mass tourism,' Léa sighed. 'People are like the pigeons in the cities, they swarm, scratching around on the same patch; they leave so much rubbish behind.' She looked up at the grimacing gargoyles lurching into the void from the octagonal tower of the basilica.

'God's enforcers. I bet they did half the work for the Inquisition, scared the people into submission.'

'More like blackmail of the soul,' said Sam,' that's why the Cathars broke away from the church.'

'Look, there, a baby dinosaur. That's unusual on a church.'

'I think it's meant to be a dragon, just hatched.' Sam had to shield his eyes against the glare. In the open square the sun already had real heat in it.

'Wait. I'll do a quick sketch of it.' Léa fanned her face with her pocket book that she carried everywhere. She seldom took photographs; she drew from life, often scribbled

9

notes indicating colour and light on the impatient sketches. Her pen captured details which passed unseen in a photograph. A series of bulging note books had become a record of the peripatetic life style of their earlier years.

'Done.' She closed the pocket book. 'Tea, Sam, somewhere, anywhere. I'm parched.'

Around the square she counted four cafés which were in the process of opening. The waiters rattled the chains that held the chairs together overnight to save them from being stolen. Somehow she didn't feel like settling down in a place dressed up for the tourists. Drawn by the Cathar myths, they had invaded this part of France in recent years and obliterated most of what had been genuine.

Sam peered through the gate of a palatial hotel to their right. The ancient building seemed to have sunk its claws deep into the highest point of the rocky hill. Whoever had built here long ago wanted to rule, or they had felt very threatened. Now this fortress for the wealthy traveller simply turned its back on the onslaught of garish, overpriced souvenirs.

'Look at that garden terrace, and the pool.' Sam's hands gripped the wrought iron gate with gilded fleur-de-lys spikes. Above gold letters announced: Hôtel de Cîteaux.

'Your big nose will get stuck between those bars.'

'Leave my nose out of it.' He turned around and leaned against the gate. His face was already tanned and his black hair was tousled by the gusts of wind driving up through the narrow alleys.

'The only thing one can say with certainty', Léa's mother had commented after they had spent a weekend at her

Paris apartment, 'is that Sam is definitely not African or Chinese.' Léa had never worked out whether this was a compliment or a criticism.

'The English,' her mother had huffed with a dismissive wave of the hand before she had met Sam, 'they're not quite …'

'Not quite what, Maman?

'Not completely…. European … floating there on that little island, always pretending they're … special.'

To Léa's mother the English had to be tall, pale and blond, preferably covered in freckles, wearing big khaki shorts that flapped around bony knees and legs so white they turned blue in cold weather. The fact that an Englishman could have black hair and get a deep tan in the summer was definitely suspect. After their next visit, when Sam had sat engrossed in conversation with Léa's mother, talking about the Cold War, she'd had a sudden change of heart about him.

'Look at his hair,' she had whispered, 'not English at all. He must have some Latin blood.'

'That's alright then with you, is it?' Léa knew that some justification had to be found for the turn-around, but that was fine. Admitting to mistakes had never been one of her mother's strong points.

The Hôtel de Cîteaux stretched along the entire South side of the square. Most of its terrace could be glimpsed through the gates. It was a fairy tale setting, an island of beauty and class.

'I'm sure they do tea in there.' Léa kissed the tip of Sam's nose and leaned into him. 'We deserve a day off, you deserve a day off. You've spent enough time in that dark chapel in the last few weeks,' she said in a fake sulk, 'and with that spooky box full of bones.'

Sam glanced at his watch. 'I shouldn't be here at all. I promised to drop in at the abbey today, give the restorers a bit of moral support.'

Léa tugged at his elbow. 'You have to make room for us sometimes. It's what they call spending quality time with your wife.'

'There isn't even a word for wife in your language,' Sam teased. 'ma femme' is what the French say. That just means my woman; it says nothing about marriage.'

'Epouse means you're married.'

'Votre épouse, your spouse, that's what the Mayor calls you,' Sam mocked. 'When a man says 'mon épouse' it sounds …, I don't know, as though he is grateful that the woman actually married him.'

'And so he should be,' Léa laughed, 'and that includes you.' She looked around the square. By the afternoon the place would be heaving with sightseers.

*

Pluck them asunder

3

Chateau de Noirlac, same day

Ophelia let her arms drop. They felt heavy and useless. De Vilmorin's son had squeezed through the gap in the perimeter wall and vanished. At her feet her lilies lay wilting in the dust. Something dripped into the collar of her dress and she realised she was crying.

Everything was going wrong since that afternoon, everything was unravelling. Was this how it was going to be when you got older? Was there nothing to look forward to but memories of the past? The thought felt like a punch to the heart. Augusto, why had he done this, now? How could she not have sensed what was happening, right here in their home? She tried to remember why she had loved him. Was it because of who he was, or because of all the good she had seen in him? For some time now, although she could not say when it had started, Augusto had been distracted, vague; she had put it down to his age. On that afternoon, after she had come upon the unthinkable, she had run to the bathroom where she had broken into spasmodic, tearless sobs until her body was heaving and she vomited into the bath tub. Her knees gave way and hit the tiled floor, but she could not put a halt to the retching which produced no more than long lines of saliva after a while.

When the convulsions had ceased she lay face down on the cool floor to offer her cramped stomach some resistance. The sun was setting. After a time she had heard Augusto tapping on the door, calling her name. In the dark she had run some water into the bathtub to clear the vomit before opening the door. He was still there.

'Come out,' he had pleaded but she would not, fearing another bout of heaving. She had sat down on the floor with her back against the wall, turning her head away from Augusto who perched on the edge of the bath, talking softly, but to her his words sounded like a father's admonishments to a child who had committed some irreparable deed, as if it was all her fault, not his. She could find no contrition in what he said; after a while she had stopped listening. At some point he must have left, because she had woken up in daylight, with sore bones from sleeping on the hard floor.

What was she meant to do now? Wipe away the past, wipe away the future? But whose past and whose future – his or hers? Her watch said five o'clock. She had opened the bathroom door a crack, in case Augusto had decided to bed down in front of it. There wasn't a sound in the house. With knees stiff and aching she had made her way downstairs, crossed the hall and used the backdoor behind the stairs to step out into the gardens.

Without intending to she found herself taking the path under the mimosas to the lake. At this end it gently lunged out, lapping on flat deposits of mud and rough sand. Reeds had multiplied and grown in great clumps; the roots threatened to suffocate the birch and willow trees growing bordering the lake. Their branches hung, brown and limp like lifeless hair. In olden days farmers would have made brooms from these flexible bundles. But what good were they now, Ophelia wondered. The gardener, who came only intermittently, would no doubt burn them. Thin branches had fallen into the lake and lay in a heap by the water's edge, swept there by the spring winds that raced over the lake. Ophelia picked up a flat stone stuck in the sand and threw it into the water. Hypnotic rippling circles began to spread. Something in her prayed for them not to ebb away, but they soon did.

She parted the reeds, searching for more stones but there were none; all she could see in front of her was her hand, moving to and fro, and her wedding ring, both looking as if they belonged to someone else. Her damp fingers began pulling at the ring, prising if off with difficulty. It lay in her palm for a moment, then she hurled it high and hard out over the lake. It hung in the air; she watched it flicker and oscillate against the sun before it plunged into the black water. The circles began, they grew and grew and time stretched. It was the rippling circles she had needed to tell her that everything died, eventually.

That I will speak to thee

4

Hôtel de Cîteaux, same day

'Come on. Let's have tea in here.' Léa took Sam by the arm and coaxed him into the hotel.

They walked straight past the hotel clerk who greeted them like familiar guests and headed straight out onto the terrace garden. No matter how exclusive a hotel, just walk in fast and look confident, like you belong, that was their motto. They had never been challenged.

In the dash through the grand lobby they caught a glimpse of a few steps leading to a mezzanine with a library filled with bound volumes. The idea of rare books was always irresistible. In the last few years they had travelled less and had accumulated not so much furniture as books and more books.

'We'll take a look in there later, let's sit outside.' Sam made for the door to the terrace.

They stepped out onto a meticulously manicured lawn. Clusters of crocus and hyacinths glowed like jewels in the crisp spring light. By the gravel path stood groups of white cast-iron tables and chairs, dainty as if made of starched lace. Just beyond the layered shrubs the light danced on the water of a swimming pool.

They were alone on the semi-circular terrace. Sam pulled one of the tables close to the waist-high rampart wall and they sat down. The waiter was already on his way, dressed in black trousers, white shirt and black bow tie. His long apron flapped in the breeze as he strode across the fresh grass. His jet black hair was plastered down and shiny, as if he had just stepped out of the bullring.

'Would you also like the newspapers, Monsieur? We have all the international papers in our library,' he announced with pride.

'Any Times will be fine,' said Sam, 'Sunday Times, New York Times, thank you.'

They sipped the tea from gold rimmed porcelain cups. The scent of warm soil rose up on the breeze. A steep bank, smothered in daffodils, fell away from the foot of the ramparts. Two large crows with mean-looking beaks strutted towards them along the wall. Sam got up and tried to approach to them.

'They'll have your finger. They don't mind what they eat,' Léa warned, 'as long as it's flesh, alive or dead.'

Sam leaned over the edge to look into the moat below which had long been reclaimed by grass. 'Charlemagne besieged this city for three years before he gave up, probably right here.'

He stretched to inspect the massive stonework of the fortifications which plunged down into the moat.

'Don't lean over so far, Sam. What if a stone is loose? I'm not climbing down to get you. But,' she mumbled under her breath, 'I would if I had to,' and she was certain that he knew she would.

He relented and sat on the wall.

'The crows must have queued up in their hundreds during the siege. Lots of dead bodies in the water,' he smacked his lips, 'delicately frazzled to a crisp in hot oil first.'

'Don't be so ghoulish,' Léa grimaced and gathered up her things. Water and drowning were inseparable in her mind. She could swim well, as long as she knew she could touch bottom. Her fear of the deep was irrational. In an unknown depth something in her body began to panic. The pull of gravity seemed to increase in deep water and she knew that she would succumb to it. Recurring dreams of her younger sister drowning woke her in a sweat and she would lie in the dark, reliving the dream in which her hands groped blindly for her sister's body which could not be seen in the muddied waters. She had spoken to no one about these dreams, but had become convinced that her sister would drown, one day.

In a bid to rid herself of the thought, she had written the dream on a piece of paper, sealed it in a tiny cardboard box and thrown it into the wild stream that toiled in the deep gorge surrounding their village. She had leaned over the stone bridge that linked Sainte Colombe with the road

18

leading up onto the garrigue and the abbey beyond. She watched the box being tossed from one side to the other. It skated over boulders, pirouetted, was swallowed by whirlpools, spat out again and finally went under when it was sodden. She had stood on the bridge for a long while, trying to etch the idea into her brain that it was the dream that had drowned, that she had made this gesture as an offering to save her sister.

Sam felt the temperature of the pool before deciding to take a look at the library. As they re-entered the hotel Léa removed her sunglasses. She stood for a moment, trying to accustom her eyes to the interior which lay in gothic darkness.

'Anyway,' said Sam. 'It's time for an aperitif.'

'Who said I'd never make a Frenchman out of you?' Léa took his hand as they climbed the steps from the lobby, pushed open the doors clad with polished brass-plates and cut-glass panels to a baronial room with bookshelves reaching up to the ceiling. To their right a barman was polishing glasses behind a gleaming bar. Gilded coffee tables surrounded by red leather armchairs were grouped on a carpet ornamented with heraldic designs. Sam scanned the book spines. They ordered Muscat and sat under the stained glass windows which filtered the light in translucent, jewel-like colours.

'Why are all these books in English?' asked Sam as the barman set down the glasses and poured their drinks.

'A gift from a British Consul, a long time ago. But if you want to know more …,' he nodded discreetly in the direction of someone who had entered behind them, 'our manager,

Monsieur Guérin, will be pleased to tell you all about it,' he whispered, 'it's his absolute favourite subject.'

A greying man in his fifties in an expensive suit with a crested tie and a silk Hermès handkerchief in his breast pocket stood by their table and gave a slight bow.

'People don't often ask about the books here,' he said with a woeful smile and a confident, transatlantic accent, 'they're always so busy . . . touristing - if that is a word.' He shrugged and made an elegant but dismissive gesture with his hand. Gold cufflinks flashed in the mellow light.

'I'm Henri Guérin,' he introduced himself and held out a hand in greeting.

Sam shook Guérin's hand. 'Sam. Sam Carter and my wife Léa.'

'Enchanté. I'll show you our books, if you like.' He clasped his hands behind his back and led Sam and Léa along the shelves. He was visibly proud of his establishment in an old fashioned way and volunteered information in the smooth and diplomatic tone more suited to guiding Royals rather than two people who had just walked off the street. 'And down there, on the bottom shelf, the tall ones, they are the hotel records for over a century.'

'May I look?' Léa reached down to pick up one of the over-sized registers.

'Let me.' He helped her lift it.

She laid it on a table and began turning its brittle yellowed pages. Spidery handwriting with nib and ink of successive hotel clerks detailed arrivals of illustrious guests, alongside the simply fabulously wealthy of the day.

'We've had some strange and wonderful guests over the years. There,' Guérin turned to a page, 'Charlie Chaplin and all these people,' he ran his finger down the list, 'even his chambermaid, they all travelled with him.'

Henri Guérin glanced at his heavy gold Rolex watch which had been concealed under the cuff of his jacket. 'I am supposed to …' he checked his watch again, 'or rather I was supposed to have lunch with a former guest, an Argentinean professor, a scientist, retired now. He stayed here for many months with his English wife and two children.' He paused. 'In fact, the younger child, a daughter, was almost born in this hotel. His wife was so very, very … young,' he added with a melancholy smile.

From his tone Léa sensed that the young woman must have been sensationally beautiful or unusually young. Perhaps she had been both if he remembered her with such feeling.

'Shortly after that,' Henri Guérin continued, 'Augusto … the professor, bought the chateau of his dreams from a bankrupt aristocrat in Noirlac, not far from here. But that was more than twenty years ago. I went on to work in hotels in Australia, the Bahamas and the States. Then I came back to manage this hotel and after all these years we bumped into each other on this very spot, quite recently. The books brought us together again.'

Guérin looked at his watch. 'I was expecting him, about an hour ago,' he smiled, 'if he comes, you can meet him. Time keeping has never been his forte.' He glanced out of the window. 'Oh. It looks like you're in luck. I think he's just arrived.'

*

Sit still my soul

5

Chateau de Noirlac, same day

Ophelia made her way back to the house. Something had left her, she wasn't sure what. A sense of detachment flooded every part of her being. From one day to the next her life had become a grotesque dance. Would her foot land on solid ground or would it fall away each time she took a step? As a child, when her father had been posted to the British Embassy in Vienna, they had gone to the picturesque Prater funfair, but all she could remember of it was the cakewalk; it was the feel of the ground tossing under her feet that now came back to her. I am a diplomat's daughter, Ophelia reminded herself.

She had grown up in half a dozen countries, learnt to deal with change, no matter how difficult. Augusto seemed to have forgotten it. She could tell no one about what had happened. Who would believe her? It seemed unreal, even to her. She looked down at herself, ran her hand through her hair to smooth it down. The fine dust from the barn itched between her fingers. Particles of hay clung to her dress and caught the light like tiny sequins. She straightened her back, took a deep breath and made her way back to the house.

Zoffia was nowhere to be seen. Augusto would be leaving for Paris. She wasn't going to tell him about the prowler or about what she planned to do, not now. He did not deserve it.

*

Then saw you not his face

6

Hôtel de Cîteaux, afternoon, same day

'I hope you've not waited long,' boomed a voice behind them as the double doors of the library were flung open. They turned. A tall man strode across the lush carpet. Despite the spring sunshine he wore a flowing Loden cape, fastened at the neck with a monogrammed clasp. His arms emerged in a dramatic greeting, parting the cape like a curtain for the opening of a play. He made a bee-line for Sam and Léa. The old man seized Léa's hand and enclosed it in both his own. She felt the cold of his bones. He did not shake her hand, but patted it and there was a caress in the gesture, as if to feel what she was made of. Strands of silver hair strayed from under a burgundy Fedora. His turquoise, watery eyes contrasted with his skin, still olive despite the pallor brought on by age. He let go of Léa's hand abruptly, as if his investigation of her no longer required it.

'Are these your children?' he teased the hotel manager.

'Good Lord, no,' said Henri Guérin, 'they were admiring our library.'

'So, you love books, eh?'

Sam nodded. It sounded like a rhetorical question.

'Most commendable! Are you staying here?'

'We've lived in Sainte Colombe for nearly fifteen years, not far from here,' Léa said.

'Ah, I know it, I know it,' he nodded, 'Sainte Colombe, very old, very beautiful, but such a troubled history. I lived in this delightful establishment,' the old man whispered as if in a confession booth as he leaned towards Léa. His eyes darted from her face to her red hair. He switched from perfect French to a clipped, almost perfect English with a soft Spanish intonation on just the odd word here and there.

'Such a long time ago. There were only the books and myself in here. And silence. There is treasure in this library . . . almost as good as mine.' 'I'm sorry, this is . . . .'

'Sam and Léa Carter. Professor Augusto Perez de Montsarrat.' Sam and Léa are book fiends, like you.'

'Splendid,' the old man declared. 'Then we must get together, no? When I get back from Paris....' He turned to Guérin. 'I shall be going soon, if not sooner. Yes,' he said triumphantly, 'I have some business with a Paris auctioneer. Who knows, perhaps I'll even bring something back.'

'Nothing heavy I hope, Augusto,' Guérin smiled, 'the airlines charge so much for excess baggage these days.'

The old man ripped off his Fedora and brandished it. 'I thought I'd go by car, stop off at a few old haunts.'

'But it's such a long drive, my friend.' Henri Guérin looked puzzled. 'I hope you'll let your wife do some of the driving.'

'Ophelia?' Augusto's eyes shifted and his brows pulled together in a sulk. He shook his head. 'She won't,' he said with a distracted air. He seemed to be talking about someone he'd met a long time ago, in a restaurant perhaps, or someone who had made little impression on him at a dinner party. He half turned away and faced the windows. The folds of his cape caught the rainbow hues of the light streaming through the stained glass. There was a sudden gap in the conversation. A fine clock chimed somewhere in the room. Someone say something, Léa prayed. Sam looked across to Guérin who raised an eyebrow. Augusto swung round and clapped his hands, turning to Sam. He bared his teeth; his mouth was smiling but his eyes were not.

'Have you a telephone number?' he asked. 'I shall invite you to Noirlac, my chateau.'

There was a hint of a plea in Guérin's eyes, a silent 'indulge my old friend'. Sam obliged with his card. Léa took a few steps back to draw herself out of the conversation. On Guérin's sign the barman filled up their glasses. Léa picked hers up and moved towards the gothic bay windows which curved out onto the high terrace with a panorama which seemed lifted from a painting by Poussin. To the left lay Mount Alaric, once the seat of the last Visigoth King. It rose sharp and black. Beyond it loomed the smoky blue shades of the Pyrenees with the rugged peaks of Spain. To the right the landscape fell away in the soft lines of endless vineyards, rolling down to the Mediterranean.

The old man's icy touch lingered on Léa's hand and she tucked it into the pocket of her jacket, as if to put it out of his reach. Behind her she could hear Augusto and Henri Guérin laugh at some joke, probably one of Sam's.

She scanned the land under the blue expanse. There was a barely visible movement in the sky high above where the air was so pure it vibrated in a violet hue. A pair of eagles, down from the high Pyrenees, were gliding in slow, overlapping circles. Their silhouettes, short-tailed with wings the shape of a straight plank, were unmistakable. How they could spot prey from that height was a mystery to Léa. She had seen an eagle pick a rabbit in a perilous dive from the rock face of the gorge in their village. Gisèle, her old friend in Sainte Colombe, had seen eagles carry away new-born boars.

'Léa.' Sam's voice sounded far away. She glanced across to the three men, silhouetted against the library windows. What had the old man wanted from her when he had held onto her hand that way?

'I think we'd better go,' Sam called as he turned to Henri Guérin.

Léa made her way back. She would have to shake hands again with the old man.

'Thank you. We'll come again,' she smiled at Guérin, as she quickly withdrew her hand from Augusto's, 'when we have more time.'

They crossed the flag-stoned lobby and returned to the square and the afternoon tourist throng.

'Do you think he has a hunchback servant called Igor?'

Sam shook his head. 'More of a touch of the Phantom of the Opera; judging by the looks he gave you he's more likely to have a nubile young virgin tucked away in the attic.'

'God, we have a nasty imagination.'

'Maybe. Don't look now. See the car on your left?' Sam pretended to look in the opposite direction.

Among the tourists following a guide manically waving her orange umbrella, Léa saw a black car parked by the hotel entrance. In the rear sat a woman in her thirties. A mass of flame-red hair framed a pale face. She was nibbling at her fingernails, waiting.

'Oh, Sam. That's probably his daughter.'

'Wrong age; and why would she be sitting out here?' He turned and began winding his way past the row of tourists pointing their cameras at the spires of St. Nazaire basilica. 'But what I saw of her, she could be your sister.'

*

Show me the steep and thorny way to heaven

7

Chateau de Noirlac, night

That night Augusto's dream was of a tumbling descent from a barren mountain strewn with furniture, objects he recognised, collected during his lifetime for reasons he could no longer fathom. He looked down and saw his silk slippers side-stepping a bulbous yellow toad that eyed him coldly. To his right his young son Pablo was skipping to and fro between piles of books, swaying as they grew higher and higher, so that the boy had to make ever increasing leaps.

They reached the foot of the mountain and Augusto felt Ophelia's hand in his. Together they were entering a huge barn filled with an overpowering, sickly odour. As his eyes adjusted to the deep shadows he saw bundled lilies, their heads the size of sunflowers, lying on their sides, stacked tight as straw bales. Ophelia led him to the wall of gaping white blooms and he saw that each star-shaped head oozed a large solitary drop of dark blood.

*

And vanish from our sight

8

Chateau de Noirlac, next morning, April 25th

Ophelia made for the hall table. The cool of the night lay trapped in the house. It prickled on her bare arms. Her espadrilles made no sound on the marble floor. There was so much to do. Augusto had underestimated her, but the thought gave her no satisfaction. He would be in Paris for the next few days, enough time to carry out her plan. She glanced at the to-do list which she had kept in her dress pocket. Her silver-grey cat sidled up to her, his purr amplified in the morning quiet of the hall. He rubbed his silken flank against her leg. She picked up the telephone and dialled, listening for it to ring at the other end.

'Si,' a woman's voice answered.

'Ariana, dear child….yes, I'm fine, sort of. How are the children?...We have just had a prowler…in the barn… no, only the flowers….no, no, I'm fine, really. I chased him

31

away… no, of course he wasn't dangerous; it was just a boy… Your father? He's going to Paris for a few days. Yes, Paris... no … on his own.'

At the other end of the line Ophelia heard voices in the background. Her daughter shushed the children.

'Maman, the twins are hoping around like excited fleas. We're just off to the zoo and the car is waiting; you know what the traffic is like in Madrid at this time of the morning. I'll call you back later.'

'No… no … don't do that. I'm going to be out and … about a lot … for a few days anyway. I'll call you when I've got things sorted. What? ….When the cat's away? Yes, I suppose you could say that. I'll call you … as soon as I can. Yes, I promise. It might be a while, that's all. Give my love to the kids.'

Ophelia hung up. Her only daughter, she could not burden her with what was happening here. She could hear Zoffia in the kitchen; now was not the time to come face to face with her maid. She could not take a crumb of breakfast. Her stomach felt hard; it pulled on her diaphragm. It's the fear, she thought, the pure fear of what I'm about to do, but do it I will. She went to the rosewood chest of drawers that stood at the far end of the hall, pulled out the Toulouse telephone directory, sat down on the chair nearby and began her search.

The house was still. Augusto descended the stairs, softly, trying to dampen the click of heels on the marble steps. From the kitchen came the clink of cups on saucers. Zoffia was preparing breakfast. He set down his travel case. The kitchen door stood slightly ajar and he could see her move back and forth. She was wearing her white Indian dress with the flowers at the hem. Her bare feet sounded like small fish slapping on the stone floor and her red hair, not yet brushed, cast a copper glow over her pale neck and shoulders.

Augusto stuck his head through the half-open door.

'No time for breakfast,' he smiled, 'I'm off to Paris, 'here,' he held out a piece of paper, 'just in case.'

A smile flew across Zoffia's lips as she took the note and tucked it into her sleeve. She opened her mouth, then closed it and the smile died as she glanced over his shoulder. Augusto turned, his eyes narrowed. Ophelia was standing in the hall, gazing at his luggage. Augusto and Zoffia froze. Ophelia's eyes seemed absent, unfocused, as if she was deciphering something in the far distance. She took one step towards them, changed direction and began to climb the stairs. Against the light streaming in through the high window on the half landing her figure began to radiate and melt. The brightness swallowed her as if she had never existed.

*

To let you know of it

9

Sainte Colombe village, same day

The invitation to the chateau came in the curt, clipped manner of an English aristocrat and he rang off.

'That was Augusto. You know, chateau man.'

'An Argentinean professor, educated at Eton, ends up in a chateau, in the middle of nowhere. It sounds like an Agatha Christie story.' Léa didn't look up from her desk. She flicked through the pages of the manuscript she was translating.

'He wants to sell some of his books. He sounded strange, as if he was phoning standing on top of a mountain in a high wind.

'Maybe he has to stand on the roof to get a signal,' Léa laughed. 'I'm out of my depth here. How did the monks make their colours for illuminated manuscripts in the 13th or 14th century? We must have a book about that somewhere.'

Sam shrugged. 'Not that I know of.'

34

'I'm tired. That's enough for today. I'll to have to find a medieval archive to solve this one. Either Toulouse or Auch.' A few clicks and the files vanished from the screen. She switched off her laptop and piled her proofs to one side of the desk. She would put some order into them later.

Sam sat down at the dining table. He heaved a sigh. His hand hovered over the photographs spread out in front of him. He had spent hours hunched over the many sections of a larger image. He began moving the sections around as if to solve a puzzle.

Although both he and Léa had their own work rooms, they tended to drift into the living room, Léa working at the dainty writing desk, which once must have belonged to a girl in a long gone century, Sam spreading his research papers and photographs on the heavy oak table which could seat eight people for dinner. When they had bought the house the removal of some flimsy partitions and the pulling down of an impossibly low false ceiling had turned three rooms into one large living space with a beamed, church-like ceiling.

Léa went over to Sam and looked over his shoulder. Although he now had a some idea of what the whole picture should be, there were still some crucial fragments missing. Something just didn't seem to come together.

The cleaning of the chapel walls at the Cistercian Abbaye de Morterive, lying in the shadow of garrigue plateau above the village of Sainte Colombe, had taken longer than expected. The restorers had to be kept on for a further four weeks at great expense to the project. As the men worked Sam had recorded the emerging lines of an ancient fresco which had been daubed with layers of chalk, over and over again for centuries. Jérôme, a specialist of medieval frescos, had been called in by the Historic Monuments Trust. His painstaking work had brought results.

'If they over-painted this wall so many times they really, really didn't want this figure to be seen.' Jérôme tugged at his dark moustache, humming to himself. Sam knew that when Jérôme did this he was thinking hard and did not want to be interrupted. 'It must have been painted with a dye which kept coming through the chalk time and time again,' Jérôme said after a long while. He had sent a colour sample to the Paris laboratories, but the results had not come in yet. His best guess so far had been that the image had been painted in blood, probably mixed with some other substance to enable it to overpower any paint applied to it subsequently. Salt, vinegar or sometimes even urine were used to fix colours.

Sam's puzzle now occupied half the dining table and was taking shape.

'That crate full of bones we found under the slab in the chapterhouse,' he said, 'it's got everyone spooked.'

'Have they worked out whose bones they might be?'

'By the number of leg bones in the box there were two individuals. The skeletons were taken apart, bone by bone, and sorted by shape and size. There wasn't a millimetre to spare in that box. The ribs were packed like those expensive sets of cutlery in a velvet- lined case.'

Léa shuddered. 'Sam. Show some respect for the dead.'

'You're wrong,' Sam said. 'They'd built the box specially and the sorting shows respect.'

'Sure. We're going to kill you but we promise that we'll make you look really tidy?'

'We don't know if they were killed or whether they just died. Not yet, anyway.'

'Perhaps they just tried to make it as small as possible. The smaller the box, the smaller the sin and the easier it is to hide it.'

'You've got a point, a very female point though. With you the emotions always come first.'

'There's nothing wrong with thinking like a woman, especially if you are one.'

Over the years Léa had become used to having her opinions tested. Even if their conversations became heated at times, they knew that honesty to each other was something they both valued. 'Murder, spontaneous or premeditated, is usually driven by emotions. Look at the Inquisition; it was driven by emotions and passions, they were just the wrong kind. What does Philippe's uncle say?'

Philippe, the current owner of Morterive had called in his uncle, a surgeon at the Cité hospital.

'Without disturbing the contents of the crate, he couldn't really say much. One set of bones is from an adult male. The other set is quite delicate; the bones of one hand was missing. It could be a young woman, or a boy.'

'A monk and his young mistress? Or perhaps she was a he?'

'Hum.' Sam was steering a picture section around the table with his index finger, trying to place it. Under cover of dark, the crate of bones had been freighted to the Paris laboratories in great secrecy. Rumours of the discovery would circulate like wildfire among the villagers. Digging up human remains in this once godly place would have been perceived as sacrilege. The village priest would feast on the opportunity to preach against such a sin in his Sunday sermon. He was a bachelor with a barrel-sized paunch who lived with his demented mother. His clothes were permanently strewn with cigarette ash; his beret was as shiny as a rasher of bacon from years of wear. And yet, the villagers of Sainte Colombe were bullied by him in all manner of ways and called upon to render services free of charge, including frequent delicacies from the grocer, butcher and baker. If one of them defaulted on these expected gifts at Christmas or Easter, the guilty would be sure to be exposed in some thinly veiled reference, in a sermon on avarice or greed by Monsieur le Curé, again and again, until they complied. No one wanted to risk eternal damnation for a kilo of Toulouse sausages, a jar of fatty cassoulet or a box of the finest patisseries.

'Imagine if guests at the abbey got wind of this?' Léa laughed, 'especially those Americans in search of a spiritual retreat, the mind and body brigade. If they hear this story they'll run all the way back home crying 'murder!'

'It would bring them back to earth with a thump,' Sam grinned. 'But I can't stop thinking about how these two people died. There were no injuries to the bones, as far as we could see. Burying them together was intentional. It means something, but what?'

'Don't most secret lovers dream of being buried together?'

'That only happens in fairy stories,' Sam mocked.

'What about us?' Léa felt something melt inside her. 'I'd like that. Just to know you're there.'

'Hum,' Sam mumbled, 'how romantic.' He got up, took one step and grabbed Léa from behind. 'They'll find two skeletons holding onto each other like this.'

She giggled. 'If they find us like this they'll get ideas, dirty ones.' She struggled around to face him. 'Like this.' They held each other, laughing, but the laughter subsided. Neither of them had ever really thought about death and where they would be buried in the end.

'I want to be with you until I die.' The idea had never occurred to her; the words had simply slipped out.

'Me too,' said Sam. He pulled her head to rest on his chest and they stood in silence for a moment.

'Can you tell whether they were poisoned or drowned, after all this time?

'Drowned no, but there might still be traces of poison in the bones.' Until the bones had been dated, preferably to some far distant century, it was better to keep the whole business under wraps.

Sam knew more than most about the Cistercian order. Although this particular abbey had been sparsely populated in the twelfth and thirteenth century, Morterive had played an unusually large part in the Inquisition in the region. Again and again Sam found that to this day the persecution and slaughter of the Cathars was ever present in the collective memory of the population in the surrounding villages. Rumours that Cistercians abducted young boys and girls for their debaucheries had survived through the centuries.

'Monks brought prostitutes and drink into the monasteries. Abbots even had their personal concubines.'

'You see, even God's power corrupts.'

'They weren't real abbots a lot of the time. They were rich kids. A father could buy a wayward son a job for life. It went on for centuries, right up to the Revolution. At the time it was rumoured that an archbishop could fornicate with a wife of his choosing, but have the luxury to remain unmarried. '

'I suppose the dark nooks and crannies of that chapterhouse were a perfect for all that.'

The first time Sam had walked into the abbey's chapterhouse he had felt it; a stifling gloom from centuries ago almost barred his way into the space with its glowering arches. Three narrow windows shed no more than the penumbra of a perpetual dawn onto the patchy stone floor. Attached to the chapterhouse lay the gloomy chapel where murderous intrigues had been hatched, much to the advantage of the Morterive abbey. Philippe de Sauterre had shown Sam around. 'After the Inquisition,' he had told Sam, 'the monks suddenly owned a great deal of the surrounding land which had once belonged to so-called heretic landowners who were hunted down and tortured to death.'

Sam did not envy Philippe for having inherited the abbey with a duty for life to maintain the fabric of the ancient buildings.

He could feel the warmth of Léa's cheek still resting against his chest.

'Perhaps the French Revolution put a just end to all that then.'

'It got rid of the corrupt clergy,' Sam agreed. 'But look at what happened to the Abbey of Villeneuve-les-Avignon.

Remember the first time we visited? The chickens still lived on the tomb of Pope Innocent, droppings everywhere'

Sam had found a box full of photographs from the 1920s in an Avignon flea market. They showed gypsies squatting in the cloisters of many abandoned monasteries and abbeys in the South of France. The Revolution had driven the religious orders out and had put them into the hands of local farmers. Abbeys were smashed to pieces and left to be trampled by farm animals. The photographs showed them roaming freely among altars and toppled statues of saints. Cow dung covered ancient flagstones of churches and chapels, pigs trotted in and out of tombs. The Converts dining halls became the home of farm machinery.

Sam had spent the best part of a month sitting by the side of Jérôme. For weeks the restorer lay on his side on a mattress, stripping away the thin layers of paint and chalk. The only sound piercing the calm of the abbey was the mosquito-like whine of his drill. Now and then Sam interrupted Jérôme to photograph a newly exposed portion.

The first indication of what lay underneath the old layers of chalk had been the appearance of a large, well-drawn eye, looking sideways out at the spectator. Half a face slowly emerged. The other half was missing.

'Acid, probably,' mumbled Jérôme, 'someone tried to etch away the image, but the acid wasn't strong enough.'

A hunched shoulder and the left side of a torso were clearly visible now. The rest resembled a somewhat larger than life-size male figure with a deformed left leg. The top of the hip, as well as the foot, were missing. The dark-skinned figure did not seem to be wearing any clothing.

Jérôme's task was to strip away the layers and expose long lost features of ancient buildings. Sam's job was to make sense of it all, catalogue it, describe it and interpret it for publication. When he had not been on site, he'd spent hours scouring the medieval archive in Toulouse and Auch for similar images. Grotesque figures were frequent in religious documents, but he had never seen anything as well-drawn or as vibrant as this. Had a monk copied a figure from a manuscript; perhaps he had incorporated the figure from the wall into a manuscript? The leg, in a darker hue than the body was what puzzled Sam most.

Sam returned to the table. 'Look at the size of the ankle. It's weird.' He showed Léa a section containing an irregular, wedge-shaped, almost black rectangle. 'We found it at ground level. And what about this?' Sam indicated a long, thick brown line with a few strands of tangled hair at the end. 'I've only got two sections of it.'

'Perhaps there was a dog or a monkey next to the figure?' Léa speculated. Poorly drawn frolicking monkeys made frequent appearances in the margins of illuminated manuscripts that she had seen. They were often half hidden among the dense foliage for the entertainment of the illuminator, whether it was a psalter or the Nativity story. Monkeys cheekily perched on a Saint's shoulder, or pinched a dog's tail whilst hanging upside down from the vines that framed the hand-scripted texts. Sometimes they had the faces of the abbots whom the monks sought to ridicule in secret.

'The tail is too thick for a monkey,' Sam said, 'it could be a donkey or a large hound walking by his side.' In frustration he pushed these two fragments, together with the wedge-shaped rectangle to one side as he couldn't place them. Léa reached over his shoulder and picked them up.

'Don't mix up my photos,' Sam pleaded.

'Look.' Léa laid a sheet of tracing paper over the lower part of the figure. She placed the tail sections behind the figure at hip height. 'And this one goes here, at the bottom.' She positioned the wedge-shaped rectangle at the end of the leg. With a thick felt pen she drew lines, linking the tail to the body and the wedge to the ankle. 'It's a hoof, Sam, a cloven hoof.' They both stared at the image in silence for a moment, checking whether what they saw was possible.

'Trust you,' Sam grumbled.

'It's the devil,' they said almost simultaneously.

'Well, a devil in any case. It makes sense now,' said Sam. The penetrating, hypnotic gaze of the face, the narrow pointed ear, the corner of the mouth with a knowing, twisted smile, it all fell into place. This was no impish monk, no saint with a wicked sense of humour.

'This monastery was a dark place, riddled with secrets; all that guilt and the fear of sexual temptation,' Sam sighed. 'Everything was a sin; so many evil deeds, most of them in the name of God. I think my work is just beginning.' His hand skipped over the photos. 'Just look at that eye.'

Léa bent over the image. 'It's so intense and so alive still.' She suddenly shivered. 'It reminds me of the old man, the way he looked at me at the hotel.'

'Hum,' Sam nodded. 'Have we become more civilised and less evil since the Dark Ages?

'I doubt it.' Léa hugged herself. 'So, what you expected to be some obscure saint turns out to be Satan.'

Sam leaned back on his chair. Through the open window he watched the first lizards of the year cling to the church wall on the other side of the street. They darted from stone to stone, disappearing in a crack, reappearing with some struggling insect in their jaws. When the last wriggling leg had been swallowed they rested on the stones warmed by the sun. Sam rubbed his chin. It felt like sandpaper and he realised he'd been so preoccupied by his work that he'd forgotten to shave.

'The old man, if he has been in Noirlac for twenty years or so he must be in his seventies. I've yet to see anyone make of good job of an old chateau around here,' he mocked.

'You're such a cynic. Ramshackle grandeur is all the rage.'

'Even if the rooms around you are falling down?'

'Why not, as long as some of them are habitable,' Léa reasoned. 'Just think, we'd get up every morning, throw open huge windows, walk down a grand staircase.'

'No,' Sam said after a while, 'Augusto with his fancy name is probably like all the others. They buy a grand country pile on a whim, then they realise that the purchase price is the smallest part of the cost.'

'Well, I'd love to live in a shabby-chic ruin.'

'Of course you would, but I'd be the one to repair it for the rest of my days.'

'Okay, okay, I give in, shatter my dreams.' He was right of course. If they wanted to pour what little money they had into a bottomless pit, there were more worthy causes than a crumbling house, no matter how grand. Léa flopped onto the old sofa by the window.

'Jesus, this has a terrible sag in it. Remind me not to offer it as a guest bed.' She sighed and cast her eyes to the ceiling like a silent movie heroine, 'Ah, mon chateau ....'

'You and your little fantasies,' Sam grinned. 'I watched him at the hotel. I bet he keeps a baroque chaise-longue in his boudoir, especially for the ladies.' He simulated an exaggerated bow, 'lie down 'ere, Madame, I am a doctor.'

'Well, he was once a professor, just like my grandfather's friends,' Léa laughed. 'People like that cling to who they once were. We always had to spend our school holidays in Paris. It was my mother's attempt to civilise me. In summer my grandparents' friends arrived in their linen suits, with gold engraved pocket watches and silver handles on their walking sticks. They let me play with them. In winter they wore fur collars on threadbare black coats and fur hats, like something out of Tolstoy. And the coats,' Léa pulled a face, 'always had the whiff of mothballs.

'How can you remember things like that?'

Léa shrugged. 'I just do. They were so ... theatrical. None of them ever sat down without kissing my grandmother's hand first. Paris was their refuge, most of them were totally impoverished. In their heads they were still promenading around like Count Esterhazy in Budapest. They used to meet in the Louvre; they had no money for coal. The Louvre was warmer than their apartments. My grandfather often took me with him. We always found his friends in one of the galleries, as near to the heaters as possible. Their talk was about Verdi's operas and Rubens and Rembrandt and all the things they'd lost. All my mother's family pretended that somehow we deserved to live in style.'

45

During Léa's childhood that kind of wealth had been a distant mirage, somewhere beyond the horizon, but nevertheless real because she knew it to have been her mother's life. The luxuries the grown-ups endlessly spoke of produced wonder in her; she could imagine all that there was to be had in the world when she herself grew up. But later, away from her mother, she began to perceive the idle rich as an affront to the life of ordinary people, people like her friend Gisèle, growing up and growing old, eventually dying in a village filled with country traditions and history. Gisèle's contentment came not from jewels and admiration at society events, but from the touch of a ripe tomato or the savouring of the sweet juice of a fig picked from the tree in her garden. Gisèle's physical comforts were the breeze at the end of a heat-pained day, the cool of the kitchen tiles underfoot, not fur coats and chauffeurs.

'God, I really hated all that make-believe when I was fifteen, but I suppose I'm condemned to carry it around with me.'

'It's not that easy to live far away from your own culture,' Sam said. 'I mean, look at me, after fifteen years. Do you think I'll ever become a Frenchman?'

'I haven't given up on you yet. But even if you don't, I don't think you'll ever be able to live in England again. France does that to you. But Augusto? Where does he belong? Definitely not in a village around here. I don't know about him - an Argentinean lounge lizard educated at Eton or Harrow; stiff upper lip versus burning passion?'

'A bit weird,' said Sam. 'Anyway, his books might be interesting. I said we'd be there next Tuesday.'

'But that's the first of May; that's a public holiday.'

'I know, but with all the stuff happening at the abbey I can't make it earlier.'

Léa cast her mind back to their meeting with the old man at the beginning of April. Her unease about him had abated. 'I expect he's selling his kids' inheritance. Perhaps that's why he was so keen, that day at the hotel.'

*

Nothing but to waste night, day and time

10

Afternoon, same day

Augusto had taken the longer route that skirted around the mountains. It promised to be less strenuous now that he was driving on his own. After his last argument with Ophelia he had not dared bring Zoffia on this trip.

The river stretched around a bend and the outline of Albi's St. Cécile cathedral rose high above him. The addition of a tower without a spire centuries ago could not disguise this medieval fortress with the long, slit-shaped windows more suited to shooting arrows at an attacking enemy than for pious prayer. Although he had driven for no more that two hours he felt that all his strength had evaporated. The town, which he knew well, seemed as good as any to take a rest. Tomorrow's drive North on the interminable roads of the Dordogne would be arduous. The brick-red cathedral loomed as he crossed the bridge and parked in the shadow of its fortified walls.

Inside the building the air shimmered in the blue reflection of its lapislazuli painted ceilings. Ambitious Renaissance popes had paid more for the precious blue than for the bricks of the entire construction. But for the glory of God nothing seemed too extravagant. Augusto had visited the cathedral before, but never alone.

He sat down on one of the dark pews at the back to marvel at the ornaments which promised the glory of heaven for the repentant soul.

He had never been able to believe in God, even as a boy, especially in one who might have looked much as he himself did now. As his gaze travelled down from the ceiling the images got more graphic until they illustrated the depth of hell and a gruesome depiction of the Last Judgment. Where would he be if there should come such a day? Was he good or evil, saint or Satan?

On either side of the gold covered arch, frescos of writhing naked bodies, some with imploring hands, were engulfed by floods. Others were consumed by flames. I know how you feel, he thought; at this moment he could identify with the suffering more than with the piety, true or false, of those desperate to enter heaven. His empathy surged like a searing pain.

His foolish pursuit of beauty and love had brought him to a kind of hell. With a shock he realized for the first time that all these tortured figures were female. Why had he never noticed this strange separation of men and women on previous visits? Painted in a band, above those condemned to hellfire, an orderly procession of apparently more virtuous women floated, with transparent naked bodies, each holding an open book to cover their breasts. What did their nudity mean? Could they hope to pass through the gates of heaven, purified by discarding all worldly apparel or was this a bit of titillation for the medieval clergy, the Playboy magazine of the time? Oddly, none of the men were depicted as having cast off their clothing.

Above the naked procession a crowd of monks and bishops were seated, with only the odd high-ranking abbess among them. The saints, who were placed under the angels floating close to the ceiling, were also all male. Who had decreed that women were damned; why were they deemed to be sinners more than the men? He had vague recollections of reading the Koran. Mohammed had likened women to dogs and devils, certain that most of hell's inhabitants would be women. If he himself had lived at the time when these images were promoted by the church, would he have blamed Ophelia for his own aberrations? Was his own story simply a modern version of the old Adam and Eve tale? Had not Ophelia brought Zoffia into his house, put temptation into his path at a time when he thought that life could not yield another great passion? Or was his infatuation some base, last-ditch flicker of the genes in his old body, craving one last chance of procreation?

An unseen hand struck up the first reedy sounds on the gigantic organ which stretched up, touching the very top of the lapislazuli and gold ceiling where four arches met. Augusto let his head drop back. In the blue haze the music floated, swirled, curled, like coloured ribbons in the cavernous space above him.

The massive central part of the organ was held up by two marble sculptures of male figures with anguished faces. Their muscular bodies and arms raised above their heads seemed to strain under the weight of the structure; their faces were carved with expressions of deep sorrow or anger.

The early evening service would soon start. Augusto could suddenly no longer bear the images of irredeemable sin. He had to find a place to stay the night or decide to move on. By the time he reached the cathedral portal, the sun was low and the decision was made for him. He would spend the night in Albi.

He had not found much sleep in the little hotel next to the cathedral where he and Ophelia had stayed years ago. The hotel had become unkempt and it seemed the beds had not seen a new mattress for years.

At daybreak, his mobile phone rang. It was Zoffia. She was whispering something about Ophelia and the house in disarray, about things being moved. He was so tired that he couldn't understand what she was telling him. She hung up in mid-sentence. He had switched off his mobile. He was too drowsy to think. Finally he had he sunk into a deep, restless sleep and awoken with every bone in his body aching. He had left before breakfast was served.

Augusto drove on. He looked at his watch; twenty four hours since he had left home. Zoffia's words replayed in his mind; he was unable to make sense of them.

There was little traffic but concentration seemed beyond his grasp. Village after village passed, houses lining the road with not much more that a café or a wine cooperative to

51

show that some sort of life was possible in these functional places. Gabled Roman church towers with bells hanging out in the open under narrow arches occasionally came into view. Other village churches held a solitary bell captive in a cage on the top of a squared-off tower. They sat squat among the houses and everything around them lay devoid of life. His thoughts, like his driving, had meandered. At lonely crossroads he decided on impulse whether to go left or right, as long as the sign pointed vaguely northwards. Sometime in mid-afternoon St.Affrique had passed by, a pile of soft orange coloured, shallow roofs on a mound across a humped bridge stradling a rubble-edged river. Soon after he became fixated on a large, dark blue mountain in the distance to his left. Was that the place he remembered, where he could join the motorway leading to Limoges?

When he reached the mountain he could find no signs to anywhere except to the next village. He drove on, taking turns randomly, up and down through tree lined mountain roads, all of which he had hoped to avoid. His arms strained to hold the road in one hairpin bend after another. The motorway was sure to lie beyond the mountain.

He was tired and his eyes burned. When he reached a sharp bend at the summit of the mountain he had seen from afar he found that the trees had been cut away on the right side of the road at the edge of a jagged promontory. A wooden platform with a rail had been erected. On a cleared patch by the side of the road he stopped and got out of the car to see what the view might be. A weathered panel pointed across the deep river gorge with the words 'Rocamadour'. On the other side of the sweep of the narrow river valley lay the town, hacked out of the rock that jutted out over the landscape. Even at this time of day the streets would be busy with pilgrims, making their way up to pray to the Black Madonna, as they had done for a thousand years. Ophelia had loved this old town, where each house had the naked rock for a back wall, with steep, zigzagging streets and endless steps leading to the subterranean church of Saint Amadour.

The sun was setting; by the minute a horizontal wave of black shadows crept up, devouring the sun-lit facades. Soon the night would swallow the whole town. Should he stop, rest for the night? Maybe not. He could not face the crooked steps to the cosy hotel where they had once stayed. There was a little time before dark to find some tranquil roadside hotel. No, he would sleep elsewhere.

It was warm in the car. He settled back in the driving seat, but made no move to start the ignition. He pulled his coat closer and watched the asthe blood-red sun turned to purple.

An oncoming car startled him as it tore around the bend, its headlamps sweeping across him like a search light. The car passed. He sat in total darkness on this moonless night; he would be going nowhere now. Shut your eyes, just for a minute, shut your eyes.

He awoke with a start. On the horizon dawn was breaking. Augusto opened the car door. The air was fresh, filled with the scent of wild thyme. He got out and rubbed his face awake. His knees had locked from having slept in the sitting position. Old age, old knees, he pondered. He walked to the edge of the viewing platform and leaned on the barrier. Below him the perpendicular rock face fell away for at least one hundred meters, if not more. It would be easy to climb through the barrier and let himself fall. It would be simple, quick and painless - death by misadventure of an old, careless man, the police report would say. He had never wanted to have to choose between more than two options. The last time the lust of old age had driven him on. He had chosen between Ophelia and Zoffia and he had made the wrong choice.

There wasn't a living soul around. Only the birds were beginning their dawn chorus. Birdsong would accompany his fall, all the way down. It was either this rock face or he would have to return home. There was enough time. His Paris appointment lay two days away. Go back, a voice whispered, go back and see what your Ophelia has done.

*

'Til of this flat a mountain you have made

11

Sainte Colombe, same day

Snow rarely fell in winter, except in the high mountains. Temperatures dropped below zero once or twice a year and then so little that Léa could leave the cacti on the terraces, covering them on the odd night when air frost threatened. Then summer arrived overnight.

On the previous afternoon a storm had been trapped in the cauldron of the Black Mountain around Marjac. During the night, with the sudden fall in temperature, it broke loose and raced down and over the village of Sainte Colombe, charging at the north-slanting roofs. Léa had huddled close to Sam as they lay in bed, listening to the violent gusts hurling the terracotta tiles into the patio where they smashed. In the next few days they would have to spend hours crawling around on the roof on their hands and knees, replacing and realigning tiles. The rain had hammered down on the village like machine gun fire until it suddenly gave way to the silence of a grey dawn. They went out onto the terrace, listening to the dripping of water in the stillness. It was too early for breakfast; they sank back into bed, grateful for some sleep at last.

They were woken by sunshine streaming into the room. For the first time since they'd had their encounter with Augusto two weeks earlier, not a wisp of cloud marred the azure morning sky and every bird and blade of grass quivered with new life.

'Let's go out for the day.' Léa stretched her limbs. Far below their terrace wall the swollen waters thundered in the shadows of the gorge. A warm wind rode up and Léa's red hair flared in the sudden gust. She closed her eyes and imagined herself standing on the prow of a ship on the high seas. Her short blue dress billowed and flapped around her bare legs. Last summer's tan had all but disappeared, except for a few cinnamon-coloured freckles on her shoulders. She examined the new shoots bursting from the morning glory winding its way along the wall. By summer she would be greeted by a sea of its blue trumpet-shaped flowers which lasted but a single day.

'We don't have to go far. How about Montferrus, my magic mountain?' A short car ride would bring them to the lake. From the rocky plateau above it there were spectacular views of the high Pyrenees, still clad in a crisp coat of snow.

They packed a picnic and set off. From the castle ruins at the top of the next village the fields and vineyards fell away steeply. Vegetation in hues of deep emerald, lime greens and acid mustard yellows formed an intricate patchwork, sweeping wide before it rose up and up to the mountains high on the horizon. 'Just look at that,' Léa stood in awe, 'beauty everywhere.'

The country roads were empty. Fresh-leaved vineyards promised the colour of wines to come. Lines of elegant cypresses laid striped shadows across the lanes leading to the wine domaines and bastides, sitting square among the fields. Now and then they got stuck behind a tractor or a farmer in his rusting car, swerving from left to the right, looking over his land.

'Beware of drivers wearing caps,' Sam reminded himself aloud. Men with hats or caps were as likely to crash into oncoming traffic as to end up in a ditch by themselves.

'It's an old French country custom to ride around looking at your fields. Farmers have done it since the Middle Ages, if not before. You English just don't understand that.'

'We English do,' Sam defended himself, 'but in the old days there weren't any cars. I mean, have you ever read anywhere of horses in a head-on collision?'

The road began its steep climb towards the village of Fanjeaux. There was a point, starting at the crossroad by the derelict monastery, where Léa felt the air vibrate, where time seemed to fall away like the discarded skin of snakes. She did not understand what this was, nor did she want to. Ahead, the road zigzagged upward through lush spring meadows, past fruit trees twisted by centuries of blistering heat and drought. Sudden slopes, at once sharp and voluptuous, ran up to the church, the final point so high that it seemed to pierce the sky. Before moving to this region she had seen landscapes with such spiraling terraces in Florentine paintings, in the Louvre.

Her mother had insisted on leading her past the great works of art every summer Sunday, talking to her about them, not as if she were a five year-old child, but in the same manner she discussed paintings with her friends.

'This is what my family, your family has lost,' she would say with resentment, 'all because of the Russians.'

As Léa grew up she became aware of the importance of these treasures. She could never quite believe that her family had ever owned *St. Jérôme in his Study* by Antonello da Messina, as her mother had implied, but in that painting, in the background of the tableau, confined in an open window and set back from the central figure, was one of those fairy-tale landscapes. It seemed no more than a throwaway gesture by the artist to demonstrate his new-found skill of perspective.

She had never found words to explain to Sam why she wanted to take this road and not another. She had no desire to take the wheel when they came this way. She was here for a different reason. As they penetrated this unruly geometry of inclines, rising, then falling away behind them, she waited for the precise moment when they passed a crippled olive tree that still clung to the stony soil good only for the growing of wine.

Now! whispered the voice in her head. Another interior eye took over and once again she saw the figure emerge from among swaying crops, always in the same place. He rode from right to left, not a hundred meters from the road, on a blond horse with a flaxen mane. They strode along together without hurry, surveying the land. His well-shaped thighs, clad in green stockings inside a pair of pointed boots, hugged the flank of his horse. His yellow doublet was stitched with gold motifs that glinted in the sunlight. A single feather of some large bird of prey quivered on a dark hat. Rooks and swifts swooped down from the church tower, circling man and horse as if to greet them. Léa knew that he had always been there and always would be. It was she who was passing through for a short moment in time. As they reached the next bend in the road the vision vanished.

They came to a fork in the road.

'There, what's that?' Sam stopped and let the car roll back a few meters. Entangled in dense undergrowth lay a wooden stake with a weather-bleached sign nailed to it. Sam got out and pulled it free. It seemed no more than an old piece of driftwood. Hand-painted black letters had faded to grey but were still legible. NOYRLAK.

Léa jumped out of the car. 'Please, let's take it home. It'll be one of my relics.'

'It's completely rotten through.'

'It'll dry out.' She ran her fingers over the crumbling lettering. 'This won't tell anyone which way to go nowadays. It's a long time since that name was spelled like this. It's a bit of history. Perhaps old Augusto will want it. He might tell us about the chateau 's history.'

'It might rattle a few skeletons.' Sam twisted the sign away from the disintegrating wooden post. He carefully lifted it into the car boot. He brushed the wood dust from his jacket. 'You and your relics. You talk about them as if they were living things.'

'Perhaps they are.'

'Hum. Perhaps one day I'll become one of them in your gallery of defunct items.'

'I'll just push it to the back.' Léa reached into the car boot. As she grabbed the sign, something made her withdraw her hand. She frowned. A rash of goose bumps was running up her arm.

'Sam?'

'Don't tell me. You've changed your mind.'

'I think maybe we should leave it here. I don't know … there is something …'

Sam was already beside her, lifting the disintegrating sign out of the boot. With a swinging motion he threw it back into the bushes and it vanished from sight. Léa turned and got back into the car and for a while they drove in silence.

*

His nostrils wide to some mysterious scent

12

Chateau de Noirlac, same day

Hugging the ground by the chateau wall, hidden by low shrubs, Romain lay on his belly. His chin touched the wet soil. It still smelled of the night rain. He strained to watch the men ferrying boxes, tables and chairs from the house to the big vans. The woman who had found him in the barn was directing them, rushing in and out of the house.

A second woman ran out, barring the way to one of the men as he tried to re-enter the house. She stood with her arms spread wide in a white tent-like dress. Her hair was red. She was shouting. Nanette never shouted when he didn't do as he was told. His mother had shouted on the day she had gone away, and in the barn; she had shouted because he had picked the white flowers for her. She had been away a long time. Perhaps that's why she didn't recognise him. Next time, he was sure, she would know him. He wouldn't let her leave again.

The woman and one the men were pushing the red haired woman back into the house.

Romain inched out from the shrubs and ran for cover among the reeds by the lake, sliding and falling on the wet sand and mud on its bank. He ran along the cypress path. Keeping low, he crawled past the pool on all fours, paused on the uncut grass to catch his breath. All the shutters at the back of the house were closed except for one on the ground floor which gave onto the garden.

He dashed across the grass. The rear door under the portico was open and he slipped into the great house. There was a lot of noise, people were manoeuvring heavy objects down the stairs.

Romain stood in the shadows by the open door that led into the hall. The men were outside at the front now. He could hear the women upstairs. He slid along the wall and went to sit in the darkness under the main stairs, pulled his knees up and rested his chin on them. His trousers reeked of mud.

The lake had been his favourite playground a long time ago. His brother Alain built little boats from tiny bundles of reed. A white square of paper impaled on a stick pierced the bundle and it became a boat that sailed along on the silvery surface. Soon Alain would come back, like his mother, and make him many boats to play with on the water.

*

It beckons you to come away

13

Montferrus Mountain, same day

The lake at the foot of Montferrus lay deserted, its water slate black and icy. Sam scanned the surroundings. He detected no sign of passing walkers. The long grasses lay in perfect parallel humps, as if a diligent wood engraver had drawn them into the landscape. Reeds leaned into the water, unbroken. No one had been fishing here. There were no foot marks at the sunny end of the lake where the vegetation gave way to a short sandy beach. He tried his foot on the rotting wooden jetty. It moaned like a beast awakened. Then it began floating in silence, away towards the middle of the lake, a ghost ship that had longed to be launched.

They walked over to the tiny beach. A few meters back stood a squat boathouse. Sam made towards it.

'We can sit on the step.'

'No we can't. That's held together by spiders' webs by the look of it. Here,' Léa pulled up a plank stranded in the reeds and dragged it onto the sand. 'We can sit on this.' She spread her shawl on it and began unpacking their sandwiches.

They settled down and watched as water hens hurried through the undergrowth to skate into the lake.

'Should have brought a fishing rod.' Léa took off her shoes and went to kneel at the water's edge. She gently dragged her hand through the shallow water. Tiny fish approached and nibbled at her finger tips, several to each finger, competing for what they took to be a new source of food. She flicked her fingers and watched as they darted away. In the water something shiny caught her eye and she retrieved it.

'I've found treasure, a ring.'
She slipped it over her finger, turned to Sam and waggled her hand at him. 'A Coca Cola wedding ring.'

A sudden gust bore down on the tree tops. Hoarse cries echoed around the lake; crows' wings beat the air. The surface of the lake shivered.

The ache in his foot reminded Sam to take it easy today. A twisted ankle was a small price to pay for a couple of days' clambering around stony vineyards, in and out of the igloo-like mounds the locals called capitelles.

Work at the abbey had halted until all the lab results were in. For once he'd had time on his hands to investigate these enigmatic constructions. They had hardly been documented and yet their strange beehive shapes could be seen at the edge of most vineyards. The locals showed no great interest in the capitelles, except to say that within memory they had always been there. To the best of their knowledge these squat constructions had been built as shelters by labourers over the centuries as they toiled between the rows of vines. The thick roofs kept men and food cool during the scorching heat at harvest times. On winter days, when shoots had to be pruned and tied, they provided a place to build a warming fire.

Sam had ventured inside the tiniest of them to eat his lunch. It was hardly high enough to allow him to crawl in, let alone sit upright. People must have been so much smaller then, he realised. He sat hunched, chewing on his bread and cheese. He'd had time to study the arched stonework and found it to be of an astonishing, perfect architecture. At the very top two stones had been tilted to leave a vent for smoke to escape, their angle preventing rain from penetrating the interior. Some capitelles were miniature cathedral domes, as if the top of a cupola had been sliced off and placed on the ground. Others seemed basic, almost prehistoric in their robustness. But all of them were constructed with precision and masterful symmetry.

Deciphering the fabric of village walls and fortress ramparts had taken up much of his time in the last three years. He had become known as something of an expert in the field and commissions of work were coming in from ever more distant places. Walls held the secrets of centuries. Léa would watch him as he stood in front of an old wall, lost in thought.

'You can read walls like a book, as long as you don't start reading them in bed,' she laughed.

Sam shrugged. 'It's what humans and many other creatures leave behind. Look at the termites, the house martins. Their nests are the same as the capitelles in the vineyards, just upside down.'

'You're saying we have invented nothing?'

'Nothing that didn't already exist in nature.'

In this part of France history seemed part of the present, like an ancient tree suddenly revealing all of its roots at the slightest scratching of the soil. Something inside him had become enthralled by so much that lay buried, but could so easily be revealed. All one had to do was look.

Their own house lay in the centre of a row of village houses overlooking the gorge with Mount Septimania beyond it and in the far distance the high Pyrenees. In all of the houses there were blocked recesses where formerly a door had led to the next building. In their own back yard he had found metal bars embedded in the walls which adjoined neighbouring houses left and right. Other walls had foot-size notches cut into them. Villagers were bemused by Sam's question about them.

'Oh, those were the escape routes,' the old grocer told him.

'From the Germans?' Sam assumed.

'Non, non,' laughed the old man and waved his dark brown, wrinkled hands, 'from the Inquisition. They were all plotting at the abbey then, deciding on whom to burn next. Here in Sainte Colombe the Cathars could climb from one house, from one roof to the next and disappear, plouff, as if by magic,' he laughed, but his laughter faded. 'We were in much danger in this village.' He chewed on the last of his cigarette. 'It was so close to the abbey and those damned plotting monks. Later on, of course, they used the steps during the Great Terror, running from Robespierre's men after the Revolution,' he added, as if he had witnessed it himself.

The Sainte Colombe church had been a monastery in the 9th century. It sat at the highest point of the village, its tall tower and broad nave now out of proportion with a modest and ever shrinking congregation. Shortly after their arrival in the village, Sam and Léa had stood behind the church on a raised cobbled square framed on three sides by the ancient ramparts. At the edge of it a large cross looked out onto the vast land running south-east to the Mediteranean. When they had stepped into the centre of the plateau directly in line with the cross, the ground under their feet suddenly swayed for a few seconds. One step to the left or right and nothing could be felt. The villagers knew about this perturbing phenomenon. They called it the Devil's Spike. Cats and dogs were seen to leap into the air when they stepped on the spot. Rumour had it that the village had been built on its rocky spine because it was made almost entirely of iron, that and the fact that many underground rivers criss-crossed beneath it. Children were threatened with the Devil's Spike and told that they would remain there, glued to the ground if they misbehaved. Someone long ago had marked the cobbles and school boys dared each other to leap over them, but the old villagers steered well clear of the spot.

Sam chewed on the last of his sandwich. He wondered whether here around the lake, half-way up to mount Montferrus, the bloody events of the time of King Saint Louis were inscribed, whether the ground might resonate somehow with the horrors of past battles.

He got up. 'Not much of a lunch.' He wiped his hands and scattered the last crumbs into the water.

'What do you expect? A three course dinner?' Léa packed away the empty sandwich wrappers. 'This was as much as you normally eat. It's all this fresh air that's making you hungry. If you spend more time at the abbey you'll go mouldy. Here, you carry the bag a while. It's half empty now.'

He swung the bag over his shoulder and they began their climb to the plateau. They followed the faint trace of an old path, now overgrown with short prickly shrubs which clawed at the hems of their trousers.

'Someone's been up here, very recently,' Sam said. He examined some lower branches which had been beaten, then trodden down. A few woollen fibres hung on a twig. 'It's not someone who came via the lake though. They came from the other side, I can't imagine how though, it's an almost vertical climb.'

'Must be someone local who knows something we don't. Maybe we're not the only ones to appreciate the view after all.'

Léa knew that like everywhere the paths surrounding the old villages had become disused. Children were now driven around in cars. Parents no longer allowed them to roam free. Léa was grateful that her father had insisted on bringing up his daughters in the country, despite her mother's constant hankering for the big city. Léa's father had reluctantly agreed for the two girls to spend half their summer holidays in Paris rather than on the mediterranean beaches. Thanks to him the sisters had grown up in blissful freedom, running through the woods, climbing onto rocks at the top of nearby mountains overlooking fields and meadows. With the village children Léa had played in streams and taught herself to swim in rivers. As long as children turned up at meal times all was well.

'The next generation will have forgotten all this. Give it a couple more years and this place will be inaccessible.' Should she be glad that nature was reclaiming what she had known as a child or sad for the loss of the next generations' freedom to explore?

The path led up through an abandoned olive grove. Now and then Sam bent down to examine what looked like sand coloured pebbles that littered the path.

'Found one.' He held out his hand. A fossilised snail lay curled in his palm.

'The stones have definitely got you again.' Léa touched the fossil, following its spiral shape to the centre with her fingernail.

'So lovely, so perfect. Just like a tiny ear. Imagine what it has seen and heard.'

'There was a huge earthquake here in the seventeenth century or it could have been chucked to the surface by a volcano even earlier.' With his thumb, Sam rubbed the grit out of the grooves. There was something irresistible about the almost human shape in his palm and as they ascended he enclosed it in his hand until it was warm and felt like a living thing.

The pungent scent of wild sage and thyme hit them as they emerged onto the scrubby plateau strewn with grey, pock-marked lava stone. In the savage bluster their clothing tugged at their bodies. A large flattened rock jutted into the void to the south. Three twisted cedars offered the only shade and shelter. With their roots anchored deep in the rocky crevasses, they strained away from the southern winds that tore at every plant that dared raise its head above ground level.

'Up here, this is the perfect place. This is where I want to be buried.' Léa threw her head back, spread her arms and whirled around.

Sam kicked the stony ground with his heel.

'There isn't any soil to bury you.'

'You could build a stony mound, like those capitelles you photographed, bury me under it.' To lie dead among the wind-beaten lavender and thyme with the wild air rushing up from below was something she could imagine when there was no longer a body to consider. 'I'd be a spirit dancing and you could come up here. You'd know that all the thrashing and swirling dust was me.'

'No I wouldn't.'

'Why not?'

'Because by then my legs would be too stiff to make the climb.'

'Why must you be such a realist?' Léa sighed. 'This is a magic mountain.'

They had first spotted it from below on their way home in a thunderstorm. An unseen force had bunched a mass of black rain clouds in a suffocating embrace, shrouding the summit of the mountain. The clouds began to coil upwards, accelerating ever faster, coming to a point, then bursting abruptly to shed their watery load all in one go. There followed a stillness, the damp air was torn this way and that, then the sun cut through the mist and in minutes the dripping landscape had dried out. All that had remained was a whispy white plume of steam rising vertically from the top of the summit.

Sam scanned the sky. 'No storm today, I hope.' This mountain could not be trusted.

Sam went to sit on the flat rock under the cedars. Léa sat close behind him, hugging him for fear of being swept over the edge. Jackdaws perched on the craggy ledges just below them. Eyes like granite beads, set in light grey circles, watched the intruders. One after another they launched themselves into the hot rising air, hovered without a single movement of their wings, before plunging towards the fields below. Their harsh caw-caw cries were swallowed by the wind that rumbled and howled in the branches overhead.

'Close your eyes, listen,' said Sam, 'you could swear that it's waves crashing against cliffs.'

Below them lay a small village with a dainty bridge and a narrow road curling its way up a hill. Farms and houses with gardens to the rear bordered the main street. A church of light stone with an exposed bell tower sat in a tree-lined square in the village centre. To the left they were looking down onto the roof of a chateau sitting in large grounds. A high wall separated it from the rest of the village with the main road hugging its perimeter at a right angle.

The midday sun cast deep shadows on the ground. The lonely bark of a dog rode up on the wind. The only movement visible from their vantage point were two figures marching back and forth, loading objects into two large removal vans parked on the forecourt of the big house.

A swarm of screeching swifts swept past them, barely avoiding Sam's feet which dangled over the edge. Suddenly there was another movement below, a black car came speeding through the village. Dust swirled as it turned into a narrow lane and through the chateau gates to come to a halt in front of the cab of one of the large vans. A dark figure struggled out of the driving seat and hurried into the house.

*

And still, your fingers on your lips

14

Noirlac village, same time

Armand Arouet hovered on the doorstep of his café. He waved across the street. A short man wearing a beret and overalls had flung his ground floor shutters open. He stood with arms braced on the window sill and was peering to the right where the black car had disappeared.

'What's going on?' he called across the street, alarmed.

'God knows,' Armand cried. He threw his hands up in outrage. 'Have they gone mad over there? Was that the old man in that car?'

At the window Paul Airvolt shrugged. 'When Louis delivered the post the maid said he'd gone to Paris yesterday morning.'

'He can't have been there and back. Impossible.' Paul glanced left and right and signaled for Armand to cross over. His shutters closed with a clang and the front door half

73

opened to let Armand slip into the dark corridor. Paul led him through the house. At the end of the garden the high chateau wall rose like a fortress. The path to it was barely wide enough to set one foot in front of the other. Paul put a finger to his lips to silence Armand's whispered questions.

The two men stealthily made their way towards the end of Paul's garden. In the corner a gnarled cherry tree was still in blossom. Paul picked up a sturdy trowel from the side of the path and ducked under the low branches. Armand heard the scrape of the tool against stone followed by a dull thud on the soft ground. Paul's arm emerged from among the blossoms and pulled Armand in. At waist height a boulder was missing from the wall. Armand followed Paul's instructions to kneel and look through. He felt sweat break under his moustache. The skin around his nostrils pulled tighter; he hardly dared to breathe.

Apart from a few tall weeds which grew on the other side of the wall, the view was almost unobstructed. Armand shifted to one side to get a better view of the chateau forecourt. Two huge removal vans stood near the main doors. Blocking their path was Augusto's black car with the driver's door wide open. A couple of men in overalls hovered nearby, glancing towards the house, smoking, waiting. Harsh voices floated out from the house, their sound too distant to be understood.

Paul settled back on his heels. From his pocket he took his tobacco tin. His roll-ups bore little resemblance to the cigarettes sold in Armand's *Tabac*. Paul's creations usually ended up as twisted white twigs and once lit they smelt like an Arab camp fire. He crumbled a few shreds of black tobacco into the thin paper and his rough-skinned fingers slowly worked it round. Something was wrong on the other side of the wall; it was just a question of watching and waiting.

*

Something have you heard

15

Chateau de Noirlac, same time

Romain sat hunched under the stairs. Directly above him there were two voices now, women's voices, one of them getting louder, shrieking and sobbing all at the same time. The shrieking voice was running up and down. A low, angry voice boomed in the hall. The women fell silent.

'Ophelia,' the man's voice shouted, 'what is the meaning of this?'

'The meaning? The meaning?' came the woman's voice from the top of the stairs. 'What is the meaning of … her … calling you to come back? It's too late, Augusto, too late for questions. Go back to Paris.'

The shrieking voice suddenly changed to a whine. Heavy footsteps made their way up the stairs above Romain's head. He put his hands over his ears, pressing hard to block out all sound. He would wait until all was quiet. His mother would come and find him when everyone was gone, put her hand on his head, kiss his forehead. He would be good and she would stay with him forever and never send him away again.

The pulsing of his heartbeat and the throbbing of his blood was getting louder as time passed. His ears were hot and painful from the pressure. It seemed he had been sitting under the stairs for hours. His knees were locking; how much longer could he hold out? He was getting drowsy.

A sudden tremor came through the wall that he was leaning against. Gently, he removed his hands from his ears. On the stairs above him heavy footsteps were descending. Dust rained down on Romain's bent head and trickled into the back of his collar. Somewhere a big door slammed shut. The house shuddered. He heard the howl of a car engine and the scraping of tyres on the gravel. His time would come, soon.

*

A pile of branches ready for the burning

16

Noirlac Village, same day

They were entering the village they had seen from the plateau. Sam slowly drove through the main street.

'Look, on that sign, it says Noirlac,' Léa said, 'there's no getting away from this place today. It's so close to Sainte Colombe. I don't understand why we've never come this way before or are we meant to be here for some reason?'

'You think too much, Léa.'

The village slumbered in the early afternoon heat. A black cat stretched on the hot bonnet of a parked car in the church square. A dog with carrot coloured fur lay on a door step opposite the café, jaws resting on its front paw, but the eyes were watching.

'I can't see a chateau.'

They were approaching a bend at the end of the village. Before Sam had time to reply a van the size of a house shot into the road from nowhere and bounced to a halt, nose to nose with them, brakes screeching. Sam slammed his brakes on to save their car from being crushed. The driver angrily waved a fist as he tried to exit from a narrow lane to their right. It was an oversized removal van.

'Someone has plenty of furniture here.' Sam's fingers were drumming on the steering wheel. Two men jumped from the cab and came towards them.

'Look at the size of them, Sam. Just be nice to them, please,' Léa pleaded and wound down her window. Sam gritted his teeth. He could be impatient, at times confrontational in situations such as these. The trouble was, so were others.

'Une seconde, ' Léa called, leaning out of her car window, 'on va reculer. Back up Sam, let them out.' She gave the two brawny men her best smile. It worked. The driver stood in the middle of the road, hands on hips, trying to assess how many millimeters he had to exit the lane. The younger of the two, wearing a Rambo shirt with biceps the size of Rugby balls, came over and discreetly signaled in the direction of the driver.

'Had a bit of stress back there today,' he smiled, 'désolé.'

'Not to worry.' Léa gave him a friendly wave.

Sam reversed the car to allow room for the truck to edge out of the lane and get around the corner. He switched off the engine and they sat and watched the driver make six or seven precision manoeuvres. In the open door of the Café-Tabac stood a man in defiant posture, tugging nervously at his moustache. The truck jerked back and forth and finally exited from the lane, barely missing the window of the café, but deeply scoring the red and white CAFE-TABAC - Chez

Armand sign. The man with the moustache took a leap backwards and watched helplessly as one of the chairs standing on the pavement was crushed against the wall.

The removal van moved off. Its driver did not take a second look at the havoc he was leaving behind. Léa watched the café owner stare after the offending vehicle, holding on to the twisted remains of his plastic chair.

Sam started the engine again. 'Bully,' he grumbled. As the car moved forward a sign came into view, pointing up the lane. Chateau de Noirlac. A second giant van was approaching the alley exit.

'It's up there, the old man's place.' Léa craned her neck.

'Let's get out of here. There's no guarantee that the second van will make it out.' Sam slowly drove on. 'You'll see plenty of the chateau next week. At least we know where it is now.'

As they passed the last house of the village, they noted that the chateau's grounds stretched a long way beyond the village. They drove along the road that hugged the boundary.

'Stop a second, Sam. I just want to have a look.'

Sam eased the car onto the grassy verge and they got out at a point where the wall was low enough to allow a good view of the gardens behind the big house. Outlines of a formal layout, with paths and roundels, trees and shrubs and water features were still clearly visible.

'Imagine living in a place like that,' said Léa dreamily.

Sam shook his head. 'A place like that is a liability.'

'My aunt Ilena had a house like that on Lake Balaton. Come to think of it, my mother's house was not much smaller. The English would have called it a manor house.

Just once it would be nice to have real space. Every time I buy a book, we have to rearrange the furniture.'

'They had a dozen servants in those days. Can you imagine the old man, pushing a vacuum cleaner around that house in his hat and cape? Perhaps if you're especially nice too him,' a hint of a wicked smile hovered in the corner of Sam's mouth, 'he'll let you have some rooms. By the looks of it he'd love to pay you a visit at midnight.'

'Sam. You've got a dirty mind,' Léa protested.

'You're wrong, you know. No matter how old a man gets, he'll always go for young flesh. You heard, his wife is called Ophelia. Perhaps he's got a thing about redheads.'

'Was Shakespeare's Ophelia a redhead?'

'Who knows, but Millais's Ophelia was.'

Instantly the picture flashed into Léa's mind; the pale skin, the half closed eyes, the lugubrious grasses leaning in on the glistening figure in the water.

They were returning to the car when a strange, hollow shriek made them look back over the wall. There was movement on the lawn. Two women were running. The first not very fast, the second with more agile steps, almost like a young girl. A line of pencil-thin cypress trees sliced their movement into a flicker. The flame red hair of the second woman flared as she ran. Her voice echoed as she called out to the woman ahead of her, but from this distance one could not distinguish whether her shrieking was in fun or in anger.

'Come on,' Sam pulled Léa away, 'it's rude to spy on people.' He got into the car and eased it off the verge. Léa looked back over the wall and saw the women vanish behind the dense shrubs.

*

81

And it must follow, as night the day

17

Domaine L'Espérou, next day

Guy de Vilmorin stood by the window of his study, fists clenched in the pockets of his tweed hunting jacket. A permanent deep furrow divided his bushy eyebrows. Every morning and afternoon his gaze fixed on the same spot in the distance. Half a mile across the vineyards the sun picked out the façade of the Chateau de Noirlac. He found it hard to realise that it had once been his. The years had passed. He felt he was looking at a stage set rather than at a solid building. Although the ties to his ancestral home had been cut, the shame of losing his century-old heritage gave him no rest. But it was more than shame that gnawed both at his heart and in his mind.

Behind the walls of his former home village midwives had helped generations of the Vilmorin family into the world, had slapped the new-born's bottoms to elicit that first vital cry. In the darkened bedrooms priests had taken deathbed confessions and their waxen hands had gently closed eyes which would never again look upon the world.

It was mostly the women of the family who had died in the chateau; many had not reached the age of thirty. Childbirth was a dangerous, almost yearly event to which a woman had no choice but to submit. Fathers and sons went to die on the battle fields, defending the honour of France. Theodore de Vilmorin, Guy's father, had lost an eye in the Great War at Verdun when three out of four of French soldiers had been killed. When the call-up came for another world war two decades later one-eyed men like Theodore had been spared.

Today something about the chateau, with its shuttered windows, looked inexplicably sad. For an instant Guy thought he detected movement across the chateau forecourt, but his view was blocked by the line of cypress trees running up to the gates. The once magnificent house seemed like a faded beauty gasping one last breath. He watched the sun's progress but had no sense of time.

A door banged and for a moment the faint sound of kitchen clatter and a woman's voice reached him through the closed door of his study. Nanette was going about her daily chores. Though she had not mentioned it the new kitchen maid was proving a bit of a handful. In his heart he knew that without Nanette's devotion he would have been utterly lost but to admit to it, face to face to his life-long maid, was simply not done.

At the other end of the hall the kitchen door opened and Biquette stood in the door looking disgruntled.

'You look just like your uncle Armand when you make that face,' Nanette scolded her. 'What is the matter?'

'I wanted to clean out the fireplaces.' Biquette dropped her metal bucket with a clang. A cloud of ash puffed up.

'Patience. You'll have to get used to how things are in this house,' said Nanette. 'You do the work when it suits Monsieur de Vilmorin, not when it suits you. This is not your house and you can't make the rules. Not even I can do that. I'm just … a maid, like you.'

'No, you're not.'

'What kind of tone is that, Biquette?

'I was just saying …,' Biquette tried to soften her tone. She was fond of Nanette, especially as uncle Armand had placed her to work for Nanette in the Vilmorin household when there was no work to be had in the entire village. 'You're the best thing in Monsieur's life since he sold the chateau.'

'Biquette!'

'He said you were a blessing, on the phone. I heard him, honest.'

'Have you been spying on Monsieur?'

'No. I was just … passing. Anyway, the whole village knows it's true.'

'Gossip, that's all it is, Biquette. And I'm sure he didn't mean it in the way you think.' Nanette turned away from the girl to hide her blushing. 'You can't go round repeating things. Try and learn that. You have no idea what Monsieur meant when he said that, do you hear?'

'Yes, Nanette,' Biquette conceded, 'but you're the only one who understands him. If he… if you…'

'No ifs, no buts, Biquette.' Nanette said. Her tone was sharper than she had intended. The girl's name was Brigitte but everyone called her Biquette, a nick name that had stuck since she was a toddler because she had a habit of kicking like a kid goat. She was fifteen now, going onto sixteen, but her temper had not changed.

'He's still in there, staring out of the window,' Biquette sulked, 'He's usually gone by now.'

'He has a lot of worries, especially now that Romain is back.'

Nanette began working the butter to soften it for the pastry. 'Didn't your uncle Armand tell you … about things? When I still lived … and worked at the chateau, things were different. Esmonde de Vilmorin, Guy's mother, you should have seen her. She was a fine lady. Guy's father lived in the past, in Napoleon's time for all we knew. He was revered by the villagers for his generosity, but he was always too severe with his own sons. He came to regret it. "It's his war wounds," Esmonde always said. I'll never know how she could forgive his unpredictable rages. You're a very lucky girl to be working in this nice house, or would you prefer washing the dishes at your uncle Armand's café?'

'Hum,' Biquette frowned. 'You told me you were allowed to do the library at the chateau when you were fourteen. Why can't I do that here?'

'Perhaps one day, when you've learnt to be a bit more careful. That library was ten times bigger than the one in this house,' Nanette added under her breath. 'Now go and finish in the salon and we'll decide what to do after that.'

Biquette picked up her bucket, pulled the kitchen door to and made her way along the hall. She halted a moment outside Vilmorin's study. No sound came from the room. After her conversation with Nanette she did not dare put her ear to the door. He was probably still at the window, gazing across to his former home. She avoided crossing paths with him. He seemed sullen and melancholy beyond all measure; everything seemed to darken when he appeared. Biquette had never set foot in the chateau, but her parents and grandparents' generation all had stories to tell about the Vilmorin family. Its enforced sale had dealt a blow to the fabric of the village community. The stranger had bought the great house before Biquette was born.

The kitchen door open again and Biquette's head appeared.

'I forgot. Uncle Armand said he needs to talk to Monsieur, before he opens the café. He'll be here soon.'

If only my mother or grandmother were here, Nanette wished, they would have known how to put everything right again. As it was her sense of loss simply festered on and had not lessened with the years.

Rose, Nanette's mother and her exotically named grandmother Amandine had spent their lives in the kitchen of the grand house across the vineyards. Nanette had practically been born beneath the gleaming copper pots dangling from high wooden bars. A vast cast-iron cooking range presided over the kitchen. The wide-hipped beast, ornamented with arabesques of ivy leaves, stood on bulbous claw feet. It spewed fire when a series of rings were removed to let the flames lick around the base of the saucepans. It had warmed the new-born Nanette as she lay swaddled on the kitchen bench near the range next to her mother who sat peeling the potatoes, watching that her precious bundle should not roll off the bench onto the hard stone floor. Ladles, knives and wooden spoons became more familiar to the little girl than her own dolls which sat forlorn on the square bed she shared with her sister Régine and her brothers François and little Henri sleeping at the foot of the bed. In her pre-school days Nanette roamed among the ample skirts of the kitchen maids going about their chores, all the while chattering like jackdaws. Every time the cook reached for the big meat cleaver, Nanette would scurry under the kitchen table, holding her ears shut while the woman's muscular arm cut through meat and bones with one mighty chop.

Her father, who was in charge of the horses and the stable boys, could rarely be found in the house, except for a drop of brandy in the kitchen on icy winter days when the master was out. When her grandmother Amandine 's body became stiff, when her feet refused to stand all day on the scrubbed kitchen flagstones, she had asked to be given the supervision of the potager, the kitchen garden which had supplied the family for generations with vegetables and herbs, winter and summer. Amandine knew everything there was to know about plants and under her orders it was one of the stable boys who did the heavy lifting and bending; the kitchen maids did the weeding

'You kill your servants with kindness,' Theodore de Vilmorin had grumbled, but his wife Esmonde would not be swayed. Amandine had been a vital part of her life since Esmonde had entered the chateau as a young, inexperienced bride. Amandine, with the dark, piercing eyes full of wisdom, had seen the young wife through difficult pregnancies, most of which had ended in miscarriages or stillbirths. Amandine alone was the reason why Guy, Esmonde's youngest son, had not succumbed to scarlet fever like his brother Hubert. Thanks to her there was a male heir to carry on the family name. The woman had done more to comfort Esmonde than her daughters who had married young and seemed too busy with their high society lives in Paris. Amandine, the sturdy country woman had an arsenal of herbal remedies, handed down from one generation to the next. She had healed Esmonde's body and soul from ailments no man could begin to grasp.

Nanette glanced at her assortment of herbs planted in long wooden troughs just outside the kitchen door. Not much compared to grandmother's herb garden at the chateau, she thought. Since Guy had lost the house, which had shaped his family's history, he led a lonely life. Nanette didn't cooked for more than three people, now that Romain was back from years in the sanatorium. When it came to Romain's reintegration into some sort of normal home life Nanette and the boy's father could only hope for a miracle.

Pictures from the past flashed by in her mind's eye and yet, that world lay in the far distance, hazy as distant trees in a foggy dawn, forever dissolving.

In the chateau kitchen the windows had almost reached from floor to ceiling. Their sills were as wide as child's cot, a space the little girl claimed as her own. When it was warm enough to throw the windows open Nanette often sat and watched her grandmother tend the kitchen garden. Bees hummed in the rows of calendulas, planted between the vegetables to ward off pests. Courgette Leaves, large as open umbrellas, barred Amandine's way. Tomatoes and peppers glowed like fiery red lanterns. Nanette would watch her grandmother move from plant to plant, filling her basket as she went, cutting and plucking with infinite delicacy, as if precious jewels were being gathered. The herbs were planted in squares and surrounded with short box hedging to protect them from the wind and scratching cats. Now and then, Amandine would rest on a low bench and contemplate the beauty around her which was entirely of her own creation.

A knock on the kitchen door interrupted Nanette's meanderings in her childhood memories.

'Can I come in?' Armand Arouet greeted her, kissed her on both cheeks twice. 'I need to see Guy,' he whispered in an urgent tone.

'He's still in his study. We can't disturb him until he decides to come out. Sit down. I'll make some coffee.'

Armand scratched his head. 'I must tell him ... things are going on ... I'll wait, but not forever. I have to open the café in an hour. How is Biquette settling in?'

'She's young, it's her first job. She needs to learn a little patience, but I'm glad I have someone to help me. Romain has been back for no more than a few days and there's trouble everyday. Guy is quite helpless when it comes to that boy. But please, Armand, don't go spreading it around and scare people.'

'I won't breathe a word,' Armand protested, '... just watch over Biquette, you can never know with someone disturbed like Romain.'

'She has nothing to do with Romain, she's not aloud upstairs on her own. Only Guy and I go to his room. When

89

we can't be with him we keep him there, except for supper. Biquette goes home before seven, he never sees her, so don't worry.'

They sat in silence for a moment, drinking their coffee.

'Something has to be done,' Nanette said quietly, 'something ....'

'Something is happening, over there. That's why I'm here.' Armand shifted forward on his chair, his face close to Nanette's. 'You and I, we grew up in a time when most masters knew almost nothing about their servants, except their function. To them a maid meant less than a piece of furniture. But the Vilmorins were an exception. They spoke about your grandmother, about your mother, and even about you, as if you were family. Of course,' he sat back and toyed with his keys, 'face to face they demanded the respect of being addressed properly. After all, most village families worked for them in some form or other. They were our employers, but in their hearts .... Even Guy, if he's so harsh to you these days, it's just to hide his feelings. He'd be lost without you. I wouldn't be surprised if ....'

'Armand. Don't talk such nonsense.' Nanette blushed to the roots of her hair. 'Guy has never said anything of the sort to me. What if Biquette hears you talk like that? Today's speculation is tomorrow's rumour and ... next it'll be in the gossip column of the newspapers.'

'I wouldn't dream of mentioning it to anyone, not even Marilou,' Armand protested.

Knowing Armand Nanette found that hard to believe. She got up from her chair and turned her back on him. She gazed out of the kitchen window without being able to focus on anything.

90

'You should be ashamed of yourself. Hasn't Guy suffered enough?'

'Precisely,' Armand said with an inflection which she understood only too well. She was glad he could not see the tears welling up in her eyes.

'The old man, he left for Paris yesterday, this morning suddenly he's back, and guess what? On the forecourt two huge ....'

A rattling against the kitchen door interrupted him in mid-flow. Biquette struggled in and put her bucket down in a corner.

'Look at the ash; so much, just from the salon. Monsieur must have had a bonfire in there last night.' She kissed Armand. 'Bonjour, Uncle.'

'Ashes were precious when I was a girl,' said Nanette. She took a tall glass from the shelf, poured a little grenadine sirup over a couple of slices of lemon and topped it up with water. 'Here, you must be thirsty.'

Biquette gulped the glowing red liquid down in one go.

'At night my mother and my grandmother used to cover the kitchen garden with nets against the rabbits,' Nanette continued as she sat back down opposite Armand, 'but the slugs could still get in. My grandmother made us collect the ash from all the fireplaces and sift it. Some of the fireplaces were huge; they could have been home for a whole family,' Nanette laughed. 'I had to spread the ash around the edge of the vegetable plot and in the mornings the slugs sat on the grey dust like tiny stranded boats. They couldn't move on the powdery surface. Guy and his brother Hubert used to throw them over the fence to the chickens. It was disgusting but the chickens grew fat and juicy.'

Armand shook his head. 'Biquette doesn't know what life was like for children then.' He turned to his niece. 'Nanette was only five, but her grandmother made her watch the herb garden all day sometimes to shoo away the cats. She gave her a palm leaf to swish across their backs, remember, Nanette?'

'My grandmother joked that she would put the cats' doings into my salad if I let them into the kitchen garden.' She grimaced. 'I was absolutely terrified. I didn't want to eat salad unless I had searched through it on my plate.'

'Ah, your mother, and your grandmother - some women they were.' Armand said with a nostalgic smile. 'Winter or summer, your grandmother always had a flower in her hair. They belonged to that grand house as much as the Vilmorins.'

Biquette's lips had turned ruby red from the juice. 'I didn't know Monsieur has a brother.'

'He did have a brother, once,' Nanette said after a while. 'Both boys fell ill with scarlet fever. They were in quarantine for more than six weeks at the top of the house. Hubert died one night, Guy didn't. Afterwards all the bedding and the curtains from that room were burned. Poor Esmonde, she never recovered from the loss of Hubert. Guy was very weak and pale for a long time after the illness.'

'He's not weak or pale now, but he's still in pain from his divorce. And now Romain brings it all back to him.' Armand scratched his head. 'If you ask me though, those troubles are as nothing compared to how he feels about losing his family's heritage, even now.'

Biquette was sucking on the rim of her empty glass. 'Why didn't they take the sick boys to hospital?'

92

'Things were different then, Biquette,' said Armand. 'They had a full-time nurse, the doctor came everyday. People only went to hospital if they were dying. Hubert died, suddenly.'

'He seemed to be pulling through and the next morning …,' Nanette sighed. 'While the boys were ill Esmonde put me on slug duty. It was revolting. I had to close my eyes when I threw them over the fence and when I looked most of them were caught up in the wire and writhing around.' She shuddered at the memory.

Armand smiled and whispered to Biquette. 'All the boys in school knew Nanette hated slugs, so one day they put one down the back of her dress and she ran around like possessed until the teacher found out. Because I was laughing loudest the headmaster thought it was me, so I got punished. Nanette was only eight or nine and I was nearly fourteen. She was a pretty little thing. All the boys had their eye on her when she got older.'

Nanette blushed. Biquette looked puzzled.

'So why didn't you get married then?'

'Don't be indiscreet,' Armand scolded the Biquette.

Nanette gave a wave of the hand. 'No, it doesn't matter,' she turned to the girl, 'I worked at the chateau along with my grandmother and my mother. Amandine's and Rose's duty was to Esmonde and Theodore; then it was my turn. After my mother had to go … after Guy married Elianne my mother's life was made hell. When she went to live in the village, my job was to look after Guy.'

Biquette's lower lip curled. She seemed unconvinced.

'That's the way it's been with all the Vilmorin's. My family has been with them since before the Revolution, if not

93

longer. Now I also have Romain to look after. That's why you're here.' She stood up and cleared the coffee cups from the table. 'Biquette, now go and see if Monsieur has finished his contemplation. And tell him Armand needs to speak with him. Say it's urgent. Your uncle can't sit around here all day.'

'I'm sorry I can't give her better work,' Nanette apologised to Armand after Biquette had left the kitchen. 'When things have settled I'll teach her how to cook.'

'She's only fifteen; she'll survive,' Armand smiled. 'Old Madame de Vilmorin was always very good to you when you were that age.'

When Nanette was fourteen, on the day after leaving the village school, a frail Esmonde had summoned her to the study. Although Theodore had been dead for two years she still wore her black mourning clothes. A gentle smile came to her bloodless lips at the sight of the girl.

'How you have grown, Nanette,' she remarked in a brittle voice, 'for a moment I thought it was your mother Rose.'

Esmonde noted that Nanette's black hair, wild and wiry like her grandmother's, had been tamed in a single thick plait and neatly tied with a green ribbon. This was surely Amandine's doing. Esmonde was surprised by the shapeliness of the girl's waist and legs. No doubt before long she would turn the heads of the stable boys and grooms, as her mother Rose had done. Times had changed and Esmonde was all too aware that Nanette might not feel duty-bound to remain with the Vilmorin family, as Rose had done after Nanette's father had died, crushed by an angry bull. It was too much to expect of the younger generations.

That day Nanette had stood in the old lady's study with her hands behind her back, nervously twisting her green summer cardigan which she had removed before entering. She was overawed by the beauty of Esmonde's chairs, by the fine rugs underfoot, by the paintings on the walls. Nanette had never seen this room. On one side of it shelves were stacked to the ceiling with dark leather-bound books. Esmonde followed Nanette's astonished gaze.

'Have you learnt how to read properly in school?'

'Oui, Madame,' Nanette whispered. She hesitated. 'It was my favourite lesson.'

'Good. It is a precious thing to have a passion for such a thing at your age. You will like the work I shall give you then. From now on you will dust the library every day. It is a big job, and an important one.' Guy's mother was sitting with a carriage shawl draped over her legs. There was a ripple between her feet, then stillness, followed by a rolling in the hem of Esmonde's shawl. A dark brown tail, a tiny paw emerged, followed by two dark brown noses. Two pairs of sky blue eyes looked at Nanette.

'Shush,' scolded Esmond as she tapped on her knee. Two tiny kittens appeared. She picked them up and placed them in her lap.

'This is Napoleon and Josephine, Nanette.' Esmonde stroked their light coloured bodies. 'They are Siamese. You like cats, don't you? Perhaps you'll have to look after them after I'm gone.'

'Madame,' Nanette remonstrated, but Esmonde cut her short with a wave of the hand. 'In the meantime don't forget the slugs. I see you have mastered the art of feeding them to the chickens.'

Guy had gone to study at university. How did Esmonde know what she did with the slugs? Nanette looked down at her feet. Her shoes were smeared with streaks of mud from watering Amandine's herb garden. And now they stood on Madame's silk rug. Nanette quickly let her cardigan drop onto them. How could she have forgotten to polish her shoes?

Esmonde did not look down where the crumpled cardigan now lay. 'You may go,' she said quietly, 'but be sure to always go into the library with clean shoes.'

'Oui, Madame,' whispered Nanette. Her cheeks were on fire as she ran out of the room.

Rose had been proud to see her daughter put to work in the library. 'You'll get an education in there, if you pay attention to the books.'

For a fourteen year-old girl the dusting of the books had been a light but painstaking task. The leather-bound volumes with their cream coloured pages attracted dust like no other thing Nanette knew. Often, when her eyes were itching from the dust as she twirled her feather duster over the top of the fine volumes, when her hands ached from rubbing bees' wax into the seemingly endless rosewood cabinets, a book would beckon. She would open it with trembling fingers, terrified of being caught. People like her had no business becoming learned by sticking their noses into the books of their masters. The wisdom of village people accumulated over the years through the hard knocks life dished out to them. Then they were old, worn out from a lifetime of manual work, with gnarled knuckles and faces like ancient tree trunks. They were left to huddle together on a bench in the village square, like black crows on a fence, talking wisely and shaking their heads in unison at the incomprehensible, new-fangled ways of the young.

Biquette was back.

'He's out,' she sighed and made a sign with her thumb as though she was trying to hitch a lift. 'Sorry, Nanette,' she apologised for the disrespectful gesture, 'Monsieur has come out, Uncle Armand. He says he'll see you on the terrace. He wants coffee. At least I can get on with his study now.' She searched for polish and duster in the corner cleaning cupboard and picked up the ash bucket. Through the half open door she watched Armand walk down the hall.

'What has my uncle got to say to Monsieur that's so urgent? I bet he's up to something, drives Aunt Marilou mad with all his secrets,' she whispered.

'None of your business,' Nanette reprimanded her, 'and don't you ever dare listen in on Monsieur's conversations again, do you hear?'

Biquette cheeks flushed pink. 'I won't, promise, but Uncle Armand is up to something, Aunt Marilou told me. He's always hatching one scheme or another.'

'That's because your uncle is a very clever man. He's wasted on that café with nothing to do all day. He would have made a good policeman. Enough talk now, Biquette. I've got an onion tart to make.'

As the girl stepped into the hall Armand pushed the frosted glass door to the terrace shut. On her way to Vilmorin's study she could hear the two men's low voices. She had to keep her promise to Nanette that she would not listen at doors.

If it wasn't for books I wouldn't have known what to do with my life all these years, Nanette mused. Her work in the chateau library as a young girl had turned her into an avid reader. The house had been silent one morning. Esmonde de Vilmorin had gone to shop in Toulouse. Only a fat fly had buzzed somewhere high up on the library window. How come I can remember a fly after all this time when I have trouble remembering my mother's face? The irony of it brought tears to her eyes.

After just a few days of dusting that awe-inspiring library, she had prised out a hand-sized book nestling between two thick faded tomes. She had waited for this opportunity. She could not tell why this thin spine was calling to her. She stood, half way up the library steps, mesmerised. Carefully she leafed through the tiny volume. The paper felt like starched linen to the touch. Heavily gilded letters with endless scrolls started each piece of text. There were pictures in brilliant colours, some covered a whole page. Tiny figures in angular postures laboured in meadows and fields, wielding scythes and sickles. They were gathering the harvest. She turned the pages, hardly daring to breathe on the fragile object in her hands. Another image showed men bowed down in a large garden, planting tender seedlings in neat rows. Standing in the foreground were three women. Their gowns were encrusted with gold embroidery, dainty crowns glowed in their hair. Nanette wondered at the incongruity of their attire amidst the men and women working the land in clothes made of sacking.

The cover of the book was made of soft leather and had a minute golden lock, but no key. She had never seen such a beautiful thing. Intricate letters were embossed into the surface honey-coloured leather. Gold highlights glinted in the half light of the library. After a few minutes she deciphered the title: Book of Hours. It had been made for a young noblewoman. The letters of the name had become illegible, erased by the hands that had consulted it on a daily basis at prayer time. She tried to slip it back into the narrow gap but something at the back was blocking the space. She removed a book on either side to retrieve whatever had become wedged. It was a slim volume, a common note book. Its cover of marbled paper was bleached and water-stained. On the first page the date of 1789 was inscribed in a shaky, unsophisticated hand.

> *A terrible fate has befallen my master's daughter,*
> *Mademoiselle Milena. Now that the house is quiet*
> *again I will record what I learned so that one day*
> *the people of Noirlac will know what happened.*

Nanette had never heard of a girl called Milena. She resolved to ask her grandmother Amandine. She turned to the next page:

> *My name is Antoine. For these last thirty years and*
> *more I have been head gardener of the chateau of*
> *Noyrlac. I swear this to be a true account.*
> *Demoiselle Milena Léanore de Vilmorin, twelve*
> *years of age, only daughter of the Comte de*
> *Vilmorin, was married to the Marquis de Pourtales*
> *on the 1st of May 1788.*
> *Three weeks after the lavish wedding, during the*
> *night of the 21st of May, a very young woman was*
> *thrown ...*

Footsteps were approaching in the hall. Nanette had quickly squeezed both of the small volumes into the gap on the shelf, pushing them well to the back. She had discovered a secret; she trembled. Never, ever again will I go prying, she silently promised. Behind her, her mother Rose had appeared in the door, come to call Nanette to lunch.

Nanette had kept her promise but the memory of the secret notebook still made her feel uneasy. At the far end of the hall Biquette was closing Vilmorin's study door. How different her own life had been at the age of fourteen to Biquette's existence today.

'Biquette,' Nanette called into the hall. 'The sheets were dry. I brought them in this morning. When you're done upstairs they need ironing.'

'Oui, Nanette,' came the girls echoing reply. It would be a while before Biquette would know what to do without being told every single thing. The world had changed; girls were no longer in service, a part of their master's household. Today, everything was just a job.

On a winter's day, when Nanette was barely older than Biquette's and she had quietly gone about her business of dusting and polishing in Esmonde's library, everything had changed. For weeks the air in the chateau had been icy as glass. The heat from the many fireplaces was losing the battle against the dropping temperatures; the cold from outside seemed to have pushed through the thick walls, instantly freezing anyone who happened to stand anywhere near them. Esmonde had fallen ill. A chill had escalated into severe bronchitis which left her gasping for breath. Just a few days later her sudden death from pneumonia drained the house of its spirit.

The intricate web of family and traditions that had held everything together broke. It blew away on the wind of change, its filaments disintegrating with a powerless, parting gesture. Four weeks passed. On a Saturday night, Amandine went to bed and could not be woken on Sunday morning. Rose and Nanette found her on her bed, fully dressed, with a flower in her hair and her hands folded, ready for Sunday church.

Guy had returned from his military service. His mother's death had changed him. He became dur and distant and was frequently absent from the house. Apart from the cook, a young maid, the gardener and stable boys, there was only Nanette and her mother Rose to care for the house. It wasn't long before Guy married Elianne.

'Sainte Marie, petit Jésus,' Nanette had prayed, hands clasped and elbows digging into the edge of her narrow bed. 'Sainted Virgin, why? What has happened to Guy?' Why had everything changed so? She was the same, or so she thought, but she hardly recognised her mother Rose.

With the arrival of Guy's new wife her mother had turned into a cowed and timid woman, no longer sure of how and why this or that had to be done in the house. Nothing she did seemed to please her new mistress. Now it was as if the house itself had become sullen, hell-bent on resisting the newcomer with her sharp-tongued, impatient orders and her obsession of dominating the servants. They had always known what had to be done and when, without prompting from Esmonde. They had been trusted, but now their diligence was held against them.

The intertwining over generations of the Vilmorin family with Amandine, Rose and now Nanette had been like a red rag to Elianne; her jealousy seeped into the fabric of the house. The air became charged with venom when the clicking of her high heels approached.

Nanette could not recall seeing Guy in the company of a single woman since his acrimonious divorce from Elianne. Had the experience of his ill-fated marriage turned him against women altogether?

Nanette stopped working the pastry. She opened the kitchen window and listened. She could hear Guy and Armand talking hurriedly in low tones on the terrace. Perhaps the girl was right; what was Armand up to?

Something brushed against Nanette's leg. She bent down and stroked the slate coloured cat fixing her expectantly with its bright yellow eyes. Her hands left a dusting of white flour on the dark fur.

'I suppose you've come in for the warmth,' she berated the animal. 'You don't know how lucky you are to be living here with us.' She went over to the sink, retrieved a metal dish, poured a little cream into it and set it down for the cat.

How strange it was to remember the smallest details from her girlhood now. There were cat people and dog people. How Guy's mother had loved her two Siamese cats. Guy's wife Elianne was a dog person.

'Guy, those slant-eyed Siamese beasts must go,' she had commanded soon after her arrival at the chateau. 'I hate the way they sit like statues and stare at me with their blue eyes. They would tear me to shreds if they could.'

On Elianne's orders there followed a frenzied rearrangement of all furniture and paintings in the house.

Guy seemed besotted with his new wife and indulged her every whim. It wasn't long before Rose and Esmonde's beloved cats went to live in Noirlac village with Nanette's ageing aunt. Nanette stood crying at the gates, watching her mother walk away from the chateau which had been her home. Under each arm she was clutching one of the sleek animals. Marco, the stable boy followed, pulling a handcart with Rose's few possessions. Elianne stood at the kitchen window, triumphant.

'One less of them in the house,' the cook heard her whisper, 'one more to go.'

On Guy's orders Rose was to be kept on as a daily help, living in the village and coming in every morning.

'But keep a little out of Elianne's way,' Guy instructed Rose with an embarrassed air, 'it's hard for her to settled into life in the country.'

Elianne bought a pair of Borzoi dogs. 'Look at their elegance,' she gushed, 'only the Russians can produce such grace. Diaghilev and Nijinsky, that's what I shall call them.'

They grew and grew; their white lean bodies floated around the house with eyes following the servants' every move as though they had been trained for it. Deposits of their long fur clung to the precious fabrics around the house. They lay wherever they pleased, taking up most of the floor space in a room. If Nanette tried to move them a low growl warned her to desist.

'Clean the room when they've gone,' instructed Elianne.

Out of Elianne's earshot Rose despaired. 'Soon they'll be lying in the beds and ringing the servant's bell.'

After a year the dogs had grown tall and long. Raised on their hind legs they stood taller than Nanette. Elianne petted them like babies, fed them choice pieces of the finest pork filet and sirloin steak. She had her portrait painted with the dogs by her side and had the picture hung on the half-landing facing the main entrance; it was the first thing anyone stepping into the hall would see. Soon she tired of the dogs, leaving them to the care of Marco, the stable boy. Banished to the stable block, their pining could be heard for weeks.

Elianne returned one day clutching a minute Yorkshire terrier no larger than an evening bag.

'So much better for travelling,' she had announced as she got out of the car, kissing and petting the hairy bundle, talking to it in a kind of baby talk. Marco and Nanette stood aside and stared after her. Neither could understand how this woman could switch her affections from one pet to another on a whim.

'Stick a handle on that new dog and you can use it as a mop,' Marco whispered. Nanette turned and went over to the two Borzois fenced in next to the stables to prevent them from entering the house. Their anguish had made them haggard; their fur looked dull despite Marco's constant care. The two dogs stood and their eyes followed their mistress's every move. Elianne's cold stare met their gaze and Nanette and the dogs knew that the same fate had befallen all of them.

With the birth of two boys in quick succession everyone had hoped that things would settle down. Nanette had remained at the chateau for Guy's sake. One day he would understand that the only life, the only happiness for him lay with his own people, within the chateau walls. Perhaps then he would make things right again.

Nanette scattered the flour on the pastry board. She spread her hands, silken from the flour, feeling the cool wood under her palms. Why was she always raking up her past? It caused her nothing but pain.

Guy's mother, Esmonde, had loved her orchard. During the endless summers mirabelles, plums and Morello cherries hung in such masses from the fragile branches that all the servants and their children were put to work in an effort to pick the fruit before the summer thunder storms. By the end of the day the acid bit into their fingers, the nails turning soft as rubber. The reward for the hard work stood on long garden benches. Piles of buttery madeleines sat beside jugs of grenadine mixed with water and lemons slices. The jugs glowed bright red in the dappled summer light.

On the next day the harvest had to be processed quickly. Women and children sat in the shade of the fig trees and stoned the ripe fruit. Meanwhile in the kitchen the cook and one of the kitchen maids fired up the big range to begin the boiling of jams, compotes and jellies. Earthenware pots stood in line, prepared with herbs and spices, waiting for the fruit which would turn into wine by the time winter came.

'Don't drink after eating the fruit, 'or you'll spend tomorrow in the *cabinet*.' Water drunk with cherries or plums caused terrifying belly cramps. Each summer Amandine warned the children who ate as many plums and cherries as they stoned. The *cabinet* was the outdoor privy by the men-servants' house next to the stables. The men's house had no bathroom, nor did it have a flushing toilet like the chateau. Despite the warning each year the long hours of picking the fruit in the scorching sun made the children forget the belly cramps suffered the previous year. After climbing down from the trees they quenched their thirst and hoped that this time they would be spared.

'Maman, ' Nanette would cry at the end of the afternoon, as she bent over in agony.

'That'll teach you,' came Rose's reprimand. But grandmother Amandine would pick her up, carry her down to the little wooden hut. When the cramps struck in the orchard, there was no time to run to the servant's toilets in the main house.

Her grandmother would plant a kiss on Nanette's sweating forehead.

'I'll bring you a hot water bottle for your aching belly.'

Sitting locked in the cramped wooden hut on a rough wooden seat laid over a stinking pit, Nanette was convinced that all the devils of hell lived down there. She imagined dozens of them dancing below, with tiny flickering flames shooting from their eyes, waiting for her to tip backwards into the heap of excrement where each devil would stick his red hot fork into her tender flesh.

At other times her mother Rose had thought it wise to chase the children down to play in the wild-flower meadow beyond the mimosas where Esmonde and Theodore Vilmorin could not hear their playful squeals. There they ran wild, away from the chateau, down the steep incline towards mysterious lake surrounded by willows and reeds. In the stillness of the sunset hour, a deep-throated toad concert began, then ceased abruptly when the hidden creatures felt the tremor of approaching footsteps. The children would stop and stand in silence for a few minutes, waiting for the throaty trilling to restart. They never laid eyes on the toads.

The croaking was so loud that in their imagination these sounds could only come from a beast as large as a pig, with a monstrous gaping mouth, a slimy skin full of warts and bulging mustard-coloured eyes that the Devil himself might have planted to crown his creation. The boys frightened the girls by telling tales of long frogs' tongues that could lash out from beneath the water with lightning speed, wind themselves around ankles and pull a grown man into the unfathomable watery grave, never to be seen again. 'The lake is full of skeletons, drifting in the weeds,' they claimed.

Listening to the boys Nanette would shiver in fear despite the summer's heat as they lay on the warm ground, chewing on stalks of grass. Images of silent bodies in the depth of the lake pursued her, of skeletons layered on top of each other, having had their life-blood sucked out of them by the hellish creatures.

Nanette rolled out the pastry. The kitchen suddenly seemed cold; a draft played around her bare ankles. The grey cat had wandered off. She opened the hatch of the range and stoked up the fire. She would have to add some coal to build enough heat for the baking.

She felt guilty. Why did she let her past cling to her like a second skin?

She had a lot to be grateful for. No one ill-treated her since Elianne's departure and Guy's move to the Esperou bastide. She had a room with a private bathroom, she had enough to eat. Guy paid her a wage which afforded her the odd new dress and pair of shoes; she could borrow any book she wanted from his library. She had even bought her very

107

own books, though with their soft and often garish covers they bore no resemblance to Guy's beautiful volumes.

From her window she had a view onto the village church with its graveyard where her mother Rose, grandmother Amandine and all her family down the centuries had been laid to rest.

When she looked in the mirror at her face her olive skin showed barely a wrinkle. People in the village often said she still looked like a girl. Would the tell-tale signs of middle age come upon her and put an end to all her hopes?

Questions, always the nagging questions that wouldn't go away.

'Wipe it all away,' she mumbled to herself as she placed the coal on the fire, 'and everything will be better.' In a flash the face of little Henri leapt into her mind. The shock made her flop down on the nearest chair. Her hands fell into her lap.

Henri was her youngest brother. They had been playing hide and seek and it was her big sister Régine's turn to find Nanette, her younger brother François and five year-old Henri. Régine had found François among the wild laurel bushes. Nanette had been discovered in the long grass by the boundary wall. Only Henri remained to be found. After a while the three children began calling, loud, then louder, but no reply came. They started to run, criss-crossing the meadow towards the shallow end of the lake.

'Here,' François yelled, ' look, he's hiding in the reeds. Come out, Henri, I know you're in there, I can see your feet.'

108

They followed the narrow trail of down-trodden reeds. Water began to squelch underfoot. Then they saw him, lying motionless in the pooling water. François lifted him, Régine dragged him onto the grass by his arms and Nanette ran screaming for their mother. Rose pumped Henri's chest repeatedly with her knee resting on his stomach. There was a splatter and a cough. Henri had been saved.

But there was another memory. It sat in a dark corner, in the way spiders roll up into a black ball, not moving and yet ready to spring. It was the memory of Henri's words that night in the bedroom by the flicker of candlelight. That night Nanette had gone to Henri's bedside to kiss him good night.

'Did you say your prayers, Henri? The Holy Virgin Mary saved your life today.'

'Yes,' he replied solemnly. He reached for her hand. 'There was a ghost in the water,' he whispered.

'Don't be silly, Henri.'

'There was!' He was vexed. 'It was a lady. She told me to go with her.'

Nanette kissed his forehead. 'That'll teach you to go near the lake by yourself then.' She decided not to tell her mother what Henri had said. Rose had had enough of a shock for one day.

Nanette shook her head. The fine flour that had caught in her hair swirled and settled on her eye lashes. She hadn't thought of Henri for a long time. He lived a busy city life and rarely saw the need to return to his roots. Here in the Esperou house Nanette's attention had to focus on Guy and now on Romain. After two decades in the care of doctors he seemed as disturbed as ever.

She hadn't made a pissaladière for a long time. It was an easy dish to make. Today the savoury red onion tart was for Romain who loved the sweet caramelised flavour of these onions.

Nanette lifted the thin rectangle of buttery pastry onto the greased backing tray. With her thumb she made small indentations all along the rim to form a decorative pattern and spread the softened, almost transparent onions onto the pastry. Cutting wafer-thin strips of the remaining pastry, she laid them in criss-cross fashion to form a lattice pattern. She stood back. It was perfect. She placed a black olive in the centre of each lozenge-shaped gap and curled an anchovy around it. A blast of heat scorched her eyes as she quickly slid the tray into the oven.

She heard footsteps approaching from the terrace.

'Nanette,' Armand called from the hall as he passed by the kitchen door, 'I've got to run,' and she heard the front door fall shut. She now had twenty minutes to wake Romain, to coax him gently out of bed, help him with his clothes and give him a little of the warmth and attention he had so sadly lacked all these years.

The old wooden steps creaked as she made her way to the first floor. She counted. The third and the fifth let out a chilling groan, resounding in the hollow space beneath her feet. She had found Romain hiding under the stairs a couple of times in the last few days. He had sat in the dark with his knees pulled up tight, as if someone had put him there as a punishment.

The stairs still smelt of the sweet bees' wax she had rubbed into them last week. Biquette would only have to dust them tomorrow.

She fished for the key to Romain's room. It had dangled on a red ribbon inside her cleavage ever since Romain's return. It was warm and damp from the heat in the kitchen. For a moment her fingers rested between her breasts. It was a long time since she had felt the hand of a man on her skin. A feeling of utter loneliness came over her.

The key half turned in the lock with a crunch and the door popped open. The window was wide open but the room smelled stale. Outside sunlight burst through clouds, bulging over the vineyards that encircled the village of Noirlac.

'God is blessing our land,' her grandmother always said. As a girl Nanette had stood in awe of the heavenly light show. Today there would be a thunder storm before the day was out.

'Romain', she called in a soft voice.'

There was a clatter in the room above Guy Vilmorin's study, then feet running down the stairs.

Monsieur, Monsieur.' Nanette gasped.

'What is it?' Irritation and resignation collided in his tone.

'Monsieur,' Nanette half swallowed her words, 'he's gone. Romain. He's not in his room, his bed and …'

Vilmorin turned. He was standing with his back against the light and she could not see his eyes.

'How did he get out?' he asked in a severe tone, as if his son's escape were her fault. 'Did they teach them to pick locks at the sanatorium?'

'I couldn't say, Monsieur.' A bright red flush rose from her throat to her cheeks. 'I swear on my mother's life the door was locked after I took him his drink.'

'Your mother died three years ago,' Guy Vilmorin said cruelly. 'Mon Dieu, Nanette. Rose, your mother is dead. If you're going to swear then swear on her grave.'

He walked past her and she trotted after him, up the stairs and along the upper hall. He examined the door lock to Romain's room.

'It's been jammed, there, with a little stone, just enough to push it open with a knife.' He turned on her. 'I thought he was not to have knives?'

'Non, Monsieur.'

He left her battling with her tears as he walked across the room. The bed was untouched. Three neat piles of clothing sat on the floor next to the fireplace. Vilmorin picked up a flowery silk shirt.

'What's this?'

'I don't know, Monsieur, I've never seen these before.' She carefully lifted the items one by one. 'They're not his. These are all womens' clothes.'

Vilmorin turned away and made for the door. 'Whatever next,' he grumbled.

Nanette stood transfixed and listened to the echoes of his steps stabbing the polished parquet, down the stairs, across the flag-stoned hall, then the slamming of the front door. She stepped out of the room. The smoke of burnt pastry curled up from the kitchen below.

*

Still, an animal gone to ground

18

Noirlac Village, same day

Armand Arouet crossed the road and stuffed what was left of his crushed chair into the communal rubbish container under the old plane trees on the street corner. He was fuming under his dapper moustache. He wiped his hands on his long apron and examined the damaged sign above the door.

'Damned foreigners,' he cursed, 'let the devil take them.' He went to the back of the café and brought out another chair and placed it on the dusty pavement. He waved to the house opposite from which Paul Airvolt had emerged.

Armand pointed. 'Did you see that?'
Paul made a fatalistic gesture with one hand, keeping the other one in the pocket of his greasy work overalls. A number of ugly parallel scrapes now ran horizontally across the centre of Armand's sign. Parts of the letters were missing and it now read CAT TAPA.

'I'll have to repaint the lot. Merde. 'Armand fiddled with the extremities of his moustache, as if to tear it off in frustration. 'I've no talent for sign writing.'

'How can people have so much furniture?' Paul crossed the road, followed by the mongrel with the carrot coloured fur. Even though the village street was entirely empty both men looked around, as if someone could overhear them. 'Do you know, my grandmother had one spoon, one fork, one knife when she was a widow and lived on her own. And only one single needle to do her mending.' Paul followed his friend into the café and went to sit at the bar. Armand poured two Ricards. There was no more to be said. They emptied their glasses. Paul slid down from the bar stool and stretched his legs. He reached across the counter and patted Armand on the shoulder in a gesture of friendly consolation.

'That's life,' mon vieux. Allez, let's go, Zozo,' he called to his dog. 'We're going for a walk now. Don't worry, I'll help you with your sign.' He turned and went on his way, the dog trailing behind him.

The dog had picked up a scent at the bottom of the chateau wall and turned the corner long before Paul. Tiny yellow flowers shone in lush, perfectly rounded clumps along the side of the road. The trees lining the road would be in leaf in a few days. Somehow they never really died off over the winter. No sooner had the leaves dropped off the plane trees than the fat buds reappeared and burst open.

Paul's gaze vaguely followed the ditches and the new growth. Ahead a dark shape moved in the middle of the road. Paul was increasingly short sighted; in recent years he had abandoned his glasses and only wore them for reading the daily paper at Armand's café. His pace quickened and as the shape came into focus he realised it was a man sitting on the tarmac. It was a young man and his wet hair was stuck to his forehead. A deep and bloody scratch ran across his right cheek. The front of his shirt and trousers were covered in soil, as if he had romped across a muddy field. He looked like a lost child. There was something familiar about the face, but Paul could not place it.

'Allez.' He grabbed the young man under the arms and dragged him to safety onto the grass verge.

The dog looked on, yapping now and then and sniffing the damp mud on the stranger's clothing, wagging his tail and licking the stranger's face.

'Hum,' Paul scratched the back of his head hard so that his beret moved back and forth. 'Do you know him, Zozo? Come on, you sit with him. Sit.' He ordered the dog to remain by the side of the young man. Then he ran as best as his ill-fitting boots allowed to fetch Armand.

Armand's old Citroen 2CV jogged to a halt. Paul struggled to remove an old blanket which covered the torn back seat of the car.

'Here, Armand, put that round him or he'll catch pneumonia.'

Armand bent down to inspect Paul's find.

'Do you know him, Armand?'

'Romain?' Armand gently touched the young man's shoulder.

'Is that Vilmorin's boy?' Paul looked puzzled. 'I thought he had been sent away, to the crazy house.'

'I went to see Guy … about something. He asked me not to tell anyone. Look at him. He's like a child. He's grown but the eyes are the same still.' Armand shook the youth by the arm. 'Romain?'

Romain looked up at the two men standing over him. His eyebrows were dark and well-shaped and knitted in the middle, but the eyes, large and trusting were those of a wounded child.

*

Let come what comes

19

Noirlac village Café, same day

'What do you suppose the row was about the other day, Popol, over there, at the chateau?' Armand wiped his shiny counter in agitation. His cigarette hung from his lower lip and he had all but forgotten it. His curiosity had been stung; there was detective work to be done.

'God knows.' Paul tried to hoist himself up onto the barstool. He was too short to perch on it and nonchalantly keep one foot on the ground all at the same time. He was badly shaven. His hands were callused, despite the fact that he had stopped working the vineyards years ago. Instead he spent a lot of time pottering in his garden. After his back fence had blown down, with a little encouragement on his part, he had dug a meter at a time, closer and closer to the chateau wall, mostly at nightfall. It had taken years, but in the end he had annexed the piece of ground which ran between Augusto's wall and his own modest property. No one came this way; if the chateau was ever sold the new owners would never know. Now his garden ended with the chateau wall which was home to his tomatoes and grapes. In the centre of the wall stood the cherry tree which had grown profusely in the shelter of the sunny wall.

'They had a blazing row, last week,' Paul gazed out at the deserted village street, 'Monsieur Augusto and Madame. The windows were open, it was so warm that night. In all the years they've been here, I'd never heard them fight.' He ran a dirty sleeve over his mouth.

'I'm sitting on the old man's bill for his papers and cigars,' Armand frowned, 'hasn't paid for months. What is it with rich people?' He wiped his sweaty brow with the red and white checked dish cloth and tucked it into his belt. 'Where do they get the money for the grand things in life but never bother to pay for the small ones?'

Paul laughed. 'You know what they say about the Queen of England. Never carries a penny.'

Armand mechanically carried on polishing the same spot on the counter. 'He sends the red-haired girl down most days.'

'Clever,' Paul grinned, 'he knows you can't say no to her. One look of her big green eyes and you turn to jelly.'

Armand looked over his shoulder towards the door leading into the kitchen. He leaned close to Paul. 'That girl is enough to get any man going. Just imagine what's beneath those plain frocks she wears. If I were the mistress of the house,' his eyebrows rose in a perilous arc, 'I would definitely not expose my husband to a maid like that. Marilou never liked her, but then,' he winked and checked the kitchen door again, 'she is the jealous type. She'll be like that when we're a hundred and five years old.' He shook with suppressed laughter. Ash from his extinguished cigarette rained down. He gathered it up with his cupped hand and began re-polishing the gleaming counter.

Paul nodded philosophically and peered into his glass, disappointed to find it empty.

Armand's wife, Marilou, was not the usual kind of village woman. She was born just down the hill from the café run by Armand's father. Marie-Louise, as she had been christened, was not a country name in those days. It was a name one could find in towns, in the rambling villas which stood in gardens with tall trees, high-ceilinged rooms, servant's entrances, with a gardener and at least one maid and cook. The 'banlieue aisée', the comfortable suburb they called it, almost as if some lucky children were eased into their privileged existence.

'Suburbs,' Jono, the middle-aged English musician had laughed. He had bought a village house to live out the years of his declining fame. His rant about the differences between England and France had become part of the evenings entertainment for many of Armand's regulars. As on most evenings Jono had clung to Armand's bar in his habitual inebriated state.

'Suburbs, suburbs, suburbs,' Jono drawled after emptying a bottle of whisky, now nursing a cognac, 'suburbs are bad places in England. 'Terrrrible,' he emphasised in French, exaggerating the French R in the wrong place in his throat. 'It's where they re-house people who can't afford to live in the cities in streets where the nice people buy houses.

119

They've stacked the 'not-nice-people' high into the sky, *dans les petits cartons,* in vertical egg boxes. The poor have no right to ground space.' Unlike in France, he said, land was scarce in England. Armand didn't want to contradict Jono's idea of France being the perfect country. In the big cities in France the same thing had happened. The poor, the maladjusted, the immigrants who couldn't or wouldn't integrate, the long-term unemployed, they all had to have a roof over their heads. Armand was often the first to spew vitriolic criticism about the government, but he would not do so in the presence of 'les étrangers'. France's honour would not be blackened in front of foreigners, neither by Armand nor by most other rural French who were passionatly protective of their origins.

'They've stopped making land,' Jono giggled in his drunken stupor.

'Ah, the famous English humour.' Armand feigned a laugh at Jono's joke. 'The client is always right,' he winked at the village men sitting at the far end of the bar.

Throughout the long summers Jono seemed to have a ready supply of English blondes, most were half his age or less. At first the villagers thought they were his daughters. They appeared at the end of June; when September came they disappeared overnight. For a few weeks Jono got a bit of sex out of it, the girls got a free holiday, or so some in the village speculated.

With Armand and Marie-Louise it had been so different. She was fourteen, Armand sixteen when they fell in love. Her father worked in a cognac distillery. Armand was taller than the other village boys, with brawny arms from humping his father's wine barrels from the delivery vans into the café cellar. His hair was shiny and thick and the village girls competed for a glance of his dark eyes. He was a good catch, with a 'situation', a job for life lined up for him when he would take over from his father. The other village girls were named Huguette, Georgette, Pierrette or Marguerite, good old country names. Marie-Louise was only one step removed from Marie-Antoinette. It was clear that by christening their girl Marie-Louise she would be destined for better things than milking goats and shooing the sheep and geese up the village street. Naming a girl Marie-Antoinette remained out of bounds. When that name was mentioned the rush of the sharp guillotine blade still resounded in the collective memory. City people had all but forgotten the lessons of the past, but in the country superstitions were alive and well. The people of the Languedoc were in no doubt that history had been known to repeat itself more than once.

A family had recently arrived on the outskirts of the village. They lived in a new single storey bungalow with a bright terracotta rendering, built to order from a catalogue, typical of so many that now encroached on the ancient villages. Its colour shone garishly among the soft greens and smoky emeralds of the surrounding landscape. The parents exhibited their offspring as others show off their china figurines in a glass case. The boy was named Orphée, the girl Salomé. But this Orphée was not the ethereal, lyre-playing creature that Armand had imagined. The boy looked nothing like the Orpheus who had ventured into the underworld to charm the king of hell in pursuit of his beloved Euridice.

'I left school at fourteen, but we had a proper education,' Armand replied when asked how he knew about Orphée.

'And I know what an Orphée should look like.' This Orphée glowered from behind strong glasses which enlarged his eyes. When spoken to he fixed adults with a frog-like stare. He was squat and blond, not very bright. Armand also knew what a Salomé should look like, and the girl passing by the café wasn't it either. The only difference between the boy and his sister were her stumpy legs, pink as the skin of a piglet under her Barbie-style dresses.

'Salomé.' Whenever Armand heard the mother trill the name, calling to her daughter on their way to the épicerie, he shook his head at the folly of such a name. Would this Salomé burn with love for an unattainable village boy and have him decapitated? Would she passionately kiss the dead lips of the severed head sitting in a pool of blood? Would she carry it down the village street on her mother's best silver platter? The girl did not look the temptress now, but Armand had long realised that it was not the most beautiful women who committed the worst crimes of passion. Perhaps the trouble at the chateau had its roots in passion gone wrong. Madame certainly was a beauty, even now. The thought of some terrible event taking place just around the corner from his café was too horrible to contemplate. As far as anyone knew there had never been any trouble with Augusto and his wife before. Madame had the expected English reserve. Somehow, to Armand in any case, she did not look as though she would lose control over her emotions, unlike Marie-Louise. That was the one thing about his Marilou; she knew how to fight. She hissed, she growled, she turned into a fire-spewing volcano when she was angry, even when she was fourteen. But all the while, he knew she

122

would always forgive. They would make up; it was just a question of time; and how sweet the reconciliations were.

'So,what happened after their fight?'

'Don't know,' Paul shrugged. His rough palms slapped down on his knees. 'It went all quiet. A couple of days later his car leaves. I couldn't see the driver but I'm pretty sure it was him. The Louis told me the old man had gone to Paris.' He paused and surreptitiously manoeuvred his glass into Armand's sight line, speculating on a refill as a reward for telling the story. Armand obliged and topped Paul's glass up again.

'And then those damned removal trucks arrived.' Paul jerked his head and gave a sigh. 'And then the old man comes back with tires screeching.'

'I'm telling you, Popol, something is going on there. The blood went to his cheeks. 'I didn't see the removal people arrive. It must have been before I opened.'

Paul swilled the drink around in his mouth.

'I did. They nearly shaved off the corner of my house. The scraping noise was unbelievable, like a machine gun going off. I nearly fell out of bed with shock. What are we supposed to do? Cut the corners off our houses because the trucks and vans are getting bigger and bigger?'

'They did that in Lamazes, to the house by the bridge. The lorries coming down that steep hill were forever burning their brakes and running into it.'

'Our villages are not built for the size of those monsters. They're made for the motorways.'

'When he came back,' Armand grumbled, 'I could hear him speeding down the hill like a madman even before he'd got to the bridge, and his driving was even worse when he left again.' He gave a sigh. 'I'll add the cost of repainting my sign to Monsieur Augusto's bill, if he ever pays up that is.' He found it hard to console himself. 'Not a lucky place, that chateau. My family has been here as long as the Vilmorin's. My grandfather, and his father before him had a few old horror stories to tell about that house, and the lake. They'd been handed down from his own grandfather and so on, all the way back to when it was a monastery. Word of mouth is what kept our history alive then, not the internet.' He huffed, mechanically drying and sorting last night's wine glasses back under the counter. 'To us the Cathars, they're not so far away. That's what it means to be an Occitan, an unbroken line reaching back to Roman times,' he said with pride.

Paul shook his head. 'Everything good went when old Madame de Vilmorin died. And all that business with her son's fancy wife. Guy thought he could be modern. He should have married a girl like Nanette, a simple honest village girl who knows what's what. She would have honoured him and his station in life. Everyone except Guy knew she'd walk through fire for him.'

'Still would.'

'I really felt more sorry for little Romain. When they all lived at the chateau years ago, when his mother left I could hear him crying for weeks from my garden.'

'Well, now Guy is on his own with Nanette. Who knows…,' Armand winked.

'No way. She still calls him Monsieur le Comte.'

'Stranger things have happened. She's still pretty. He might come to his senses.' Armand returned the Ricard bottle to the shelf behind the counter. 'Women have their ways. Who knows what she's capable of? She'd make him happy.'

Paul slurped his drink, a little at the time, making it last. There probably wouldn't be another refill. 'I think Romain is a gentle soul.'

Armand tut-tutted. 'He's not been right in the head since the day his mother walked out; he thinks and acts like a five-year old, except that now he has the body and the strength of a man. No, there's no telling with people like that. I reckon even Guy is scared to have his son in the house.'

*

And it must follow, as night the day

20

Domaine L'Espérou, same day

Sitting slumped on the floor of his room Romain shivered and stared at the floorboards. The mud on his clothes had dried to a bright ochre crust. Nanette was gently removing his trousers. Bloody scratches criss-crossed his lower legs where the blackberry bushes by the chateau wall had caught him as he clambered through. Nanette drew the curtains half shut. The darkened room would help to calm Romain. If she could clean him up and put him to bed everything would be fine.

The door opened and the silhouette of his father stood against the glare of the sunlit hall.

'Dear God,' Vilmorin put his hand to his brow. 'What are we to do with him? Will he never understand that he can't keep going over there?'

'I don't know, Monsieur.' Nanette went to the tray on the table by the window, took some fresh gauze and dunked it in a bowl filled with warm water. 'He can't tell the difference.' Her voice was hushed, taking care not to aggravate Vilmorin. She turned away from him and quickly wiped away tears collecting in the corners of her eyes. How could Guy, the kind-natured boy she'd idolised, grow into this sour, harsh man?

'Don't ever, ever dare think about it,' her mother Rose had reprimanded her, 'there are no Cinderellas in real life.' Even at the age of fifteen Nanette had known her mother was right. Her grandmother Amandine had been all too quick to spot her granddaughter's teenage infatuation for Guy, the master's heir. Amandine's eyes had turned dark with warnings of the dire consequences of Nanette's foolishness. But things weren't always as they should be, not in young Nanette's heart. One look at Guy and a hundred birds had fluttered to the roof of her stomach. They turned and churned and knocked so hard in her chest that her heart was squashed like a soft rubber ball. Why was the front of her dress not heaving from the turmoil inside her? No matter how long she searched for some evidence if this, no lumps or bumps could be seen where those birds pushed with their bony wings. What if they escaped, suddenly flinging themselves up her throat and out of her mouth? Whenever Guy was home on holiday he had been playful as ever; he seemed unaware that something in Nanette had changed since they were children. He had grown into a young man, she was still a child, to him anyhow. And yet, despite her struggle, despite the dread of being found out, she had longed for him to guess how consumed she had become by her delicious agony.

'It'll pass,' Rose had tried to appease Amandine's foreboding. 'We've all been there,' she sighed, 'but we all had the good sense to remember our place.'

'Times have changed,' grumbled Amandine, 'today young people no longer know their place. They think love is everything. But when the heat fades away....'

In time Nanette had grown ashamed of her girlish dreams. To Guy she would probably always be a maid; she would never rise above her station. But his wife Elianne had been gone for such a long time. All Nanette wanted now was to see Guy restored to his old self, content once more. She knew little about the world outside the Vilmorin household. She had never been more than fifty kilometres from home. How could she give him back what he most wanted, his ancestral home?

Nanette was kneeling in front of Romain. 'He thinks his mother is still over there.' She tried to keep her voice steady to hide her emotions from Vilmorin. 'He told me he saw her, over there, at the chateau a few days ago. He says he picked flowers for her, but she got very angry. Sometimes he thinks I'm his mother. The word will get round in the village.' She carefully dabbed the bloody scratch on Romain's cheek. 'You want your Maman, don't you.'

Behind her Vilmorin's feet shuffled.

'Well, we all know where she went to,' he said harshly. 'For heaven's sake, Nanette. Stop treating him like a baby.'

Vilmorin was bitter about Romain's illness, bitter about Elianne leaving him alone with the two boys from one day to the next. He had given her everything, a life in his chateau, his status, his heritage. At first she had been flattered by the family title, the respect and advantages it had brought with it. His family was of Spanish origin and one of the oldest in Southern France. The name said it all: Vilmorin, town of the Moors. And he had loved Elianne to distraction, until it was too late.

*

It leads the will to desperate undertakings

21

April 29th

The sky to the West was sinking under a mass of slate grey. *And all the clouds that lour'd upon our house*, Augusto whispered.

He had eventually made it to Paris and to his meeting at Drouots, despite his brief return to the chateau after Zoffia's frantic call. As he drove he could not rid himself of Ophelia's face, her contorted expression. What had he done to her? He felt as though he was driving with her ghost beside him.

When he had stormed out of his house, the first of the furniture vans was fully loaded and ready to leave. By the time he had reached the Paris auction house he was no longer sure whether there was anything left to offer them. The auctioneers had pored over his snapshots of valuable antiques, taken before he had left home. Halfway through the discussion panic hit him, so he had held meandering, hypothetical discussions before he could extricate himself. He made a more or less dignified exit, explaining he had to consult with his son about the estimates and potential sale of the items. He meandered around in the streets down to the Opera, finally sitting on a bench in the Jardin de Luxembourg to watch old men playing chess. In days gone by he might have stayed in a fancy hotel in the Faubourg Saint Honoré. Now all the formality of being fussed over like a VIP held no attraction. He booked a room in the narrow Rue de Seine on the Left Bank in a noisy hotel which was populated by a group of young ballet dancers running on the stairs in dance attire. Somewhere in a room someone was doing voice warm-ups. His mood lifted at the insouciance of youth. His fifth floor window looked out onto attic rooms of the buildings opposite where once a painter might have suffered for his art. The street market below and the quaint square at the end of the street where he could sit on a bench in the shade of a chestnut tree, watching other old men, brought no solace. His whole being seemed hollowed out; he had become no more than a walking shell of a man. Several days went by; Paris had lost its fascination.

He paid his hotel bill and collected his car. After what seemed hours he finally escaped the Paris traffic jams and found the motorway to the South. After another night's restless sleep in a hotel in a picturesque town he set off at dawn, determined to reach Noirlac by evening.

Ahead the outlines of the mountains lay leaden like an exhausted beast. How many times had he driven down this road with a quickening of the heart beat at the thought of

coming home to the house of his dreams? Today anticipation
had turned into a thumping of the heart which threatened to
lift him from his driving seat with every beat. His brain
fizzed as if plugged into an electric current. He was going
back to Noirlac, but it no longer felt like a homecoming.
Soldiers must have felt this way, he thought, following an
irresistible urge to return to their village which they knew to
be in ruins after a long war. What was there to rebuild out of
the ruins he had brought about himself? After a few hours he
had left the motorway somewhere in the North of the
Dordogne, prefering the quiet country roads.

He forced himself to blink to keep his eyes fixed on the
rapidly darkening road. The light was turning everything to
slate blue. In front of him the white central line swung left,
then right as if some invisible hand was pulling a ribbon in
front of his eyes. Occasionally a broken horizontal line
commanded him to stop.

At a crossroad he came to a halt; there was not another
car in sight. Signs pointed vacantly in all directions;
Carcassonne, Toulouse, Revel, Foix and under it in smaller
letters, Noirlac. The familiar road rose and stretched over the
hill. In the drawings of his children's Disney cartoons years
ago a panicked Donald Duck would have come racing over
the hill, with webbed feet flailing on a perfectly smooth, blue
tarmac.

It had taken him time to unravel Zoffia's confused,
whispered telephone call that had woken him in Albi.

'Ophelia, she's going mad, moving everything….,'
Zoffia had sobbed. 'Why didn't you tell her you wanted to
marry me?' Augusto had been unable to make sense of what
she was saying. 'Come home, now,' she had pleaded before

the line went dead. It wasn't until the morning when he had stood on the pavement outside the hotel, with an empty stomach but too impatient to wait for breakfast, that he began to imagine what might be happening at the chateau and with Ophelia. He had interrupted his journey to Paris to return to Noirlac, raced down that hill and through the village only days before. He'd had some vision that Ophelia, in a fit of anger, was moving the furniture, maybe throwing his books out of the window, or burning them, or moving her belongings into another wing of the chateau, perhaps even wrecking Zoffia's room. When he had driven through the gates he couldn't understand what was happening. What were those giant removal vans doing on the chateau forecourt? He could not have imagined that Ophelia would attempt to remove all their possessions; he had not thought her capable of such cold enterprise. All that appeared untouched was his library and the books within it. After he had set foot into the house everything became abstract; all reason ceased. There was just humiliation and the haze of fury. When the door fell shut behind him, after his desperate attempt to reason with his wife, his only instinct was to get away. He had resumed his planned trip to Paris, but it might as well have been to the end of the world. Now he was forced to return for good. On the way to Paris he had stopped at a resting place on a mountainous road and made an appointment with the Carters to sell some of his books. They were coming on the 1st of May, his birthday. If none were left to sell he would have to cancel their visit.

Once over the top of the hill he had a clear view onto the village of Noirlac, lying in a hollow at the foot of Mount Montferrus.

That it should come to this

22

Domaine de l'Esperou

Guy de Vilmorin watched as Nanette cleaned up his son with infinite tenderness. He stood in the door, not committed to entering the room. Where did the girl get the patience from? He had always thought of her as a girl, but as he watched he saw not a girl, but a woman kneeling in the room and what he saw was not duty but something altogether different - it was devotion, it was love. He felt a confusion he could not explain. The sudden realisation made him take a step back when Nanette looked up. There was such pain and longing in her dark eyes. It was not a look he had ever seen in Elianne's eyes. Nanette was crying. Had Elianne ever cried? He could not recall it, unless it had been about money. Elianne had had such grace, such beauty. Romain had her eyes, her dark, perfectly traced eyebrows. Both he and his brother Alain were handsome, but now Romain's resemblance to his mother caused Guy to feel uncomfortable whenever he faced his son. Alain was just two years older than his brother. Somehow he had coped with the impact of Elianne's desertion, but Romain had never recovered. At first they had diagnosed a breakdown, a regression into early childhood. Then they gave it a name. Autism was the new mystery label. Vilmorin couldn't make sense of it, didn't know where the term came from or what it meant. All he knew was that his son, now a young man, saw the world through the eyes of a five year-old, a rejected, resentful five year-old.

Vilmorin caught himself staring at Nanette. He realised that for years he had let his raw anger about Elianne's desertion flood and dominate every part of his life. Being tied down by two young boys had been a strain for Elianne, no matter how many staff he had put at her disposal. She didn't want to be needed. She was hungry for distractions, and most of all, she adored to be entertained and admired. The boys needed more than nannies and maids. For Elianne's birthday the grand salon had been turned into a forest of long-stemmed red roses. Among the invited guests had been Céline, Elianne's childhood friend. Céline arrived, accompanied by Bruno, tall, tanned with a shock of blond hair. Throughout the evening Céline showed him off like a trophy.

'This is Bruno, an absolute genius, when it comes to living the good life,' Céline flirted. She had moved close to Elianne, as if to whisper, but had intended it to be heard by the whole room. 'He's always rushing between his properties in Spain and the Bahamas, or he's out on the town in the Big Apple.'

Bruno's hand had rested on Céline's shoulder, but his eyes were on Guy's wife.

Céline and Bruno turned up at the chateau more and more often, as Elianne's house guests. Vilmorin did not object.

'You are so anti-social, my darling,' Elianne cajoled him in cat-like tones. 'I'm trying to make you just a tiny little bit more gregarious.'

Guy knew that frequent house guests where a way to quell Elianne's lust for distractions. But despite his generosity she increasingly craved spending time away with her friends. Vilmorin had found Bruno and Céline strangely over-familiar in their demeanour, in the way they gradually treated his house as their own. During their frequent stays no room was out of bounds to them and Guy was deprived of the privacy he was used to. The city life was Elianne's natural environment and she had little understanding of the duties that Guy's position as landowner and employer of most of the villagers involved. He had responsibilities to his farmers, to his tenants who tended his vineyards. The success of his farming depended on them. It had been so for centuries and the villagers expected no less. Elianne could not begin to understand that these symbiotic relationships could exist in the age of the internet. No one knew exactly how Bruno earned his money, but his lifestyle implied he had plenty of it, or so it seemed. In a very short time Elianne spent a great deal of money shopping and staying in Paris, Barcelona and Rome.

As she was sponging Romain's knee Nanette could sense Guy's unease, that he wanted to leave and yet he remained.

'Do you remember that day?' he suddenly asked.

'Which day?' She knew which day he meant but would not say so. 'There were so many….'

'That day,' he insisted, 'when she left.'

'How could I forget, Monsieur.'

Three days after her return from a trip with Céline and Bruno, Vilmorin's study door flew open. Elianne caught her reflection in the Napoleon mirror over Guy's fireplace. Her cheeks had flushed and her eyes were black with anger.

'Why do you summon me like a school girl, in front of the servants?'

'Here.' Guy waved a handful of bank statements at her. 'This is why. And it's not in front of the servants, it was Nanette.'

'Precisely,' Elianne stamped her foot and her high heel crunched into the wood of the parquet floor, 'the servants. You and those ... people, you' re all in the same bag. They mean more to you than I do,' she raged. 'Since you've brought Rose back she spends so much time creeping around the house, she might as well live here again. I suppose she's here for … for reinforcement?'

'Don't be absurd. Nanette needs help with the housework.'

'The boys love Nanette more than their mother,' Elianne growled.

'Are you surprised? You're never here.' Guy turned back to his desk. 'This has to stop, now. Give me your credit card.'

Elianne swallowed. Despite the heat of anger she suddenly shivered.

'Don't be silly, Guy,' she tried her honeyed tone to placate her husband. 'What else can I do in this God forsaken village except to try and enjoy myself?'

'Your card, Elianne,' Guy had repeated in a dry voice. He didn't have the heart to fight, but she gave him no choice. 'The bank has blocked our account and cancelled our overdraft arrangements.' The papers rustled in his hand as he shuffled them. 'Hotel... hotel... Galerie Lafayette... jewellers in Barcelona, Bulgari, more designer boutiques. Anyone can see what you're spending the money on. I'm not surprised they won't let it continue.'

'I don't believe you,' she had shouted. 'Whose money is it anyway? Look at this house, your property, your land. Don't they know what that means? It's our money.'

'Not our money, Elianne. You've been spending their money. I can't repay the bank by sending them a pig. Not even my best wines can placate them nowadays. Times have changed. My great-grandfather could have done that, perhaps even my father. It's not going to be a good year for wine and the price of cattle and wheat has dropped. It'll be months before any money comes in.'

'What has that got to do with me? Since when do I make the weather? What do you want me to do? Put on clogs, dig the ground, feed the chickens, slaughter and skin the rabbits? Do the cooking?'

'When you married me, did you really think that the life of a châtelaine was all parties and shopping? Don't you see how I and all my people work? Are you totally blind?' Guy's shoulders slumped in exasperation.

'Well,' she swung around, 'they say shopping is better than sex,' 'with some people in any case,' and she slammed the study door shut.

Nanette had been kneeling at the far end of the hall, polishing the marble floor.

'Spying on me, are you?' Elianne spat. 'You're all the same round here. You and your precious master. All you think of is that pathetic patch of sun-baked land you were born on.' She open her handbag and threw her credit card at Nanette.

In her mind's eye Nanette could still see the shiny slice of plastic as it skipped on the polished floor and disappeared under the carved oak chest in the corner.

Next morning the kitchen door had opened. 'Rose?'

'Yes, Monsieur.' Rose did not meet Guy's gaze. Nanette had remained in her room, still upset by the row she had witnessed.

'I have to go to Paris,' said Vilmorin.

He stood there, looking grey and drawn. He indicated two large parcels leaning against the wall in the hall.

'Fetch Marco. I need help to load those into the car. I'll be back in few days. I'll be staying at my cousin's house in Paris if there is something urgent.'

'Yes, Monsieur.'

Rose had watched as Vilmorin's car crossed the bridge and disappeared over the hill beyond the village before she went into his study. The Napoleon mirror and the two drawings by Delacroix were gone. All that remained were three empty rectangles on the wall. Tears welled up in Rose's eyes. Behind her she heard her daughter's footsteps. Nanette laid a hand on her mother's shoulder.

'Napoleon himself had sent that mirror to the Vilmorin's,' Rose whispered, 'it's been hanging over that fireplace ever since.' Then they both wept.

The money from the sale of the mirror and the drawings had barely sufficed to wipe out Elianne's debts. When Guy returned to the chateau, Elianne had gone. Rose and Nanette were left in charge of the boys. Romain was in a hysterical state. He had watched his mother pack her bags and walk out of the door. He had clung to her coat. His grip loosened a split second before Bruno's car door threatened to slam shut on his hand. Elianne's last message to her husband read: 'As you don't want me to be happy I am leaving you.'

The family doctor had sedated the traumatised boy. After some weeks Romain became completely withdrawn; his speech ceased and he spent most of his time sleeping or sitting on a low velvet nursing chair, rocking back and forth, refusing to look anyone in the eye. Elianne could not be found. After six months, the doctors advised that Romain should be sent to a sanatorium for a sleeping cure.

'He will forget,' they had promised. But the boy had not forgotten. He was moved from the children's sanatorium to a home for disturbed adolescents, then to a home for young adults and on to another sanatorium.

The humiliation of his failed marriage had drained Guy de Vilmorin of his energy; things went from bad to worse. After several poor harvest years the upkeep of the chateau became too great a burden. A staff of eight was needed to keep everything in good running order. In winter it took nearly a ton of coal per day to heat the house. After a particularly bad year in which many of his vines became diseased and the grain harvest was savaged by hail storms,

140

Guy was bankrupted. He sold the house to the Augusto Perez De Montsarrat, the man with a fancy name. After debts had been paid off most of the money from the sale went into a trust to provide for Romain, if he were to outlive his father.

At first the old bastide of the Domaine L'Espérou, which Guy had inherited from his uncle a couple of vineyards to the West of the chateau, seemed a compromise which would cause least upheaval. It was a building of lesser stature constructed in the 16th century with a square footprint, built of heavy stone. It was workman-like and purpose built for a wine grower. It squatted on the land with more outbuildings than living quarters.

Back then the name of the property, L'Espérou, derived from an old Occitan word for hope, held promise. Guy could stay close to his vineyards and to his people. When the burst of winter sun painted the February snows flamingo pink the land would still be his to gaze at. His would be the sultry July nights when thousands of sunflowers turned their eyeless faces to the full moon. They would stand guard, giants in the silver light on his night time strolls between the fields vibrating with the rasping of a million crickets.

His move to the smaller property had not been a total loss of face. At least keeping the land had saved the family honour; the villagers continued to work it as they had done for centuries. They were fiercely loyal to Vilmorin still; some had voiced open relief to see Elianne go. But over the years the ghost of what he had lost began to loom larger and his pain burned like a fierce love sickness.

Every day his eyes scanned the jagged horizon in the emerald distance as his ancestors had done since before the Middle Ages. But it was the view from his window of his

141

former home that drew him in like a magnet. From the Domaine L'Espérou Guy de Vilmorin kept watch. It was a daily, melancholy vigil. Augusto Perez de Montsarrat had a big name. To the best of Vilmorin's knowledge there was only one maid and an occasional gardener left to do all the work. The great house and its grounds had become more and more dishevelled.

La citadaine, the city dweller, as the locals nicknamed Augusto's wife Ophelia, was liked well enough in the village, though her English reserve was perceived as snobbery by some.

Ophelia let the formal gardens become engulfed by shrubs that went untrimmed. There was no traditional kitchen garden filled with sweet smelling herbs and Mediterranean vegetables. Instead fields of flowers appeared. In the first year a large pool was dug, just beyond the cypress path, half way to the lake lower down. Guests' laughter could be heard throughout the village as they took midnight swims in the pool after their many noisy parties. No one seemed to swim in the lake. Its banks had become overgrown and strangled with matted reed and broken branches, blown across the water during the November storms. Now the chateau facade seemed to be peeling and lately even the exterior shutters with the grey zinc cladding had remained closed on all but one of the windows.

There had to be a way to save the house, to make it live again. The honour of the Vilmorin family deserved it. When Guy had sold the house to Augusto it was in good condition, the gardens were preened, the interior polished by Rose and Nanette. Now it looked shabby and dead. If Guy wanted to buy it back, even in this condition, its market price would force him into heavy debt. The whole region had become infested with holiday-home owners, mostly foreigners or Parisians, the most reviled of all. Prices had rocketed and derelict barns were being sold for the price of a family house. If he wanted to return to his ancestral home another way had to be found. And what was he to do about Romain?

'Try a period at home. Just to see if your son will adapt to the world again,' the doctors and psychologists had said. 'It's part of the program to re-socialise him. We can safely assume that he does not present a danger.'

Only a few days after the boy's return home it became clear that without a normal family structure, Romain could not be kept. He could not be left to run free and he could not be confined to his room day after day. Guy de Vilmorin knew it was not safe, neither for his son, nor for anyone else.

So much time had passed; he had wrapped himself in his grief. And here, at the sight of the woman attending to his son, something inexplicable had happened. The simplicity of Nanette's humanity overwhelmed him. He felt faint. He closed his eyes and his hand gripped the door post.

'Monsieur, Monsieur...?' He felt Nanette's hand on his shoulder. 'Guy? Are you unwell?' Her other hand now took his hand. How long had it been since someone had held his hand?

'Look at me,' he heard her say. He opened his eyes. She stood close, looking up at him, her eyes searching his face.

'I'm sorry ... I thought you were going to faint,' she stammered. She tried to withdraw her hand but he held on to it. They gazed at each other in stunned silence. As they stood there, so still, she realised she had not been this close to him

143

since they were children and she was surprised to see that the hair of his temples had turned grey.

There was a look of total confusion in Guy's dark eyes, as if he had never seen her before. At her touch the age-old boundaries between them had crumbled in an instant and with a sudden shock it dawned on Guy de Vilmorin that he was glad of it.

Romain stirred and Nanette turned her back on the boy's father. She pulled a clean T-shirt over his head and he let her handle him like a rag doll.

'Whether you like it or not,' she glanced at Vilmorin who was now leaning against the door post, 'he is a baby for all intents and purpose, or nearly.'

From the entrance hall came two voices.

'Yes, Uncle, wait here, I'll get him. Monsieur …, Monsieur,' Biquette's call echoed from below. Nanette heard the girl's footsteps rushing up the stairs. 'It's Uncle Armand. He needs to see you.' Biquette stopped at the top of the stairs. She had been instructed never to venture as far as Romain's room. 'Uncle Armand says it's urgent, really urgent.'

'I have to go.' Guy suddenly sounded apologetic. 'Watch over him, Nanette,' he said softly without looking at her, 'I'll see what I can do. We can't lock him up here forever.' Nanette listened to his steps fade away along the upper hall.

She took a soft towel and rubbed Romain's hands.

'Poor, poor boy,' she whispered, 'one day you'll be home, one day we'll all be home again, I promise.'

*

144

There's nothing either good or bad,
but thinking makes it so

23

Chateau de Noirlac, 1st of May

The narrow lane leading to the chateau lay in shadow, hemmed in by towering stone walls smothered in wild ivy.

'One to you. Ramshackle,' Léa smiled. She took a look in the mirror and ran a hand through her red hair, tousled from the wind rushing through the open car window. An overpowering scent of lilac in bloom filled the air.

'Smell that. Divine. It must be coming over that wall from the garden we just passed.'

As expected, arched wrought iron gates announced the entrance to the life of the privileged.

'That's weird. He hasn't got around to changing the old family crest.' Léa craned her neck to read the faded coat of arms topping the elaborate gates. 'It says Vilmorin. I thought old De Montsarrat has been here for twenty years or more. Vilmorin must have been the original owner, whoever he is.'

The tyres crunched on the white gravel of a semi-circular forecourt. Sam parked the car next to what appeared to be the only door in use. A brass handle dangled on a chain. Sam gave it a half-hearted tug. They waited.

'Pull again'.

He did and they waited some more. 'I suppose it takes longer to get to the door in a chateau than in our hamster cage of a house.'

'Shhh. I can hear chains rattle!' Léa put a finger to her lips and pointed to the door handle which was now being turned from inside. They tried hard to suppress a giggle.

The door opened. Augusto's large rectangular face looked out from the darkened hall. The turquoise eyes with a touch of the bloodhound about them flicked to Sam and then back to Léa, assessing. He seemed to have shrunk since they had met him in the hotel library; his head protruded from a shirt collar which looked several sizes too large. He was wearing an apron over blue Indian silk trousers, a black velvet waistcoat, embroidered with blue and gold arabesques and a pair of pointed turquoise slippers with gold stitching. His outfit, no doubt once deemed exotic, reminded Léa of the man with the monkey she had tripped over in the shadows in Carcassonne, the man who had vanished in seconds. Standing there, face to face with Augusto, she suddenly wondered what she had seen that day in the square, or had it been a premonition?

'Welcome, welcome, thrice welcome,' the old man proclaimed. He wiped wet hands on his apron. 'I thought you were the postman.' There was the theatrical hilarity

146

again. 'It's May the first, my birthday. I might even get a birthday card today.' He raised a bony index finger – 'I hope! Enter, children.'

As in Hansel and Gretel, Léa thought and felt his gaze rest on her longer than it should have. There was a melancholy hunger in his smile as he bid them in. He averted his eyes, but she sensed that somehow he was still watching her.

'Were was I?' He thought for a moment. 'Ah, mon Dieu,' he clapped his hand to his forehead, 'the telephone! Excuse me a second. Pablo, my son is on the line. From New York.'

He made his way across the hall in no great haste.

'Yes, Pablo. Well, no, it wasn't like that... Yes, she did. Yes...well …, you don't understand. I did, I did, but …,' he said in a contrite voice. 'I can't …, no, I can't explain. Just please, please, Pablo, don't tell Ariana. Not yet. You know, women … promise?' He hung up.

They felt like school children standing in the cavernous hall. He hurried back to them.

'My wife has left,' he announced with bravado. He gestured to an open door to his left, 'we will look at books later. First we must eat.'

This was unexpected. 'No, Monsieur, 'Sam protested, 'please don't trouble yourself.'

'Call me Augusto. And it's no trouble. I don't want to eat alone, today of all days.'

Sam and Léa exchanged quizzical looks. Inviting total strangers to one's birthday lunch seemed a little eccentric.

Sam shrugged his shoulders. Better to give in than to make a fuss.

'That's very kind.' Sam took Léa by the arm and they followed him.

'This is the new kitchen. Formica and such, but so convenient. So nice, *and* small.'

Good God, Léa thought. I never stop howling about the lack of space in our house and he relishes small spaces, with all this. Do people always long for the opposite of what they have?

'No servants to work the big kitchens now, of course.' He shuffled ahead, his slippers clapping on the tiled floor.

How many kitchens, she wondered.

'Three kitchens,' he answered her unspoken question. 'Thirty eight rooms, all in use at one time. Plus the servants quarters under the roof, of course, and the stable men. That takes some cooking.'

'No servant, no wife, no-one', Léa whispered.

'Shut up,' Sam mumbled under his breath.

Augusto made his way across the kitchen to the French windows, turned the oval brass knobs and flung both of them wide open. Outside the outlines of an old potager were still discernable but instead of herbs and vegetables dense groups of lilies in the palest yellow stood in the centre of the box hedge squares. Their scent burst into the kitchen; the intoxicating perfume flooded the room for a moment. At the foot of the chateau wall beyond clumps of hyacinths. Elegant tulips in acid lemon and mustard hues stood in the shade of the wall. They seemed like a row of exotic parrots as they lightly swayed in the breeze. Seeds of wallflowers had burrowed their way into the cracks of the old wall and were now sprouting, their thick blooms the colour of egg yolks. Nature and the wind had created their own hanging garden.

'This was Ophelia's yellow garden,' Augusto waved, 'the white garden with the lily field was lower down, towards the lake, inspired by that strange Sackville-West woman.' He sighed. 'Ruined now by some idiot vandal.'

Iron spikes ran along the top of the boundary wall as if to fend off even the boldest intruders. Driving up to the chateau they had spotted an old iron door hanging open on rusted hinges. Beyond it a village garden ran right up to the chateau wall. In times past no chateau owner would have tolerated a villager's garden to creep up so close to his wall and invade it with grapevines and tomatoes. The boundary's purpose was to separate two very different worlds, to keep the common people at bay. This chateau owner no longer dominated the village; now the spiked walls locked him in.

'Forgive me, my memory goes AWOL, absent without leave, as they say.' Augusto gazed at Léa. 'Remind me of your names, was it Sam and Eleanora?'

'Léa,' said Sam, 'Sam and Léa.'

The old man busied himself around the kitchen table laid with ham, peas and crisp bread which, to their surprise, he stuck into the toaster standing on a side table. The kitchen did not smell clean. The grand proportions of the room looked insulted by the vulgar Formica cabinets and work tops running along it on the far side.

They talked as they ate. The old man was witty, well read and well traveled and seemed to relish their company. He had bought the chateau with his family inheritance.

'Doesn't simply *everyone* dream of owning a chateau in the South of France? At least once before they die?' He stared across to Léa, expecting a positive reply. Both Sam and Léa ventured a non-committal smile. They knew only too well that most great houses in the area ended up looking like this one – flaking, fading, surrounded by rolling thickets of thorns and thistles.

His wife and two children had lived here for two decades, he confided. Zoffia had cooked and kept house for the family.

'Zoffia was just for us, our personal maid. My wife found her in Barcelona, an orphan, half Spanish, half Irish.' He swallowed.

'Her fault all this. . .' His eyes flickered and shone and with a flourish he continued, 'Zoffia was my MISTRESS.' Having made this momentous announcement he laughed and again leaned across the table, fixing his limpid eyes on Léa. 'You see,' he said with heavy innuendo, 'I've been a very naughty boy.' He played with the peas on his plate. 'Now you may think it improbable…,' he pursed his lips, 'I'm over seventy and my wife was … so much younger than myself … thirty years or thereabouts .' He pondered on his statement for a moment, almost surprised, as if this particular truth had only just sunk in.

Léa glanced over to Sam. The old man was speaking of his wife in the past tense.

'She never thought,' Augusto continued, 'that at my age I could . . .,' his tongue ran over his lower lip as a mixture of guilt and wonder flew over his face, 'and then, whoosh, the women, both gone on the same day.' He seemed amazed by this fact, apparently making light of it, or perhaps he was just a convincing actor.

'Where is your wife now?' Sam was trying to make small-talk.

'Most likely with her sister, in London I should think. It's an excellent place if you want to disappear. And Zoffia . . .,' he looked to the door as if he expected her to appear, 'Zoffia vanished into thin air. She had no relatives that we ever knew of, no friends; we were her family. Adored the children when they were still around. I doubt whether anyone really knew she was here at all. She loved this house, hardly ever went out, except to the café, for the papers. Sometimes I hear her still.' His voice trailed off and he seemed to be listening.

'Alas, alac, Ophelia could not forgive me,' he wailed as if on stage. 'But not to forgive is to deny human weakness, and to deny THAT,' he opened his eyes wide to emphasize his point, 'is to deny our very humanity!' Before they had time to reflect on this profoundly biblical question he said, 'come. Seeing is believing.' He went into the hall ahead of them.

Sam cupped his hand in front of his mouth. 'Here goes,' he whispered, 'the hard luck story of a man with a chateau.'

'Embarrassing.' Léa pulled a face. 'Just don't get involved.'

'Come along, children,' Augusto's voice echoed in the empty hall. 'See that. Took every stick, my Ophelia; left me a couple of baubles she apparently considered worthless. And the books.' He raised his arms as if receiving an ovation at the Scala in Milan. A vague flick of the old wrist indicated large paintings which hung all around them. Their heavy gilt

151

frames caught shafts of light streaming down from a domed sky light above marble stairs leading to a sunlit half-landing.

'That was my great-grandfather. A Duke ... and the little one here,' his hand brushed over a small painting in a caress hanging slightly apart. A boy with wild, dark curls and luminous, turquoise eyes had been painted in a bold Expressionist style. Léa stopped in front of the small portrait.

'That's me. My father commissioned it before I went to Eton.' He paused, watched them while they appreciated the boldness of the artist's brush strokes.

'My son, oh, my son Pablo ... hates that picture,' he volunteered suddenly. He had an abrupt way of throwing his life's intimate details out into the open which would have been embarrassing from a younger man. Perhaps he has nothing to lose, Léa mused.

'What kind of painting does your son like?'

'No, no, it's not the artist's style he hates. It's something else. Never said what it was.' He stood, contemplating the picture as if he were alone. 'I'll give you a tour,' he waved and began climbing the stairs gripping the solid brass banister sweeping elegantly to the first floor. They followed.

'It's all a bit barren now,' he continued, making light of the lack of just about everything one could expect to find in a house, let alone a chateau. He commented on the painted portraits left and right as they went. On the first floor an expanse of parquet floors laid in an elaborate pattern stretched on either side. At each end oval windows framed the landscape. All but one of the doors to the rooms stood gaping open. The vast bathroom, decorated in exquisite green and cream tiles, was a reminder of what this house had been in centuries past. An old fashioned roll-top bath tub with its gilded claw feet looked naked and forlorn, untouched by the dramatic exodus of all other items.

They came into the centre room. A row of French windows looked out over the village huddling just a few hundred yards away. Beyond the shallow roofs fields and vineyards rose to the snow-capped Pyrenees shining on the horizon.

'See that house between the cypresses, there?' asked Augusto. That's the Domaine L'Espérou. Guy de Vilmorin, the man who sold me this house now lives over there. Every day, morning and afternoon I see him standing by the window, looking, staring at us... at me,' he corrected himself and turned to Sam. 'Why would he do that? Even when I don't look, I know he's there,' he complained. 'His family had this chateau for centuries, why shouldn't I have it for a while?'

To the left in the grand room the shoulder-high fireplace was flanked by dark marble columns wrapped in gilded vine leaves. A giant mirror with a damaged ormolu frame was propped up on the mantle piece. Perhaps its condition had made it unworthy of a space in the removal truck. This room too was devoid of furniture. The door facing the main room was closed.

'You must have a wonderful view onto the grounds from this room,' Léa hazarded a guess. As she moved towards the door she could hear a faint noise of water swishing and the clinking of china. Augusto swiftly moved and stood in front of her, blocking the door.

'We can't go in here,' he said with in a sudden rush in his voice. Léa glanced down and saw his hand on the brass door handle. His knuckles were turning white. He averted his eyes to escape her puzzled look, 'come, you'll get a better view from the next room.' He let go of the door handle and wiped his hand on his trousers. He seized Léa's elbow, squeezing a little too hard and guided her into the next room. The handles of the two French windows were stiff and he struggled with them for a moment. He unbolted the heavy zinc-clad shutters, flung them open and let Léa and Sam step onto a balustraded semi-circular terrace over a portico. From here the lines of the original garden layout could clearly be seen.

'Now that's something worth looking at, is it not?'.

Sam and Léa nodded their appreciation.

'We had planted a field of glorious white lilies between the pool and the lake, not far from that beautiful old barn on the right there. A prowler broke into the enclosure, decapitated the flowers, just before Ophelia … just before … all this. Great houses like this attract that sort of thing, all that space in the garden to creep up, so many windows to look into.'

'That's a strange thing to do,' Sam remarked.

'He laid the blooms out in a circle, in the barn entrance, some sort of bizarre ritual. They're still there, all shriveled, couldn't bring myself to clear them up.' Augusto shielded his eyes and pointed down to the lake to the left. 'What's that, there, by the lake,' he cried. He appeared to be straining to identify something in the distance.

Sam peered into the direction Augusto had indicated.

'I think it's a small dog, ginger. I can only see its rump and a wagging tail,' he laughed.

'That damned dog again,' roared Augusto. His eyes popped and his face became flushed with rage. He turned on his heels and ran out of the room. 'He's digging up the lake again,' he yelled, running down the stairs with his fancy slippers clap-clapping on the marble steps. 'I'll get the rascal for good this time.'

'Over-reacting a bit, the old boy.' Sam looked puzzled. 'His garden is not exactly Hampton Court.'

Léa watched the old man hurry down past the pool with a stick in his hand. 'Oh, my God, he'll kill that poor animal.'

The dog heard Augusto approaching. It jumped up onto the bank of the lake and bounded across the meadow which stopped at the wall bordering the road. From the terrace Léa noticed a head with a beret peering over the wall. It was the same spot from which they had looked into the grounds and seen the two women running when they had passed through the village that day. The man with the beret was whistling. The dog ran towards him and on reaching the wall, scrambled onto it with a messy leap and into the arms of his waiting owner. The whole episode seemed comical until they saw Augusto, feet planted apart, standing on the path half way to the lake, waving his stick in anger.

'That dog wasn't digging for flowers.' Sam turned. 'We'd better go down.'

They left the room and stood still for a moment. Léa looked back at the closed door.

'Did you hear that noise, in there?' she whispered.

'What noise?'

She signaled to him to put his ear to the door. Léa's hearing was very acute. At the fall of night she could hear the high pitched squeaking of bats or the soft swish of an owl's wings, hunting low over the gorge below their terrace.

'Shush. There.' A faint, intermittent splashing could be heard.

'I hear it. Perhaps the maid came back.' Sam took Léa by the arm and they tiptoed down the stairs. 'Let's wait for him here.'

They stayed in the hall and studied the magnificent portraits of eminent men in statesmen-like poses.

'That's some family gone to pot,' Sam said sadly.

They heard the echoing sound of Augusto's slippers approach. Sam coughed to signal to the old man that they had come downstairs. Augusto reappeared and seemed to have regained his composure. The only sign of his agitation were the throbbing veins on his temples.

'Where were we?' he said as if nothing had happened.
He showed them into the room across the entrance hall. More old family portraits, looking down onto a single very threadbare Persian carpet. They followed Augusto from room to room. Here too there was not one piece of furniture to be seen. Augusto caught Sam's astonishment. His ability to anticipate questions was disconcerting.

'My ancestors are the only thing she didn't dare rob me of. Surprised she didn't destroy them really.' For a moment he pondered the fate he had apparently escaped, just.

The door bell rang.

'Huh! The postman, that mountebank! Spends most of his mornings chatting or drinking. Falls off his bicycle. Always late.'

'I wonder whether she left him a bed,' Léa whispered.

'What a woman,' grinned Sam in disbelief.

Augusto returned holding an arm full of publicity brochures which he simply let fall on the floor.

'Ah! This handwriting I know only too well …, this one too straight for the bin?' he asked rhetorically and held a light green envelope between thumb and index finger as if it were a dead rat. 'Hum.' He cocked his head. 'To bin or not to bin, that is the question!' He giggled at his own pun, but proceeded to slice the envelope open with a short hunting knife which he produced from his trouser pocket. He pulled out a number of hand-written pages, then stuffed them back into the envelope. 'Very rude to read in the presence of visitors,' he apologised.

'Now.' He clapped his hands. 'The garden salon. Books, glorious books,' he exclaimed triumphantly as they entered yet another room. Near the French windows, on the barren parquet floor, stood a ping-pong table loaded down with books, stacked in neat piles. The windows looked out onto a sizeable lawn. At the lower end of it and half hidden by grasses grown wild, one could make out the edge of the pool.

'She left the books. And you.' He stooped and inspected a silver grey cat with luminous yellow eyes which had been following him around. He roughly shoved it away with his foot, a gesture at once resentful and impotent.

'My two children are scattered all over the world,' he said cheerily with an impish grin, 'so what would they do with all these books?'

How can two people be scattered all over anything? Léa smiled at the image. Picking over words and sentences had become second nature with her, a professional obsession.

'My will,' said Augusto suddenly. 'I must make it now. Momentous decisions have to be taken. I'm glad you came.'

Sam wondered what his will could possibly have to do with them. Augusto didn't look at death's door. Perhaps he would turn out to be the rich uncle they'd always dreamt about.

Sam cast an astonished eye over the books heaped on the table.

'Which books do you want to sell?'

'Help yourselves, children, everything or nothing, as you please.' Augusto described a generous, inviting arc with his bloodless arm. He gathered up a pale turquoise cardigan lying on the books and pulled it closed around his shoulders. He had been handsome once, perhaps slightly drooling, almost pretty in a feminine way, as some upper class young men could be in their first years of adulthood.

'This will take a while.' Sam contemplated the sorted volumes. Augusto wistfully fingered a leather bound volume.

'One of the best, The Name of the Rose. Ophelia had it rebound for me. The first edition hardback was so terribly banal, so . . . *modern*,' he said with distaste. He stroked the calf skin cover, with the title embossed in gold on the spine. Léa was astonished that he would want to sell this book. It was one of her all-time favourites; she would gladly have paid a very good price for it. As if he had read her thoughts he held the book at arms length in her direction.

'Here, my dear. A gift. Important book this. And oh, so relevant today. Suppression of information only works for so long. Look at Russia, China. Argentina too. The lid will blow, even in North Kroea, you just wait.' He waved the book at her, 'and haven't I learned that lesson now.'

158

It seemed immodest to put out her hand to receive something she so badly wanted. He noted her embarrassment and, keeping his gaze on her, put the book into the empty box at Sam's side with a gentle, sensual gesture, as if laying down a child on a soft pillow.

'My Ophelia,' Augusto sighed with a listless gesture of the hand, 'took my 18th century bound Shakespeare folios, the complete works, each volume heavy as a sack of potatoes. And a giagantic historical atlas. Why? I can't imagine. Who would want to be weighed down by those?'

Léa touched Sam's arm, trying to look casual. She needed to feel that he was near. Something was closing in on her. She cast her eyes around the room, as if the paintings might answer her question, yield up the secret of the strange events that had taken place in this house. What happened here?

'What?' Sam turned to her and she realised that she had spoken her question aloud. Opposite the carved mirror, on the darkest side of the room hung a large tapestry. Again Augusto appeared to sense what puzzled her without lifting his eyes from the table.

'That tapestry. She left it, as a final rejection, I suppose.' His lower lips curled in a childlike sulk. 'I had it made for her fortieth birthday. Ophelia for Ophelia.' He gave a cackle which was hard to interpret. 'Italian. Cost a fortune. It took four people two years to make.' He paused. 'Or was it two people and four years?' With a distant look he continued to explore the permutations of the numbers and years in a hushed voice, walking up and down with one hand on his hip and the other playing with his left ear. 'And does it matter, les enfants?' he concluded and joined Léa in front of the tapestry. It was a breathtaking copy of Millais' painting of Ophelia floating in shallow water, drowned. Contrary to the painting the Italian craftsmen had had the delicacy to depict her with her eyes close rather than half open as in Millais' painting. This Ophelia looked asleep. The water and plants around the figure were rendered in subtle greens, transparent as a delicate watercolour painting.

'That is incredible, a masterpiece,' whispered Léa in admiration.

'Yes!' said Augusto. He defiantly straightened his back. 'Perhaps my daughter will want it?'

As Léa gazed at the tapestry she became aware of a constant flicker, running over its surface, like a breeze skimming the water in the embroidered surface, bringing it to life. The ripple travelled and Léa realised that it extended beyond the cloth and onto the ceiling and now she saw that the entire room was gently glinting like an aquarium. It came from the open French windows. Near the house two silver birches rustled in the breeze. Their leaves fluttered, catching the sunlight like tiny mirrors, reflecting their specs of light into the room.

Her shirt was sticking to her back. She went over to the windows looking out over the grounds.

'You'll break your ankle if you go out there; the steps are broken. Quite dangerous'. The old man stood close behind her, too close. She made a little move away, but he continued.

'Ophelia planted hundreds of red climbing roses at the foot of those apple trees. They wound their way into the branches; a little paradise, a garden of Eden she used to say. The only thing missing was Grünwald's Adam and Eve.'

160

Léa saw it, very faintly at first. Then more and more red seeped into her mind's eye, until everything out there seemed to be dripping blood red. She turned, not understanding what her imagination had conjured up. Augusto's turquoise eyes gazed past her out into the garden, as if to decipher some illegible message.

She felt removed and icy. She needed air and sun on her skin. In an effort to reconnect to reality, to fill the silent space she asked, 'Do you still use the pool?'

Augusto sighed apologetically. His expelled breath smelled sour. At lunch he had drunk almost the entire bottle of Chablis by himself. The acrid odour nauseated her. He continued his blank, unfocused stare into the distance.

'I didn't notice until later. Ophelia let all the water out of the pool before she left.' He pulled his turquoise cardigan closer around his shoulders and crossed his arms over it. 'I can't think why.' He looked down at his fancy slippers. 'Still, it's being used, in a manner of speaking.'

Perhaps he parks his old limousines in the empty pool, perhaps he keeps potatoes or coal in it, Léa wondered, like some hill farmers did in their bath tubs.

Not long ago, she had seen it with her own eyes, in a house in Sainte Colombe. Old Antoine lived a few doors away in her narrow street. His front door always stood ajar. Léa had been watering her flowers in front of her house. Her new kitten, which followed her everywhere, had made a mad dash into his house. Antoine gave a wave and she followed him. The tiny animal had scrambled up the stairs and into the first open door to a dark room.

'Ah, la salle de bains,' Antoine reassured her, 'we'll soon have la petite bestiole.' Cats were beasts to him. They were good for catching vermin and got no more than a saucer of milk, if any was left over. They were locked out of the house at night and if they had the audacity to venture into a bedroom they were sure to be chased out of the house with a broom and a volley of curses. Léa's cat was black and that meant bad luck to the old villagers.

Antoine reached into the darkness and pulled a light switch and there, in the windowless room, was the kitten, sitting in the bath tub on top of a pile of neatly stacked potatoes. Strings of onions hung from a drying rack above. At Léa's startled look Antoine's mouth opened in a wide grin; his face creased like an old leather handbag. 'Les patates,' he chuckled, 'they stay cool here.' His scientific approach to potato storing was obviously something to boast about. 'Who spends more than five minutes a day in the bathroom, eh? It's a waste not to use it. They're much better here than in the cellar, it's too humid down there, and the slugs get them.' Evidently, he was happy to put off his next bath until he had eaten all the potatoes, probably sometime next spring.

Throughout France rusted bath tubs ended their life in wild flower meadows as water troughs for grazing cattle. These and rusty cars were icons of isolated farms. Usually the cars were full of hay. Chickens clucked in and out through the broken car windows, using the vehicles as a day roost or nests, balancing on the edge of the windowless doors. Their white droppings transformed the car body paint into zebra patterns.

'Maybe Jackson Pollock got his inspiration from French chickens for his paintings,' Sam remarked on a particularly

162

well frequented car wreck, 'that belongs in the Tate Modern. It would probably win the Turner Prize.'

Sam was sorting through the piles of books. Léa needed to get out of the room, into the air, away from Augusto's intrusive stare. Slow down, she thought. Discreetly she made for another one of the French windows to the garden.

'Go through the library,' Augusto waved, 'at the back, the low door. It opens outwards, needs a good push.'

She caught a glimpse of herself as she passed the foxed mirror above the fireplace. Her discomfort was pulling at her face. Lift up you mouth, damn it, she told herself, we'll be out of here soon. Her shoe kicked something hard which bounced and skidded on the parquet floor. It sounded like a large pebble. She went after it and picked it out of the dark corner. At first it looked like the fossilised shell Sam had found on the path above the lake. But it was not; it was a tiny marble ear resting in the palm of her hand. She placed it on the table.

'Broken, but still so life like.' Augusto reached for it and gently stroked the tiny object with his thumb.

'There were two exquisite marble busts of my son Pablo and my daughter Ariana, here,' he crossed the room and let his hand rest on the mantelpiece where they had stood. 'Perfect likenesses. We had them made for their fifth birthdays, a time of transition from fantasy land to the real world. You can always see it quite clearly,' he pondered, 'suddenly, from one day to the next the world of magic and wonders vanishes from their eyes.'

Was the regret in his voice for the vanishing childhood dreams, Léa wondered, or for the loss of his children?.

'She took the busts. Very thorough, my darling Ophelia. I don't expect Zoffia swept up in here. She too had gone by the time I got back. This,' he said with absolute certainty, 'is Ariana's ear, 'must have dropped the thing in her rush to get out.'

With great care he balanced the ear with its broken edge on the mantelpiece, so that it was facing into the room.

'There, my child,' he said tenderly, 'you can listen to the proceedings.'

Sam looked up. His eyes met Léa's; he gave a shrug.

'I'll go and get some more boxes from the car to pack these.' As he passed her Léa instinctively reached out for his arm to hold him back. Sam slightly pursed his lips as if to say, 'it won't take long now'.

Get out of here, Léa pleaded with herself. The boundaries between reality and something beyond it were becoming blurred. She felt that she was being jostled back and forth through some invisible wall.

She turned into the library. It was darker here than elsewhere. The room was much smaller than the others but almost double the height and hexagonal, as if it had once been part of a tower. Every inch of wall space was covered in shelves with rails and sliding ladders reaching up to the last row of books just under the ceiling. By their leather binding it was obvious that Augusto was not ready to sell these, not yet perhaps. The old dog must be more agile than he looks, Léa thought, either that or he risks his life each time he climbs to the top shelf.

A small writing desk stood under a high window in the corner of the room with books, papers, photographs and press cuttings untidily piling up. On the window sill sat a row of specimen jars. They were filled with a dark brown liquid. Only one of them contained an object, some kind of flattened, dark shape. She bent down to look at it from the side. A brown toad with yellow eyes stared back at her.

'Don't worry, he's dead,' Augusto's voice came from next door, 'in time his eyes will shut.'

Léa straightened up abruptly. From her footfall he had heard exactly where she had stopped.

In the corner, partially hidden by a faded velvet curtain there was a low carved door. Léa turned the rustic ring handle and pushed. The door was heavier than she had expected. It suddenly gave way and she stood outside on a patch of white gravel, taking a deep breath at last.

The uncut grass softly brushed her ankles as she walked around the side of the house. Each step released an earthy aroma beneath her feet; humidity rose, thick in her nostrils, up into the narrow passages just behind her forehead. It made her giddy. Time assumed a different shape in this house; she felt as though they had been with the old man for hours, but her watch only showed a quarter to two.

The sun had moved to the back of the house. The three main floors were topped by a row of smaller windows under the roof. Apart from the room in which Augusto and Sam were dealing with the books the shutters were firmly closed on all other windows, a house blindfolded. On either side of an Italianate portico stood a row of bulbous blue portugaises planters. Each one contained an orange tree. Their new growth needed trimming. The grounds swept away from the house in terraces of shrubs and groups of mimosas, interspersed with fountains and stone carvings to mark the focal points.

The pressure Léa had felt in the house was subsiding. I'm just hungry, she comforted herself. Neither she nor Sam ate meat and she had eaten no more than half a plate of the peas. Augusto had forgotten about the crisp bread in the toaster.

Bumblebees grumbled among the grasses. The sun's heat beat sharply on her face. There was another faint, indefinable noise, short and guttural. It came from the pool. She went to its edge and peered down. Round black objects were scattered across the once turquoise pool bottom. So he does keep coal in it, she smiled. But the shapes moved. They hopped, made small leaps, climbed over the top of each other. She took half a step back and bumped into what felt like a billowing cushion.

'Frogs,' said the sour breath, now beside her. Augusto's bony hand slipped in between her body and her arm and held her elbow.

'With all the water gone it was brown and stinking. After the warm rain a few days ago I heard a multitude of little voices.' He put his other hand to his ear. 'The pool was full of them. They sit and croak and call their mates and next season there will be thousands more. The rain collects at the deep end. It's Frog Nirvana to them. I shovelled them out, put them into a bin bag and took them to the lake, but the next day they were back. Not the same ones, I'm sure, but if one of them starts calling they all come running.'

Léa shook her head in disbelief. She felt a sudden twisting pang of pity for Augusto. This place and his life seemed to have been visited by a succession of absurdities.

'So! You see,' Augusto sounded almost amused, 'this then is what my son will inherit.'

Puffs of white clouds were drifting into the perfect blue of the sky.

'What's over there?'

A number of crows circled lazily over a depression below them. Their mournful calls carried up on the breeze.

'They've been there for days, over my lake. It's a magnet for mosquitoes, but oh, so exquisitely savage.'

'Do crows eat mosquitoes? I thought they fed on carrion.' Where was Sam? He was taking a long time fetching his boxes.

'Perhaps there is a rabbit or a dead fox down there.' Augusto's detached voice sounded as though he was speaking from a hollow space. 'They'll eat anything; just like vultures really.'

Léa followed him back to the house. Stay back, she whispered to herself. She tripped on the loose step to the library. He had waited for her inside the door and caught her by the hand. He held it in his for a moment after she had regained her balance.

'What happened here, Augusto?' she asked, at once regretting her intrusive question. He lightly touched her red hair to push it out of her face.

'Spun copper.' He exhaled the words almost in astonishment. Slowly, he lifted her hand and kissed it. 'I'm so sorry, my dear, that you have to know me like this.'

167

Léa stepped past him and made her way back into the house to where Sam was still sorting the books. The slapping of Augusto's slippers followed her across the library. She felt his body close behind. The sound of his steps ceased and she heard him mumble something but did not look back.

Sam had begun packing the boxes. She put her hand on his shoulder.

'I'll help you. I want to have another look myself.' She delved into the piles of books, picked out a few, but the bulk of them were more Sam's province.

Augusto had remained in the library. They could hear the rustle of papers. Léa was glad of something to do. She felt a need to stay close to Sam instead of drifting around the desolate house on her own. She picked up a slim volume. The cloth of the binding was embossed with a colourful William Morris design.

'Kelmscott Press. God. It's the real thing, Sam,' she whispered, 'how can he bear to part with this?'

'Ask him if he really wants to sell it.'

'You ask him. Please, Sam.' She took his hand and ran it over the goose pimples on her arm.

'That's what he does to me. He stands too close to me.'

'Okay.' Sam held out his hand and took the book. The library door was not closed. As Sam reached it he saw Augusto hunched over the desk in the corner. His chest and back were pumping hard and his legs were positioned at a peculiar angle, trying to keep his balance. Spread across the desk lay the pages of the pale green letter the postman had delivered earlier. One of the pages fluttered in his hand like a dying bird. His breath was loud and rasping and he was unaware of Sam's presence. Sam quickly stepped back and tiptoed back to the table.

'There's something wrong with him.'

'You've finally noticed.'

'No. Really.' Sam's whisper was urgent now. 'He's reading that letter and virtually heaving up over it.'

Léa was struck by Sam's sudden panic. 'Let's get out of here.

If he keels over we'll have a corpse on our hands.' She stopped, horrified at the cruelty of her remark.

They silently gathered up the remaining books of their choice, hardly daring to breathe, listening for the old man's moves. After a while they heard his footsteps pacing up and down in the library. A few minutes elapsed, then the library door fell shut and the shuffle of his feet came towards them.

'How are you getting on?' It was meant to sound casual and friendly, but Augusto's face was flushed and he was still breathing hard. Léa put her head down. Let Sam handle this, she thought, he's more inscrutable than I am.

Sam and Augusto settled on a price for the books. They packed the last remaining ones into Sam's boxes. Augusto pointed to yet another door they hadn't noticed before.

'Your boxes are heavy. Take a shortcut through here.'

He beckoned them through the old chateau kitchen. Two long oak work benches faced each other in the centre. Antiquated cooking implements and a multitude of objects dangled from two rails bristling with hooks. A massive tiled kitchen range took up half of the back wall which was clad in tiles that had once been white. The walls were lined with glass-fronted cabinets. Racks and shelves were laden with bowls, stacks of meat plates, serving dishes, sauce boats, wine and water jugs of all shapes and sizes. There wasn't a thing under the sun that could not have been boiled, steamed, fried or roasted in this kitchen. Pots and pans hung in rows, as if the cooks of a castle of centuries gone by had just finished their shift.

'You could feed an army out of here,' the old man gestured with the look of a sleep walker. 'She must have forgotten about the kitchen. Not really her province.'

As he walked he began humming a tune to himself, '*Oh, Du lieber Augustin, Augustin, Augustin,*
Oh, Du lieber Augustin alles ist hin.
Oh, Du lieber Augustin ....' His words trailed off into the vast stillness of the hall.

They ran the gauntlet of Augusto's ancestors watching from above with haughty expressions in their painted eyes. Augusto opened the main door. A breeze had sprung up from the mountains. The sudden bluster nearly took their breath away.

*

As hush as death, anon the dreadful thunder

24

Noirlac Village Café, 1st of May, afternoon

As they drove down to the gate Augusto raised his transparent white arms and waved good bye.

'You're the linguist,' Sam said. 'What was that he was singing?'

'It's a German children's song. Oh, my dearest Augustin, everything is lost.'

'Maybe he regrets the loss of the books more than the rest, said Sam. 'We shouldn't have come.'

'I wish we hadn't. How could we have known? I'm going to faint with hunger.' She looked pale. 'Let's eat something at the café? I only ate the peas.'

'A piece of crisp bread wouldn't have made much difference.' Sam too needed to give his stomach something to do. He parked the car by the side of the café under the suspicious gaze of Armand Arouet who stood in the open

171

door, smoking. Armand hastily crushed his cigarette underfoot and disappeared in the darkness behind the counter where he polished his already clean glasses, trying to look as if he'd just waved good bye to a bus-load of customers. Until it was time for the half dozen villagers to take their evening aperitif these two could turn out to be his only customers of the day.

The breeze was turning into a fierce wind and they decided to sit inside to escape the swirling dust of the café terrace.

'Can we eat something?' asked Sam pulling out two chairs by the window table. Armand nodded.

'Pizza, Croque Monsieur, quîche aux poireaux, or a sandwich, Monsieur?'

'Two tuna sandwiches, a café crème and a pot of tea, please.'

Armand called the order to someone over the saloon doors. From the kitchen a shrill voice answered.

'C'est bon, c'est bon, j'arrive. Is the house on fire or what?' followed by the clutter of pots and pans in acknowledgement of the order. Armand returned to lean on the counter.

Paul Airvolt had crossed the road, shook Armand's hand and went to half perch on a stool by the bar.

'Salut, Armand. Customers?'

A dog with orange fur stood in the café door and raised his nose to get the scent of the newcomers. The two men chatted, unaware that Léa and Sam could hear their conversation.

'You never liked the old man. Can't blame you really. He doesn't belong in these parts.' Paul cast a conciliatory look at Armand, 'but his wife, c'est autre chose. She is a real lady.'

'Well, then they should pay their way, like proper lords and ladies. I've been waiting for them to show their faces again.' Armand picked up a slice of salami from his aperitif dish.

'Viens, Zozo,' he called to the mongrel who was chewing clumps of earth out of his paws in the centre of the floor. Deciding that it preferred sausage to wet soil, the dog got up and gratefully took possession of its tasty treat and trundled over to settled next to Sam's chair.

'Look at the mud in his paws,' Paul pointed with the glass in his hand. 'He keeps digging for something, down by that lake. 'Méchant Zozo,' he pretended to scold the dog, but his heart was not in it. 'He's just a poor dog,' Paul sighed philosophically. 'Today I had to chase all the way round and whistle my head off before he came back over the wall. He's totally obsessed with that lake. And then he only came back because 'his lordship' stormed out of the house with a great big stick.'

'So that's the intruder,' Sam whispered. 'I don't know what Augusto got so mad about. This is not exactly the Hound of the Baskervilles.'

As if to prove the point the mongrel raised its head and waged its tail. Sam patted its head.

'All dogs dig up gardens. They usually come back with no more than a pathetic old bone,' Sam smiled at the man with the frayed beret.

173

Léa licked her lips. 'I wish someone would bring me a bone to chew on right now.'

Armand reached for the broom and swept up the dried soil the dog had left on the tiled floor.

'Zozo adores the maid,' Paul grinned at Armand, 'sneeks after her like a love-sick detective all over the village. He knows she's coming long before she turns up. But the old De Montsarrat, he scares Zozo out of his wits.' He had an air of a wise politician predicting the end of the world.

'Have you seen Madame since the row that night? It's incredibly quiet up there.' Armand's broom swept on mechanically as if of his own volition, wafting the man's brawny arms this way and that. 'The redhead hasn't been for the papers either.'

'Haven't seen either of the women,' Paul contemplated his glass, 'but then Madame never came to the village much.'

'To be honest, I don't know how they can afford to keep up that house. Louis says it's getting really run down and he should know. He's up there delivering the letters almost every day.' The broom stopped and Armand rubbed his stubble chin. Léa could hear it chafing like coarse sandpaper. Goose pimples sprang up on her arms as they had done when her teachers made the chalk screech on the blackboard. Armand cupped one hand over the other on the top of the broom handle and rested his meaty chin on them.

'The old man used to give Louis a drink when he delivered the letters most days, but yesterday he said that he wouldn't let him into the house anymore.'

Armand turned and disappeared into the kitchen through the flapping doors. Paul, with his hand casually tucked into the pocket of his worn-out overall eyed up Sam and Léa for a moment. He climbed down from his high stool and strolled over to their table.

'Viens, Zozo.' He took the dog by the scruff of the neck. 'Mes excuses, Madame, I don't like him making a nuisance of himself.'

Léa shook her head. 'Don't worry, your dog looks like a very nice dog to me.' She bent down and stroked the dogs head. She felt the grease of the coarse, unwashed fur deposit itself on her fingers. Remember to use the other hand to eat the sandwich, she reminded herself.

'You're not from round then?' Paul asked casually. Retrieving his dog had obviously been a pretext to enter into conversation with the newcomers. Sam and Léa exchanged looks.

'We live not far from here, at Sainte Colombe.'

'Ah, just the other side of Montferrus then.' Armand came out of the kitchen with two gaping baguette sandwiches the size of an arm. Léa put a hand to her stomach at the sight of the approaching food.

'Are you going to buy the chateau then?'

'Popol, alors! Don't be so indiscreet,' Armand pretended to admonish his friend, but in his eyes burned the same unbridled curiosity as in Paul's. Sam laughed and took a bite of his sandwich. He shook his head.

'No, we're not buying the chateau. Even if we had the money we wouldn't,' he reassured Armand who cast his eyes to the ceiling in apparent relief at Sam's sensible point of view. Armand and Paul exchanged looks. Sam knew that the two men had to decide whether they were in the presence of two untrustworthy strangers or not.

175

'Can I buy you a drink,' Sam smiled at Paul and Armand. 'What will you have?' There was a slight pause in the conversation. More than an offer of a drink was needed to gain their trust.

'I am Sam Carter and this is Léa. I'm a journalist, a writer. I'm doing some research at the abbey of Morterive. Léa is a translator. She partly grew up in this region and spent her school holidays with her grandmother in Gruissan,' he added.

'I went there once to see the flamingos,' Armand sighed. 'We stayed in one of the beach houses on stilts. It was so exotic.'

'We've been living in Sainte Colombe for fifteen years,' said Sam between two mouthfuls. 'For some reason we've never been through Noirlac until recently.'

'Ah, bon,' Armand's eyes glanced over to Paul who nodded. 'It's easy to by-pass this village, we're so put of the way. Everyone is always taking the big roads to Carcassonne and Narbonne or Toulouse. It's the lure of the cities these days.'

It seemed the two men had proof enough that the visitors could be trusted.

'This is my good friend Paul Airvolt.' Armand placed a fraternal arm on Paul's shoulder. 'We call him Popol. He lives across the road.'

Léa sipped her tea. She turned to Armand.

'We were passing on the day when that truck nearly demolished your café,' she laughed. 'In fact, it nearly flattened us too.'

'That was you in the car?' Eyebrows arched like a comic in a silent film and he slapped his forehead in a gesture of recognition. 'Mon Dieu, it all comes back to me now. In that case the drinks are on me.' Now that he had decided that they were both victims of one and the same truck it was a different matter.

'I'll fetch the Ricard.'
He poured out a double measure of the drink into four glasses. He obviously felt there was something to celebrate or perhaps he just wanted to loosen their tongue.

'Are you friends of Monsieur … at the chateau?' he asked casually. He put the glasses down on the red Formica table.

'Not at all,' answered Léa, 'we met him once in a Carcassonne hotel. Today we came to buy some of his books.'

'Looks like he's selling every stick he has got. Perhaps he'll pay his bill now?'

'He said his wife had taken everything,' Sam said to Léa in English. Léa shrugged and silently continued to munch her sandwich.

'Huh! Wonder what his wife will say about that!' exclaimed Armand, rolling up his shirt sleeves and crossing his hairy forearms, Oliver Hardy preparing for a fight. The two men were making all the running in the conversation, eager to impart their hot village gossip.

Sam and Léa were used to village rumours and all the posturing that went with them. Today's remark on the most harmless topic was tomorrow's innuendo and a proven fact the day after that.

They had arrived in their new home in Sainte Colombe on a Tuesday. On Thursday Sam answered the door to a hill

177

farmer who asked if they needed a ladder or tools for their renovation work. After an exchange of a few friendly words the man could contain his curiosity not a second longer.

'Sans indiscretion,' he ventured with a conspiratorial, near toothless smile, 'without wishing to be indiscreet, will you have lots of young ladies like this one visiting?' And without pausing for breath he added, 'and how much did you pay my cousin for this house?'

The man's question about the house was most likely motivated by jealousy of his cousin who had probably boasted in the village that he had sold the house for twice the price Sam and Léa had in fact paid. But the man's first question was to establish whether or not Léa might still be available, apparently with his mountain-farming sons in mind. They had accompanied the father on his mission. Sunburnt and raven-haired, they stood well back, arms crossed and legs assertively apart. From their young but already weather-hardened faces coal black eyes hungrily stared at Léa standing on the doorstep next to Sam.

'This is my wife Léa, 'said Sam with an almost apologetic smile.

'Bon Dieu!' the old man swore in exasperation. 'At this rate I'll never find wives for those two. All they do is tend their sheep in the summer; they drive them so high up, practically into the clouds where we never used to go when I was young. In winter they mend the barns and stables and never leave home. I sometimes think they prefer the sheep to women. Who's going to take over the farm when I'm gone and they're old? I need grandchildren, and soon.'

The sons' plight was a real one. The story was not new to Sam and Léa.

178

'These modern village girls,' the man dug his calloused hands into his pockets as he looked down the street, frowning, 'they think they're better than their mothers.'

The new breed of girls wouldn't dream of sharing the meagre existence of a simple mountain farmer, surrounded only by hundreds of bleating sheep, Léa knew, but to confront the man with the blunt truth would have insulted him. It would have invalidated his life-long struggle in what she knew to be a hard life. Girls today received a good state education, which often took them to university level and beyond by the time they reached the age to marry. Only the slow learners stayed behind with their parents and their harsh, rustic way of living.

'Girls, they want to strut around in high heels all day,' the old man complained, 'but who will do the work?'

The new kind of village girls preferred the shiny shopping malls in town to wading through sheep dung in wooden clogs or gum boots. In winter mountain farms could vanish for weeks on end in clouds of freezing mist. Houses were cold, beds got humid and icy draughts froze the feet. Clothes took on the acrid smell of damp wood smoke and soot from being dried by the open fireplaces which consumed huge logs that spat and sizzled with resin and sap.

'Our neighbours across the mountain, his son married an American last year.'

'So we heard,' Sam nodded. The old man continued to look accusingly at his sons. The girl, a tall blonde American, had been one of a string of female visitors to an ageing rock star who indulged in a great deal of drink at the Sainte Colombe village café. Léa and Sam also knew that the American girl had not lasted the year. After nine months she had given birth to a boy in primitive conditions on a sheep farm. Two months later she and the baby were gone. Her mother had turned up. There was a violent argument during which the men locked the girl and the baby in. They were rescued by the gendarmes who had to struggle up the mountain in a pick-up truck in a storm. The weeping daughter and her baby sat with the gendarmes at the front. Amidst raging thunder and lightning, the mother endured the trip back down, tossed around on the open back of the truck under a tarpaulin, as it descended the steep rocky paths which were turning into mud slides.

Only madly romantic foreign women had been known to go native. The old man's assumption was that Sam, being English and in his thirties, might have passing girlfriends to stay, like a number of expat men in the area. A single man with a house in France seemed to be a magnet for holidaying pretty girls. His sons could be in luck the old man had reasoned. A wife for one year was better than none. Léa was not offended. She felt sorry for the men. They were handsome enough as they stood there, smelling of wood smoke, sheep dung and strong tobacco. She could see why some romantic foreign girls would see these testosterone charged young men as an exotic adventure for the duration of a summer season.

'It wasn't always Monsieur Augusto's chateau,' Armand imparted with an almost superior air, 'but,' he smacked his lips, savouring the next titbit,' the previous owner was not a lucky man either, with his wife that is.'

'She ran off with her lover,' Paul butted in. 'One of the boys went mad, had to be put away.'

'He is grown now, though no better. Never got over his mother rejecting him like that.' Armand licked his thumb and forefinger and teased the ends of his Dali-esque moustache. 'Sad, sad story,' he sighed with pathos.

'Madame's car hasn't been there since the day the removal truck left, but Monsieur Augusto's car is there.' Paul wagged his index finger. 'He's not fit to drive anymore.'

'He shoots down the lane and around the corner, engine howling in first gear,' Armand joined in, describing a demented trajectory with his hand. 'On the way back several times now he nearly missed the corner altogether.' He flicked his checked tea towel over his shoulder in a gesture of resigned disgust.

'Ça alors.' Paul greedily gulped down the remainder of his free drink. 'I'm not surprised. The women usually do the driving.'

A pregnant silence hung in the room. Armand and Paul looked from Sam to Léa and back. They were obviously expected to divulge secrets about what they had seen at the chateau in their turn.

Paul cleared his throat. 'Is Monsieur Augusto alright?' he asked with unconvincing concern for the old man's well-being.

Léa checked with Sam but he shook his head. They tacitly agreed that it would be unwise to reveal details of their visit.

'He seems fine,' said Sam. 'We didn't meet anyone else.'

'We only went to look at his books.' Léa picked up her bag. 'Time to go.'

'Let me pay for the drinks.' Sam held out a note.

'Ah, non, non, non. Absolument pas, Monsieur, I won't hear of it.' Armand went into an unconvincing swagger. With a smile Sam laid down an appropriate amount on the counter. It was not refused.

'Thank you very much all the same. This is a beautiful village. We'll be back.' They shook the warm, rough hands of the two men. As they emerged from the café a frontal gust assaulted them.

'Be grateful for the wind,' Léa brushed herself off before getting into the car. 'That dog was home to a million fleas.'

*

Hold off the earth a while

25

Chateau de Noirlac, Thursday, May 5th

Augusto shuffled to the dark end of the hall. There was a mark on the wall where Ophel rosewood chest of drawers had stood. He opened the back door to the garden but could not bring himself to step outside. The light fell into the hall; in the dust under the stairs there were foot prints. Nothing but dust, he grumbled, she's left me nothing but dust. He closed the door, retraced his steps from room to room, at last returning to the hall. He had kept the library door closed in the last few days, trying to contain what lay within. Again and again he stood with his hand on the cold china door knob but could not bring himself to turn it. Fear clawed at his stomach at the thought of being confronted by Ophelia's letter in the very room which had been his favourite all these years. He turned his back to the library. The ping-pong table with the pile of books no longer looked so intimidating. Sam and Léa had bought a fair number, not that the sale could save him from his predicament. They had chosen some surprising volumes. Were they truly interested in the construction of pre-medieval fortresses and the life of monks or had they bought more than they wanted out of pity? To sell the chateau would take months, endless paper work, Pablo would have to come from New York, Ariana from Madrid, the inheritance taxes would be huge.

He felt drained. Sit down, sit down somewhere, he mumbled, but there was nothing to sit on. He wandered across the empty rooms to the kitchen for one of the last remaining plastic chairs and positioned it by the French windows in the garden salon.

It felt as though the air had been sucked out of the room. The brass handle of the French windows was stiff; he pulled hard and both panes flew open and slammed into the plaster surrounds. In the grounds there was not a breath of wind. The leaves on the birch trees were motionless. Everything appeared somehow fixed, glued into place.

It was past noon. He shivered. A few days ago, when he had closed the doors behind the couple carrying away the books the cold had descended on him. Ah, he thought, the English man and that French wife of his. The shimmer of her copper coloured hair had stirred up something deep within him. He had spoilt it all by making her so wary. It was as if she had sensed his thoughts, his desires. Perhaps, a long time ago, when he was younger .... Now there was no more. Sam and was it Léa? Short for Eléanor or Léonora? They were the last people he had seen. He had been unable to face anyone else, to be humiliated by his absurd predicament, by his downfall.

He sat and waited in the silence. Gloom hugged the ceilings; it hung in the corners like damp and dirty drapes. On this sunny day the night had entered the house at three in the afternoon.

*

If she unmasked her beauty to the moon

26

Auch library, same afternoon

Léa parked the car in the cobbled square. The Place Bartas was devoid of trees. Many of the tall buildings on either side, once built of flat Toulouse bricks and cream provencal sand stone, had been rendered. Most of the pale blue shutters were closed against the sun. At the far end of the Place Bartas the high frontage of the library looked as if plucked from a Venetian square and dropped into the largely medieval Auch. A recent over-zealous restoration had left the elegant building so clean one would have thought it had been dipped in an acid bath; all patina accumulated over the centuries had been meticulously erased. The bright pink of the bricks radiated and was almost blinding in the early afternoon light. The elaborate carvings of the sandstone mullion window surrounds had been scrubbed back to almost white. A brash, incongruous modern entrance announced the current use of the building – *Bibliothèque Municipale de la Ville d'Auch*. I suppose the people of Auch deserve to have some concession to living in the twentieth century, Léa mused, as she pushed through the gleaming glass and chrome revolving doors that propelled her into the building. She could feel the swish of air on her naked ankles as the doors behind her continued to turn for a few seconds before they came to a halt.

She looked around the flag-stoned library reception. At the end of the hall squatted a Gaudi-esque reception desk with a bronze-tinted glass top. With its surreal curved shapes the whole construction looked as if it could take flight at any moment. Behind it three housewifely women peered in her direction. They reminded her of chickens watching a worm. All that was missing were the indignant little clucking noises.

She had telephoned the previous day with her apparently unusual request.

'I called yesterday, about your medieval archive.'

All three nodded vigorously, making a sort of Mexican wave with their heads. Léa politely waited for it to ebb away. Perhaps she was the only visitor of the day with the exception of a couple of school groups who didn't want to be there anyway, but who were overjoyed to have a day out to tumble about in strange places, pushing and shoving each other and giggling noisily.

The blonde woman with the frizzy perm smiled. Her doll-like cheeks puckered; bright pink flushed from the neck up into her face.

'It's so rare that anyone asks to see the archive.' She rose but stayed behind her office chair as school girls do in front

187

of teachers when they don't know the answers. Her hands were gripping the back rest of the chair and she swivelled it this way and that in a little dance. Léa tried to fathom the women's excessive curiosity. Perhaps they had so few visitors that she was the nearest thing to an event.

'My name is Marie-Ange. This is Christine and Jeanne.'

'I'm told you have the best archive outside Paris,' Léa smiled.

'We do, we do,' said the pink-faced woman and heaved a nostalgic sigh, 'but you know, most people today want their history 'prêt-à-manger', so to speak. They don't want to spend time searching for anything much.' She made her way around the desk. The broad behinds of the two other women meanwhile remained firmly on their respective chairs.

'I'm not going in there,' sulked the elder of the two.

'Nor am I,' the second joined in.

'C'est bon, c'est bon,' Marie-Ange waved to calm their remonstrations. 'I'm the only one who can stand the strong-smelling chemicals used to protect the books from insects and such like.' She walked around the reception desk and indicated an archway and the end of the hall. 'This way, please. Jeanne and Christine are allergic to all that,' she whispered, 'but they do make such a fuss. Five minutes in there and their eyes are streaming and their skin is aflame. My predecessor fainted the first time she went in. They call it the evil spirits, silly girls. Follow me, please.'

She padded across the hall. Beyond the arch they snaked through the lending library with shelves filled with French translations of Agatha Christie, Jilly Cooper, Stephen King and Jackie Collins. Léa wondered how the latter might translate into something comprehensible to the housewives of Auch. Marie-Ange caught Léa's surprise.

'English and American thrillers and crime are much more popular than Victor Hugo or Balzac, even Emile Zola sits on the shelves mostly untouched. You get too much of them at school, so in the end you don't want to read them at all. As for the new French writers…,' she came to a halt in front of a heavy oak door with a deep relief carving of a large crest, 'all they do is write about their own little lives, with a few exceptions.'

From a recess in the wall she picked a form, filled it in and handed it to Léa to sign.

'Léa Carter,' she spelled out on a visitor label and pinned it to Léa's shirt. The form was slipped into a folder and returned to the recess.

'Take a couple of deep breaths,' she advised, 'the air is a bit foul in there.'

Two large iron keys turned in vociferous locks, one above the other and the door opened with a groan into a vast room lying in a yellow haze. A wall of musty humidity enveloped them. Here and there a loose flagstone rumbled underfoot as they made their way across the dimly-lit space.

'This is the oldest part of the building, ninth century'. Marie-Ange pointed to the vaulted ceiling. 'The beams have settled a bit since then. Un peu comme moi, at bit like me,' she tittered and patted her hip.

She directed Léa to the left side where a steep lectern ran the full length of the room. Heavy tomes were displayed on it, as if the monks had just gone to pray at vespers.

'The index is at the end here. But first let me show you our oldest book.' Marie-Ange steered Léa into the corner.

'No more than a handful of people have seen this in the ten years I've been here, and most came from the Sorbonne University in Paris.'

In the half-light stood a pulpit in the shape of a life-size lioness carved in black wood. The animal stood on its hind legs, holding an inclined desktop between its front paws. On it lay an open book.

'What were these holes for, at the side of the desk?' Léa asked.

Marie-Ange opened the pulpit drawer and produced two cow horns.

'These are inkwells,' she glowed, 'and they sit in the big holes. And these go here, into the smaller holes.' She inserted a pair of large feathers, which had been trimmed and cut in a sharp slant. 'They were the only writing tools then, although some of the poorer monasteries often had to use bevelled wooden sticks when they ran short of good feathers.'

She was obviously keen to use this rare opportunity to impart her knowledge. 'The desk is much older than the book, maybe even from the seventh or eighth century. I should think it came from the Middle East, Persia or even ancient China. It would have reached France via Spain. It was probably war booty. Or it may have been left behind when the Moors were driven back across the Pyrenees into Spain.' She stroked the beast's toothy smile like a mother would her beloved child. 'Pity no one really sees you.' She turned to a volume displayed on the next shelf.

'This book is my favourite. Twelfth century, local history. Books produced outside the church were extremely rare in those days. But we know that this one was written in secret by a local monk over his entire lifetime in a monastery and then hidden.' She was in full flow now. Léa didn't want to interrupt.

'He compiled it page by page. His illustrations are no better than a child's, but there is a great honesty in them. He had the pages smuggled out by his family as he turned them out. He was probably the only one in the family who could write so they must have supplied him with all the gossip on visiting days. Few people in Europe could write or even had access to writing material at that time. It's full of local anecdotes, rumours, scandals, illicit love affairs, even murders. Some are amusing, others are very cruel and some downright pornographic,' she giggled. 'People haven't changed that much over the centuries, have they?'

'The tools have changed, but not much else.'

'None of the content of this book had a place in a monastery,' Marie-Ange added. 'The author would have been tortured and burnt at the stake for being in league with the devil if he had been discovered. The book wasn't bound until more than three hundred years later.' Marie-Ange carefully turned the pages for Léa to see. 'Imagine, the poor man never saw more than a couple of pages at a time, never the whole thing.'

A bit like life, Léa thought. Each event is but a fragment at best, until later it all comes together, for good or for ill.

Marie-Ange led Léa to the index. 'Take care how you handle it, it's quite brittle in the binding. I'll leave you to it. Take your time, if you can stand the air in here. Ring the bell by the big door and I'll let you out.'

She turned and her rapid footfall echoed under the vaulted wooden ceiling. With a grinding yawn the great door fell shut, keys turned in the locks and something inside Léa trembled.

The index was the largest book in the room. Titles listed were mostly entered in Latin and she had to guess at some of their precious contents. Old French replaced the Latin titles as the centuries passed. Tomes on nature, science and the humanities crept in among the missels, psalters and personal prayer books, once the cherished possessions of the Languedoc and Spanish nobility. Further into the index more and more illustrated books were listed about all manner of medicinal plants and exotic beasts.

Léa heaved the Grand Bestiaire off a shelf. She'd been awestruck by such books in the British Museum, had leafed through some in the reading rooms at the British Library.

Handwritten descriptions above drawings of creatures with long necks and sharp teeth were the most intriguing. A cow's body with an extraordinary long, thin vertical neck and a camel's face was subtitled 'giraffe'. A striped dog with a rabbit's face was identified as a tiger. Most were drawings made after travellers' colourful hear-say of fabulous beasts in strange lands. Even an elephant looked more of a cross between a cow and a pig. But the sketches had been made with such devotion and zest that they became credible creatures in themselves.

For her translation she needed to consult the famed *Musterbuch*, the only comprehensive technical manual for illuminators produced in the Alsace in the tenth century, recopied in the fourteenth. She scoured it for the techniques of producing inks. Here were the recipes for the colours, jealously guarded by the apothecaries. They dispensed them with utmost precision to the illuminators who produced books for kings, queens, princes and God.

Black or dark brown inks were made from walnut shells, from soot or by burning pine wood, others from blackberry wood, cut in mid-winter, dried, beaten, soaked and boiled over months, thickened, dried in the sun, mixed with wine and if not black enough, torched with a red hot poker.

She made notes, fearing there would not be enough time in a day, in a week, to soak up all this knowledge.

Luminous verdigris was obtained by oxidising copper sheets with wine and vinegar, arsenic, mercury or sulphur. Other greens were made from veal bile, goose feathers or sturgeon's bladders. Saffron produced golden yellows, boiled beetles and human blood made reds, blues were extracted in minute quantities from the rocks of Africa and Asia, ochre gleaned from iron. Some colours were concocted from boiled, dried parsley and leeks, honey, urine and other mysterious ingredients.

And then the ultimate recipe for 'Spanish gold'. It claimed to have been produced from red copper, human blood and vinegar. The Saracens' recipe gave the gruesome instructions to lock cockerels in total darkness until they mated, their eggs hatched by toads until chicks with serpents' tails emerged. These were to be sealed for six months in pewter vases filled with powdered basil and hidden deep underground.

Alchemists were incited to capture a red-haired virgin and have her deflowered by a sage. In a complex ceremony her throat was to be cut, her red hair reunited with the flames of the fierce fire used to heat copper plates:

'Boil the virgin's blood with one hundred leaves

of fresh basil and vinegar until thickened to a heavy syrup,
spread the solution on the red hot copper plates until the
desired gold appears.'

Léa took a deep breath. How many decades of experiments by quacks would it have taken before these men realised that gold could not be manufactured from other metals? How many red haired girls were cruelly put to death for the glory of illuminated manuscripts made for the church, for the glory of God? She shuddered at the gruesome thought. Or was the recipe made deliberately impossible, banking on the fact that few would be willing to kill an innocent virgin in order to produce the philosopher's stone? She instinctively ran her hands through her hair, bundling it at the side as if to hide it from the greedy gaze of some hidden quack resurrected from the pages of the book she was holding.

She had entered a world she had not known, an age in which no sacrifice was too great, no task too long or too laborious to obtain what one desired. Alchemists had been prepared to make a pact with the devil for centuries with nothing to show for it.

Léa examined the book, page by page. At the end of the volume, at the bottom of the last page, meticulously scripted in a stiff gothic hand, a nameless monk's rhyme about the strain of hand-penning whole books in the tenth century:

'Three fingers write,
but all the body suffers the pain'.

Léa closed the hefty tome. She struggled to squeeze it back into its slot on the shelf. She made her way back to the book so precious to Marie-Ange.

As she passed the shelves a dainty vellum-bound book on the shelf immediately above the pulpit caught her eye. There it was, in a similar spelling to the sign Sam had spotted in the bushes by the side of the road, just one word: Noyrlacque in gothic letters, finely painted in gold on a pencil-thin spine.

She carefully extracted the frail looking volume from the shelf. It creaked a little as she opened it. Had no-one had ever looked at these pages starched with animal glue?

Léa pulled up a chair. On the title page *La Desmoyselle de Noyrlacque* was scripted in an accomplished hand. Beneath it a drawing depicted a young woman, half emerging, or half immersed in water. Her long hair flowed and spread on the water's undulating surface.

The image formed an oval. In the distance between the reeds stood the figure of a bearded man. On his left a slope ran down and ended by a straight row of willow trees. To his right the ground rose and butted onto a high rock topped by three wind-blown trees. The date of 1229 was penned at the bottom of the page in the spidery hand of someone very old.

The following pages were almost impossible to decipher as the text was written in a mixture of old French and Occitan, which was closer to the Catalan language of northern Spain than to French.

Léa carefully turned the stiff, wafer-thin pages, hoping to glean some reference dating back to Augusto's chateau which had begun its life as a monastery. As she bent over to read her eyes began to burn. A tear fell onto the last page of the book. She watched in horror as the hand-scripted words began to dissolve.

She sat back down, clutching the slim volume to her chest. She squeezed her eyes shut. Hazy images began to dance behind her closed lids. A full moon lit up the scene. She saw the old man from the drawing clad in a long robe held around the middle with a thick rope. It was a monk. He was wading into the shallow lake. He moved further into the clouded water, as if drawn by an irresistible force. At the foot of the girl's figure he came to a halt. He looked around furtively, then lifted her white sodden dress. The girl was now floating with her pale secret quite exposed. The monk reached for a twig, touched her breasts with its tip before gently dragging it down to her golden pubic hair. Moisture glistened on the bloodless skin; the young face was a motionless silver mask under the cold moon. The monk's other hand felt for his lower belly and he began a frenzied kneading which culminated in a mournful, shuddering bark. He was still for a few moments. There was a rustling behind the old man. The reeds parted and a young monk stood, staring at the girl. The boy let out a cry, then turned and ran across the meadow and leapt over a low stone wall crying, 'murder, murder!'

The cries died away in the distance.

The old monk knelt, still, like an animal gone to ground. They would believe the boy. The priest would tell the abbot, the abbot the cardinal, the cardinal the judge, the judge the inquisitor. It was 1225, four years before the completion of the little book.

The old monk gave a soft sigh, then he sank down on the top of the girl's body. Léa felt herself ducking down. Rough material was scraping against her thighs and in horror she realised that she too was wearing a monk's habit.

'This isn't real,' she heard herself say. Her voice seemed to be coming from some distance behind her. 'It's a nightmare.' A hard knot under her stomach began to uncoil, faster and stronger, rising up into her throat. It erupted from her mouth in an uncontrollable roar. Her eyes sprang open. They were burning but she found herself back at the table among the book-lined walls. She gripped the ancient book, as if to test whether it was real or part of the nightmare.

'Get out, get out of here,' she repeated. Her voice rang shrill in the quiet room, reverberated under the wooden ceiling. She slammed the book shut, pushed her chair back and stood away from it - was it in fear or disgust? She didn't know. She hastily slipped it back onto the shelf, pushing it as far back into its slot until it could hardly be detected.

The desire to flee from the room, from the burning, etching stench in her nostrils became unbearable. Clutching her notes and her shoulder bag she dashed across hall. As she stepped onto the loose flagstones their vibration bounced back into her legs. Through tear-filled eyes she could barely locate the glint of the brass bell beside the oak door. She must have rung the bell hard because she heard urgent footstep approaching, a clatter of keys and the door opened. She felt a hand on her arm.

'Are you alright?' she heard Marie-Ange ask.

'I think so …I'm fine, really

The reception desk and the two women behind it were a blur.

'I told, you. I told you,' she heard one of the women say.

'Wait a second.' Marie-Ange took a tissue from her desk drawer and offered it to Léa.

'It just suddenly started to burn.' Léa ran the back of her hand over her eyes to stem the tears. 'I'll be alright in the fresh air. I probably spent far too much time with your wonderful books. I have to go now. Thank you so much.'

'I'm glad you've had a fruitful visit,' Marie-Ange beamed. 'Take a walk,' she called after Léa. 'Go and see our cathedral. People say it is a miracle of Renaissance beauty. Behind the altar there is a fabulous crucifixion.'

Léa gave a nod, trying to keep up a smile. The revolving doors swallowed her up, then spat her out onto the hot cobbled square.

*

The effect of this good lesson keep

27

Auch cathedral

Léa's hand trembled as she struggled to unlock her car.

'Christ. You don't believe this kind of stuff.' She got into the car but couldn't remember how to start it. Talking to herself was somehow reassuring. 'Calm down, go home and everything will be normal.' She gripped the scorching steering wheel, leaned forward and rested her forehead on her hands. They were hot and itched in the spaces between the fingers. I can't drive like this, she thought. She got out of the car and put her shoulder bag into the boot.

Across the square the cathedral sat on a raised plateau surrounded by a balustrade. A fountain set in the wall by the steps spouted a trickle of fresh water. Léa took a few deep breaths, crossed the square and cooled her itching hands in the water before climbing the massive stone steps. Under the old plane trees surrounding the cathedral she had expected an empty, reflective space, perhaps with a few benches in the shade, the silhouettes of old men wearing berets, smoke in the air from their Gauloises cigarettes, pinched between thin lips, as they played their early evening game of boules on the sun-baked dust. But here, as everywhere else, the parked cars and their drivers, who cared nothing about the labours of the Renaissance master builders, laid siege to the once holy ground. Her disappointment stung as if something had been desecrated. The gargoyles high above had reason to spew anger.

The interior of the cathedral was bathed in a soft afternoon gloom. The mist of incense clung to the carved oak pews, telling of a midday service of perhaps a funeral earlier that day. In the side chapels the stained glass windows stretched up almost out of sight. On either side rows of virgin candles in boxes waited to be lit for the price of a few coins.

She was alone in the church. The only sounds were the wings of pigeons, flapping somewhere above the altar. She picked up two candles but put no money in the box. As in all countries the church pleaded poverty, despite all the riches it possessed. In some remote recess of her conscience it gave her a twinge of satisfaction to take from the church and its fat priests and popes who had kept people in the fear of fabricated sins for centuries. And God didn't need her money, if there was a God, which she had doubted even as a child when her world had been filled with talk of the horrors that warring nations inflicted upon each other. If there was a God, why was the world a place of such anguish and suffering?

She lit her candles on another which was still flickering. They would go out soon. Gisèle had told her of the rumours that, on the order of some Vatican accountant, the candles were manufactured in such a way that the wick would burn out long before the candle wax had melted.

She sat down on a sculpted oak bench. The burning in her eyes was now abating and she could see the images of the stained glass windows clearly in all their colourful glory.

Behind the altar a window in the shape of giant fleur-de-lys in golden hues loomed over what Marie-Ange had called 'a fabulous crucifixion'. How could a crucifixion be called fabulous? It was certainly beautifully sculpted and painted, with Christ's body standing rather than hanging under a decorated arch of opulent Renaissance architecture. To the left a window depicted Moses and the burning bush. To her surprise she noticed that the bearded shepherd in the foreground sprouted two red horns.

It was hard to get enough distance from the gigantic windows to have an overall view of them, so details imposed themselves all the more on the eye. Ahead of her there was a sumptuously coloured window which seemed much older. The glass and leadwork were almost crude, with the panes divided horizontally by thick black bands. To the left of the image stood an old man in a blood red robe topped by a cape of radiant emerald green encrusted with precious stones. His chest-long beard stood away stiffly from his chin in a crescent moon shape. His hand rested on a rustic stick with a phallus-shaped handle. He contemplated a young woman facing him. She was looking directly at him with promise in her eyes. Her robes were sheer and tight over her breasts and body down to the onset of her thighs. Directly below her lower belly her white hand held a draped blue cloth to strategically hide what the old man seemed to desire. A plaque beneath the window read – the prophet Jeremia and Sibylla of Agrippa. Léa felt her fingers grip the notebook she was holding on her lap. Jeremia was looking at the young woman as old men do, not with testosterone charged lust, but with the melancholy and wonder that she had seen in Augusto's eyes. Prophet or not, the story of this old man seemed no different to Augusto's or that of the old monk depicted in the book about Noirlac in the Auch archive.

It was late afternoon as she settled into her car. The seats had soaked up all the heat from standing in the sun for hours. She opened the windows. A car engine roared next to her; one of the librarians was going home. The woman smiled at Léa and waved good bye.

Léa shook her head. There was no lake, there were no monks that came alive from books. She looked down at her cotton shirt and jeans, her bare ankles in her red shoes. Everything was as before.

*

Be wary then, best safety lies in fear

28

Chateau de Noirlac, sunset

The outkirts of Auch, with their rows of low houses lining the road, passed in a blur; they finally thinned out to give way to the main *départementale* road. She had forgotten that it was the end of the working day for many now eager to get home. She drove for a while, her small car boxed in by trucks and delivery vans. Exhaust fumes from the truck in front enveloped her and forced her to close the car window. On impulse she took a turning off the busy main road.

The quieter route back to Sainte Colombe would give her time to think. The hours spent cooped up in the foul-smelling archive had left her with a headache and the taste of chemicals biting in her throat. She opened both car windows and let the air fill her lungs. It had the savoury scent of grass and freshly ploughed soil. She had calmed down. Driving along deserted roads, flanked by greenery, always gave her space to think.

She stopped at a crossroad on the top of a hill. Four wooden signs each pointed in different directions: to Carcassonne, Toulouse, Albi and to Revel. A fifth, inserted under a larger one read: Noirlac. She scanned the landscape in that direction and saw the village of Noirlac below, no more than five minutes' drive away. As of its own volition, her car set off almost silently down the steep hill and across the narrow bridge.

The main village street was lifeless. It wouldn't be long before a handful of villagers, mostly men, would amble to the café-tabac for their nightly exchange of gossip over an apéritif. The café was all lit up as she passed but she could see no one in it. At the bend of the street the lane to Augusto's chateau came into view. She slowed the car down to walking pace, looking up the lane before turning into it. The spring growth of the ivy had engulfed the high walls on either side even more since she had been here with Sam. Halfway up the lane she pulled up close to the wall, unsure of why she was here at all.

Ahead, beyond the chateau gates, burned a dim light behind one of the ground floor windows. She got out of the car. To her right a rusted door giving onto a vegetable garden stood open. On a wheelbarrow parked across its threshold sat a dog with ginger fur; it was the dog that had been digging at Augusto's lake that day. Two hushed voices came from behind the wall. Perhaps someone was gardening until daylight faded. Léa hurried past the door unseen

The high wrought iron gates were open just enough for her to squeeze through. She made her way across the gravel of the forecourt. It was quiet, dream like; there was a knot in her stomach but she felt unable to stop herself from moving forward. The light she had seen from the car was to the right of the door through which they had previously entered. She remembered, it was the window of Augusto's 'small' kitchen. A single curtain was gathered untidily to the left.

Inside she saw him pacing up and down. To the right she could see him, but the left side of the kitchen was obscured by the curtain. He was pacing back and forth, vanishing from view for a few moments, then returning and vanishing again.

She waited for him to reappear. The front door suddenly opened, he looked out, as if he had sensed someone near the house. There was no escape, no shrubbery for her to hide behind, only the open space of the forecourt.

'There you are,' he said softly, as if he had known that she was coming.

'I didn't want to disturb you,' she managed to stammer.

'You are not, dear child,' he smiled, 'come in, come in. I was just wondering whether I should have some tea.'

There was no way out of the situation. A lump in her throat threatened to choke her.

'I was just passing … on my way home, Sam is expecting me…'

'Nonsense. One cup of tea, that's all it takes to make an old man happy.'

He held the door open for her and she stepped into the house. Standing in the entrance hall the house felt even emptier than when they had come to buy the books.

'How is your beautiful cat?' she asked for want of better conversation.

'Gone I'm afraid, gone like all the others. Away, away. C'est la vie.' He shrugged his shoulders which seemed skeletal under his light shirt. 'Alas. I could offer no future sanctuary to a pet ....' His voice faded.

She recalled how he had kicked the cat aside during their visit. Something in his tone stopped her from asking what had happened to it.

'Tell you what,' he perked up, 'let's have tea in the library, such as it is now. The kitchen feels so cold, with those neon lights. Just go in, you remember where it is?'

'Yes, I do.' She remembered the yellow frog in the jar, the high shelves, the desk where Sam had seen the old man, stooped, reading the letter in his trembling hand.

All the top shelves in the hexagonal room nearest the ceiling had been cleared. It was astonishing that Augusto ventured so high up on the library ladder that ran around the room on a rail.

Outside daylight was fading. Léa took a couple of steps towards the window with an urge to open it to make her feel less trapped. On their first visit she hadn't noticed that the window, which was high off the ground, had bars on it. No doubt Augusto had installed it to protect his precious volumes from burglars. Now that she scanned the room it was clear that Augusto's library had once been part of a tower.

The clinking of cups made her swing around. She tried to adopt a relaxed posture; looking nervous would be a bad idea right now.

'Here we are.' He looked around. 'Just move those papers from the little desk to somewhere else, so I can put the tray down.'

Léa picked up the handful of papers scattered over the desk, searching for some other surface. She was arranging them on one of the half empty bookshelves next to the library steps when she saw the light green envelope with its the handwritten letter among them. It was the letter that had arrived on the day of their visit which had caused Augusto's alarming reaction.

'There,' Augusto said, satisfied.

He settled on one of the plastic garden chairs she had seen in the kitchen, she perched on a foot stool in the corner, next to the empty bookshelf where she had placed the papers.

'Tell me what you've been up too since I last saw you.' His hand shook as he held out a paper plate with two biscuits. Blue veins on the back of his hands stood out like swollen rivers.

'Nothing much,' said Léa. It dawned on her that what had brought her to Augusto's house tonight was one single question; it had been swirling around in the back of her mind since her discovery in the Auch library. What had caused both his wife and maid to vanish? Was this frail man capable of a vile act? Gisèle's warning about the chateau's history came back to her and she nearly spilled her tea.

'Come, come,' Augusto smiled, 'nothing much? That's hard to believe from a beautiful girl like you.'

The eerie cold she had felt in his presence during their visit was suddenly back. Her question would most probably not receive an answer from him, but she could not leave without having asked it.

'I went to Auch library today,' she began, 'for some research. I have to translate a text about monks and the work they did on manuscripts.'

'Fascinating. Oh, how I loved doing research when I was young. I simply couldn't bear not knowing things. Even when I was six years old I'd go scuttling to my father's shelves full of encyclopedias. He had dictionaries in all languages imaginable and the most wonderful collection of enormous atlases.'

'I found something strange.'

'Do tell. I love a good mystery.' He stretched forward, keen as a dog for a special treat.

'I found it in their archives. It's something to do with this house, something that happened here when it was still a monastery.'

He raised his eyebrows and pursed his lips as his head pulled back. 'Oh, yes? And what was that?'

'Are you aware that this house has a …history of …'

'Of what?' His tone was defensive.

'Of course, I don't know whether what I found is true or whether it's a piece of fiction, made up by a monk with an over-active imagination.'

'I'm not aware that fiction writing was what they indulged in to fill their idle hours. Gossip, yes, sexual fantasies, yes ….' He glanced at her, almost looking through her. He appeared to be retrieving some distant memory.

'I suppose there was some of that in the story,' Léa conceded. 'The book tells of a girl, murdered by the lake.'

'Which lake?' He sat bolt upright.

'This lake, your lake.' It was out, she had said it. There was no way back now. 'Did you know about it?'

He leaned back on his chair, looking up to the ceiling, idly inspecting the empty shelves.

'Hum. Did I know about it?' He glanced over to her. 'As you like research, almost as much as I do,' he said slowly and got up, 'I do have some old papers about this house. Haven't looked at them for decades. I may be able to find something for you. I keep most of my stuff by my bed now - so much more convenient. Wait here.' He shuffled past her. As he got to the door he turned.

'Ah, better take these.' He reached across her and scooped up the green letter that Léa had placed onto the book shelf.

The door closed. After a second or two she heard a clicking noise. She tried the door knob and pulled, but the lock wouldn't give. She tried again.

'Don't worry,' she heard Augusto say from the hall, 'the door sticks. I'll have to find a screwdriver. That usually does the trick. I won't be long.' She heard the echoing clap of his slippers on the marble stairs. She put her ear to the door but could hear no more footsteps.

Do I wait or what? she wondered. It was now almost dark outside. She searched for a light switch near the door but could find none. A cord with an enamelled weight dangled against the wall. She pulled it; an overhead chandelier lit up but provided no more than a gloomy light reminiscent of a prison cell. She put her ear against the door again. There was a muffled sound, rhythmical, shuffling, like someone pacing up and down, quite near to the door. What was he doing? With the house almost completely empty, how hard could it be to find a screwdriver? Was he looking for one at all?

The realisation that he might have intended to lock her in suddenly hit her. She knelt down, trying to see if the door had been locked or whether she might be able to push it open with a knife. She turned and tore open the two desk drawers, hoping to find a penknife or a letter opener. The drawers were empty. Her shoulder bag lay on the floor beside the library steps. Attached to her keyring was a metal nail file. She knelt by the door again. Her file was thin enough to be wedged into the slim gap between the two parts of the lock. She wedged it into the tight space; the file bent and snapped.

She listened against the door again. The sound of feet had stopped. Perhaps her scratching at the lock had alerted him. Panic stopped her from breathing. The window was barred. It offered no chance of escape. She knew she had to get out of the room.

Stop, she forced herself to think - you've been in this room before, think. Then it came back to her. There was the red velvet curtain at the other side of the room, it hung limp, fully drawn across a corner. She had gone into the garden from this room during their first visit. She tore the curtain aside. A cloud of dust flew into her face. There was the low carved door where she had tripped over the uneven stone threshold and Augusto had caught her. The dust from the curtain made her cough; she put her hand to her mouth to avoid giving away her position in the room.

The door didn't have a handle, but a large brass ring. It had been open when she had been here with Sam. With both hands she slowly turned the heavy ring it as far as it would go, pulled then pushed against the door. It groaned but refused to open. Behind her she heard scratching, then knocking at the library door. Augusto would be in the room any second. She threw her entire weight against the oak door and it gave way suddenly, opening outwards and taking a stone from its step with it. She landed on her hands and knees on the gravel. She was outside. Her bag fell open beside her; some of its contents spilled out. Grabbing her belongings she ran around the house and across the forecourt, without looking back. Whether Augusto heard her now no longer mattered. Squeezing through the gap in the gate she ran down the alley.

Two men stood peering into her car. She recognised them; it was the café owner and his friend with the ginger dog. They stepped away from her car and watched as she ran towards them. The dog wagged its tail as she approached.

She managed a breathless 'bonsoir' as she jumped into the car. The engine howled and she reversed out of the alley faster than she should have. She caught her wing mirror on a house corner as she swung into the main street and drove off at speed. It wasn't until another car came towards her on the road running along the chateau perimeter that she realised that she had not switched her headlights on.

She stopped the car by the roadside to inspect her knees which had taken her full weight when she had crashed onto the gravel. Her jeans had taken the brunt of the fall. She dusted them off. They didn't look any worse than usual. She took her mobile and punched out a text: be home in 15, was delayed. XX L. How could she explain all this to Sam? Perhaps it was better not to.

Sam was leaning in the open door and watched her get out of the car. He scrutinised her in silence for a long moment as she retrieved her shoulder bag from the boot.

211

'Where have you been? You look terrible. Seen a ghost?' She felt caught out, unable to reply for a few seconds. 'I think I have,' she conceded and dropped her heavy bag on the hall floor.

*

No more be done

29

Chateau de Noirlac, early morning, May 7th

The celebration of his defeat had mapped itself out, as if predicted in some long forgotten book. Augusto stared across the chateau forecourt towards the gate.

The early sun glittered on the sharp gravel. He set his left foot onto it, then his right. The glare hurt his eyes as he willed himself forward. It took all his strength to heave the gate shut and to make his way back to the house. A heap of publicity leaflets lay jammed under the half open door. He gathered them up and pushed the door with his heel until it closed with a shudder. He held the papers up to the light, opened his hand and watched as they sailed to the floor. His foot brushed over them, spreading them out.

'The wretch.' He kicked the brochures, sending them skidding across the marble floor. A sudden rage threatened to burst his temples. He no longer plied Louis the postman with a glass of Ricard. Now Louis was having his revenge by stuffing the letterbox with anything he could find. The man was pernicious; he had taken to hiding Augusto's occasional letters and frequent bills, tucking them deep into the folds of junk mail advertising ladies underwear, plastic toys or body building equipment, mail he knew the old man would be sure to throw straight on the fire.

*

Let's have no words of this

30

Sainte Colombe, same morning

Léa opened her front door. She blinked into the morning light. The frail figure standing at the threshold was dwarfed by an enormous bunch of yellow broom blossoms.

'Did I wake you?'

'Gisèle? ...no, well, not really.'

'I went up to the chapel first thing this morning, on the south side the broom is already in flower. I thought you'd like some.'

'How lovely. Come in.' Léa stepped aside to let her friend in. 'I'll take those,' she took the blooms from Gisèle, 'before you break a leg. I just couldn't wake up this morning. I've had a strange couple of days. And I went to bed too late.'

'Modern life,' Gisèle teased her. 'In all the villages around here our parents used to throw us out of bed before dawn to milk the goats and by the time it was getting light kids were on their way to the vineyards. But then in those days children's evenings were short.'

They went into the kitchen. Léa retrieved an old fashioned enamelled jug she had bought in a fleamarket, arranged the broom blossoms in it and stood it by the kitchen door to the lower terrace.

'Look at that, isn't that colour unbelievable. It lights up the whole room.'

She put the kettle on and they sat at the kitchen table. The window stood open onto the terrace overlooking the gorge and Mount Septimania beyond.

'So? what happened?'

Gisèle's delicate, sharp-featured face was dominated by inquisitive coal black eyes. She was the youngest of a family of eight, all but one of them resting in the Sainte Colombe graveyard. Her mother had lost many more children in miscarriages and still births. In Gisèle's childhood only the strong survived. Her tiny frame and even tinier legs belied an unexpected strength and a steely intelligence. She had an infallible instinct which detected the slightest nuance in people's moods. They had met the day Léa arrived in the village and instantly felt as though they had always known each other.

Gisèle's house stood in a cobbled alley further down in the village. It had once been part of the old presbytery, for centuries the home of village priests. When the revolution chased the clerics from their grand abode the house had come into Gisèle's family and been divided up between successive generations. Her grandfather had retained the large walled terrace garden with the same views as Léa's house - Mount Septimania with the chapel and on the horizon the snow-capped Pyrenees.

'I went to the library in Auch,' Léa said after a while. 'I found a manuscript … it was really weird. I don't really know what happened there.'

Gisèle laughed. 'Too much reading late at night, that's your trouble.'

There was no way Léa could tell anyone about the sensation of turning into a monk, let alone by simply looking at a drawing in a book.

'We went to Noirlac the other day. It's funny. In all the time we've lived here we never went that way. I suppose it's because it's hidden on the other side of Montferrus.'

Gisèle looked up. Her expression changed.

'Where in Noirlac?'

'The chateau. The current owner invited us. He wanted to sell some books.'

'Have you never heard about the Noirlac chateau?'

'What about it?'

'It is not a good place,' said Gisèle. 'Unlucky. For people, for women. Sometimes places can be like that.'

'Isn't that just superstition?

'Who can say? People round here just know is that there is something in the ….soil, if you like. Things can be quiet for years and then ….'

'Then what?' The image from the book about Noirlac resurfaced in Léa's mind.

'No one knows how and why. There is a house just up the hill from here. It's the same there. Things happen ….'

'Gisèle. Things have happened in this house. People must have died in this house, right here where we are sitting now. Maybe a housewife died at the stove, maybe her husband had a heart attack in his bed, maybe a child or a mother died in childbirth. In fact, I'd say it was practically guaranteed. When we lifted the floor boards in the attic I found piles of dust and a huge rats' nest full of shreds of cloth, and even a piece from a handwritten village news sheet. And right at the bottom three tiny skeletons. The mother rat must have been killed and the little ones died. I don't know why, but suddenly I panicked. I thought I'd dug up the bacteria from the time of the black plague. I couldn't nail the boards down fast enough; it was completely irrational; it really frightened me, but here I am. I didn't die a horrible death, did I?'

'It's nothing like that. All we know is that sometimes there is … something in the ground that makes people do the same things over and over again, across history.'

Gisèle rubbed the back of her hand flecked with liver spots. 'Like with my Eugene,' she said finally.

They had buried her husband Eugene at the height of last summer's heat.

'Oh, Gisèle. I didn't understand that. Wasn't it just a coincidence?'

'No. I don't think so. His grandfather died up there under the peach tree, so did his father, and now Eugene. My only son will probably do the same … if only to please his ancestors.'

'Sylvain is much too sensible for that,' Léa tried to reassure her.

Gisèle managed a smile. 'There is just something in them …. 'Her gaze remained fixed on the view in the distance. 'Everyone in my family has this panorama from

218

their terraces. You bought my sister's house, that's why you have it too. The family would never have sold that house, but her children, well, they'd left the village. They just wanted the money.' She glanced across at Léa. 'And then when I met you I knew you were the right person to have it.' She pointed to the mount with the chapel. 'That there is our heritage. We have a duty to it.'

'Why is that chapel so important to you?'

'It's not the chapel,' Gisèle shook her head, 'it's the graves under it. There are eleven of them, from the 8th century.'

They had known each other for years. Léa had heard stories about Mount Septimania and its chapel. This was the first time the old lady spoke openly about it.

'They are women's tombs, from the time when the last Visigoths were running for their lives. There was a building there, probably something like a temple, or a sort of monastery. They were worried that harm would come to the women. At first they hid them there. When they were surrounded, they killed and buried them in the secret passages under the mount rather than have them defiled by the advancing Moors. Some of the men fought their way out, others died trying.'

'How do you know this?'

The mount and the chapel were the first things she and Sam saw from their bed when they awoke in the mornings. The village was built on a rocky spine. The houses on its south side had a view of the mount, on the northern side there was a view to the high garrigue plateau sheltering the Abbey of Morterive in its shadow.

'The story has been handed down through our families,' Gisèle said lightly, as if such events were part of her own lifetime.

Léa felt as though a huge chunk of history had been hurled at her and now it was directly connected to her. It was heavy and humbling. She shuddered.

'I feel like that too,' said Gisèle, 'in the middle of the night sometimes, when I really think about it. You get used to the responsibility, in time. They were the last Visigoths in France. This part was called Septimania then, a sort of independent province of seven cities that worked together. Mount Alaric is named after their king. His son Amalric never became king.'

Léa had heard the name before. 'The domaine Amalric belonging to Amaline Sabarda, the lady on the hill with the peacocks, is she related to him?'

'Her husband was a direct descendant of King Alaric.'

'So who has seen the tombs?'

'Amaline saw them when her husband died. There is an entrance, but at any one time only three people in the village know where it is. It's the only way to protect the graves. Otherwise we'd have all the treasure hunters here, like at Rennes le Chateau. Everyone is obsessed with the Cathars and they've done so much damage to the sites already,' Gisèle sighed. 'Do you know, two Englishmen even bought a capitelle, one of those little stone huts in one of the vineyards from a farmer, just to dig the place up. It was just next to a Cathar castle ruin. From the there they dug like moles to get under the mount. No one found out until the tunnel collapsed on one of them and the fire brigade had to get him out. The internet has made it worse. And the

English, the Americans, they write books, they make Hollywood films about mysteries they don't understand, my history,' she tapped her chest with her flat hand, 'my ancestors' history is being cannibalized by people who can't even speak French.'

'But how do you choose these three people? How can you keep a secret for over a thousand years in this village? It's unimaginable.'

'The chosen ones are not always the first born of the families. We choose the wisest children, boys or girls. They are quite easy to spot, especially when they are very young.' Gisèle glanced across at Léa. 'If you'd been my child I would have chosen you.'

'What if you didn't have a child? So many children died.'

'Then we jump to the cousins. Families were so large before birth control. Most families had twelve or fourteen children; only the strongest survived.'

'Have you seen the tombs?'

'Not yet. I'll do so before I die. That's the privilege of the chosen. They carried my grandmother all the way up there at dawn on a stretcher as she was dying. For now it's enough for me to know where the outer entrance is. There are three doors, three different locks, each person has a key to one of the locks, so I can only unlock one of the doors.' She got up. 'We are who we are because of what we remember, individually and collectively. For us a place, a building or an object can have memories. That's what foreigners don't understand.'

Gisèle only had one son. Her daughter had died of a brain fever at the age of three months. Perhaps her son

Sylvain, a music teacher in Lyon, would be the holder of the ancient secret soon. He had two small boys, so they would inherit the secret in the future.

Léa poured the verbena and ginger tea into the large bowl-shaped cups. The fresh aroma rising from the pot seemed to clear the air.

Gisèle took a sip of tea. 'You haven't asked me about Noirlac.'

Léa gave a sigh. 'I found something strange yesterday, in a book in the Auch medieval archives. It was quite a horrible story, but that was from long ago.'

Gisèle nodded. 'Some things happened long ago, but the Noirlac villagers always say that if the chateau falls into the wrong hands the whole thing starts all over again.'

Léa remained silent. She had no proof that anything untoward had happened to Augusto's wife, or to his maid. Wives left husbands all the time, some in more vengeful ways than others. There was no point in adding to the old man's predicament with her own suspicions. The Noirlac villagers were bound to get the rumour mill grinding.

Gisèle drained her cup. 'Change the water of those flowers every day. If you dip the stalks in boiling water for a minute or two they'll last much longer. I'm glad I've brought you a bit of sunshine today. I have to go now.'

At the door Gisèle gave Léa a peck on each cheek.

'Just take care when you go … there. Don't get involved,' and she nimbly slipped out of the door like a sparrow.

*

What is the reason that you use me thus

31

Sainte Colombe, Tuesday 8th May, before dawn

Léa slept, aware of her stillness in her dream. Her body was a leaden mass. She saw herself in a white room, in a large bed with Sam. Crisp sheets rustled as their bodies moved against each other. She recognised the dream; it was always the same. But this time there was something different, outside the window. Silver foliage fluttered in fitful gusts, whipping the window panes with a sound of rice grains pouring onto a tin tray. White light streamed in, blinding, hissing. She could hear rumblings, sounds coming and going, distant voices. She listened hard; she thought she could distinguish the odd word, but they became scrambled, overlapping, becoming louder, then louder still with the rush of an approaching train until they reached a crescendo of screams mixed with a repetitive clapping. She no longer felt Sam's warmth against her skin. In her dream he lay facing the wall, not hearing the din outside. There was a loud splash, a dull explosion followed by a growling gurgle. Léa jolted awake and found herself leaning out of the wide open window, gasping for air.

She closed the window and returned to bed. In the darkness of the room Sam's rhythmical breathing calmed her. He seemed to sleep through the night, almost as if it were an act of the will. And if he did have any dreams he could not remember them when morning came. In earlier days they had stayed in so many places, slept in so many rooms; at times when she awoke Léa kept her eyes shut, trying to guess in which bed, in which room, in which city she would find herself on finally opening her eyes.

Sam slept on, still beside her now. He lay between the sheets and blankets like a neatly folded letter in an envelope; in the morning it was barely detectable that anyone had slept there at all. Lately her side of the bed was a heap of tangled sheets, crumpled under a collection of pillows. Her dreamtime was like a multi-screen movie house, raging in full-colour images and searing emotions.

Far away somewhere Léa heard the sound. Her hand found the telephone receiver with her eyes still closed.

'Allo..., âllo …?' She could hear music.

'Allo?' said a familiar voice, 'who is that?'

'Maman? It's me, Léa.'

'What are you doing on the phone? It didn't ring at your end.'

'Why else would I pick it up if it didn't.'

'Heaven knows,' her mother lamented, 'I dialled your number but you picked up before it rang.'

Léa ran her fingers through her hair. It was too early for amateur dramatics.

'Maman, why are you waking me up at this time of the morning?'

'You sound strange, my child. I didn't recognise your voice. Are you alright?'

'I always sound like this when I'm asleep.' Not as hoarse as I used to sound when I smoked; don't say it, Léa reminded herself, just don't; one thing at the time, even that's too much right now. She squinted at the clock. 'What time is this to call people? It's a quarter to seven, Mamoutchka.'

'Don't call me that. I'm not a Hungarian peasant … and you're not people.'

'Normal people are still asleep at this time ... except the peasants, Hungarian, French or otherwise. You must have got up with the chickens this morning. '

'We have no chickens in Paris.' In the art of contradiction and feigned indignation her mother was streets ahead.

Léa took a deep breath.

'Your mother.' Sam rolled over and buried his face in the pillow, 'a debating society on two legs, day or night.'

Léa slapped his pillow with her flat hand to silence him.

'I couldn't sleep,' her mother complained.

'Is that a reason for waking everyone else?'

There was a pause at the Paris end. Her mother was playing music, rather loudly.

'Maman, turn the music down, you'll wake your nice neighbours.'

'It's your favourite, *Ah, perdona al primo affetto*, you remember? From Mozart's La clemenza di Tito?'

Léa remembered; the duet about an impossible love had always made her cry. Perhaps her mother was just trying to soften her up.

'I had a dream.'

'So?'

'I had a dream ... about you.'

'You're my mother, is that surprising?'

'I dreamt you fell out of the window. In the dark.'

Léa's stomach tightened. This was not the first time that her mother knew what was happening to her, though she had never once admitted it.

'Right. I fell out of the window, into the gorge. That's where I'm talking to you from now. The phone must have jumped after me.'

'Don't mock. I just got upset. I had to check that you're alright.'

'Yes, Maman, I'm fine, very fine. And so is Sam. And he needs his sleep.' She looked over to Sam who was laughing into his pillow. 'If you must phone me in the morning, please don't do it before nine.'

There was a vexed silence at the other end of the line.

Léa sighed. 'I'll phone you, at about ten, when I'm awake properly. Really, tout va bien, I'm fine, Mamoutchka. Bisous, call you later.' She hung up.

She wasn't in a fit state to talk at length now. She propped herself up against the headboard with her pillows. Why did she always feel guilty when she hung up on her mother? After all these years it still seemed disrespectful. Her mother had many friends. Paris was littered with those who had been lucky enough to flee Budapest from the advancing Russian tanks. Her friends were émigrés who, like her, had left their fortunes behind. They relived the good times in their never ending, melancholy conversations. But the thought of her elderly mother, alone in the third floor apartment with creaking parquet floors and high echoing rooms after prematurely losing her husband, the love of her life, made Léa sad. Her parents had married late; Léa had been a surprise for them both, quickly followed by her sister Arielle. Only fifteen years later Léa's father had suddenly died.

Perhaps one day she herself would have to learn to live without Sam. She tried to breathe evenly. She was awake now. Her nights were more exhausting than her days at the moment; lately sleep had been hard to come by. As soon as the lights went out questions about Augusto and the two women piled into her mind, hard and fast, leaving no room for any other thoughts.

On the wall beside the window she had hung her family photographs before her mother's last visit to avoid discussions about forgetting - forgetting the family's past was unforgiveable in her mother's eyes. There they sat, her ancestors, in a park surrounding their massive house with outbuildings that housed the coachmen, stable boys, gardeners; the in-house tutors had their quarters on the top floors. Under the roof were the maids' and the cooks' rooms, who, unlike the tutors, were not honoured with carpets, bookshelves or writing desks. In the group photograph her mother, aged three or four and wearing a flowered dress with an intricate hand-made lace collar, sat astride a huge St.Bernard's dog. Her mother's sisters sat on fancy garden

227

chairs, each holding a bouquet of white flowers; between their dignified parents sat their only son and heir. The grandparents, both smiling happily, perched at either end. At the rear stood the great-uncles, clad in the uniforms of high-ranking Hungarian officers. Léa had never found out what the ranks were, but there were sashes made of leopard skin and breast-plates of some shiny, embossed metal. A single portrait of Léa's grand-mother showed her in a large hat dressed with sweeping ostrich plumes, a silk gown and a double row necklace of emeralds and diamonds which Léa remembered seeing as a child. It had been promised to her. It was family legend and rumoured to be worth the price of two grand houses.

'One for each of you girls,' her grandmother had promised. When they came to clear the old lady's apartment only one link of the necklace had been found. Léa's remark that Grandmama had dismembered the priceless jewels in order to finance her passion for the finest veal fillets was met with outrage, followed by a wall of silence.

Behind Mount Septimania the sun was coming up. Its rays touched the bedroom ceiling, slid down until the golden light invaded the whole room. She was surprised to see the window open. She was certain that when she'd woken from her nightmare she had closed it. Perhaps Sam had opened it.

He turned over and blinked into the sunlight. 'She's right.'

'About what?'

'The phone didn't ring.'

'It must have, why else would I pick it up.'

'Don't know, but it didn't. I swear. Your mother pulses these messages out across the ether, like a witch. It's not the first time you phone each other at the exact same moment.'

'It always rings, either at my end or hers.' It felt quite ghostly but Léa could not deny that this link between her mother and herself existed. Some umbilical mental cord bound them together, reached across great distances. People questioned too much. Some things were best left alone. When she and Sam had met there was an instant recognition of something in each other. It was so sudden, so unexpected, but neither of them questioned it. Friends and family were waving warning signs. Neither Sam nor Léa had ever felt the need to perform an autopsy of their relationship. It worked, that was all that mattered.

'Léa Chevalier and Carter,' her mother had sighed, 'that's the horseman and the cart man. Mon Dieu, what a union.'

'Horse and cart, it's the perfect team, Maman.' Léa's riposte had reigned in her mother's disapproval for a time.

Perhaps there was such a thing as fate, everything laid out in advance, predetermined. What had turned Augusto's recent months into a bewildering misadventure? His marriage to Ophelia sounded like a fairy story – rich man marries young, beautiful girl who adores him. Did he have to have a mistress at the end of all that? What drove him to risk everything so late in life? Perhaps Sam was right about men's gluttony when it came to young flesh. That last fling had proved irresistible for the old man, but to do it under his wife's nose seemed naive. Or had Noirlac chateau, with its overbearing presence caused it all to happen?

Léa could have told Sam about her dream, about the window, but what was the point? The dreams she wanted to come true never did. Luckily, neither did her nightmares, but some of her mother's dreams had the annoying habit of doing just that.

Sam had drifted off to sleep again. He looked calm as he lay there, but his nights had also been agitated recently. Léa slipped out from under the blankets so as not to wake him and sat on the edge of the bed. The morning sun was warming the honey-coloured floorboards under her bare feet. White mist wafted low over the vineyards. The cypress trees surrounding the chapel on Mount Septimania were emerging, slim and sharp as pencils.

She took her striped jersey dress from the back of the chair, pulled it over her head, slung a cardigan around her shoulders and went down to the kitchen. There was not enough bread for breakfast.

She closed the front door softly. The housemartins and swifts were back, shrieking as they hurled themselves from the top of the church tower into the shadows of the village streets, barely missing the heads of passers-by. Vanilla, sugar, apricots and hot, fresh bread - she could smell the boulangerie before she reached the corner of their winding street. Five crooked steps from her street led onto the Place de l'Eglise. Pigeons bathed frantically in the fountain. The tips of their wings sent beads of water flying in a blitzkrieg on the insects living snug in the warmth of their plumage.

'Bonjour, Colette.' In the narrow shop the baker's wife was already busy with the morning rush. Léa picked up two sticks of bread from a basket by the shop window, caught Colette's eye over the heads of several elderly women patiently waiting their turn and signalled that she was putting the right money on the counter. Behind her the shop door open and Gisèle came in.

'I'll wait for you outside,' Léa kissed Gisèle on both cheeks, 'it's a bit crowded in here.'

The village was waking up. A dog bounded over to the fountain. He rushed the pigeons at its edge and the clapping of their wings, heavy with water, echoed against the church wall. Léa ripped small pieces of crust from the tip of one of the bread sticks she had tucked under her arm. The fresh golden crust was irresistible. At this rate there wouldn't be much of it left by the time she got home.

'You're early today.' Gisèle struggled out from the cramped bakery. She held her large jute bag open for Léa to see what she had bought. It was filled with bread and pastries.

'Sylvain is bringing the kids, they're coming down from Lyon.'

'My mother threw me out of bed this morning,' Léa smiled ruefully, 'she's in Paris but she wakes me up all the same.'

'It's the 8th of May. Don't forget to come to the ceremony in the monument square. We may not have covered ourselves in glory in the wars, but we can celebrate the armistice all the same. I'm sure the mayor's heroic speeches will wake you up,' Gisèle grinned. 'It takes four hours from Lyon. They'll be here for lunch. Sylvain wants to go up to the chapel this afternoon. He hasn't had a chance to do that since last summer. He thinks it's time his boys got to know the place. Come to my house, now, for a quick coffee on the terrace. It's nice and fresh there.'

Gisèle walked beside Léa with dainty, bird-like steps. The top of her head barely reached Léa's shoulder. Her bag almost dragged on the ground.

'Here, let me carry that.' Léa put out her hand and took the bag. They walked down the main village street. Wooden shutters open with a groan and were knocked back onto the house walls. The street rang with a hollow, syncopated clatter.

'Concert pour volets,' Gisèle chuckled, 'the shutter concert; that's what my Eugene called it. They all do it at the same time. It's a sort of competition. They don't want their neighbours to think they're lazing around in bed. In my grandfather's time, after the shutter ritual there would be a cry of "Garde à vous",' Gisèle giggled, 'to warn passers-by that the contents of a full chamber pot were on their way down.'

A loud crackle came from the village loud speaker.

'That'll be Gérard,' Gisèle smiled. 'The mobile clothes merchant is coming today and you know how Gérard enjoys his announcements.' Her cheeks blushed slightly.

'Allo, âllo,' blaired the voice of the village secretary over the roofs, 'the clothes merchant is about to arrive. Ladies, hurry. On sale today will be aprons, underwear, stockings, suspender belts, girdles for the fuller figure and brassieres in the largest sizes.'

'There,' giggled Gisèle, 'you can hear him grinning behind his microphone when he says these things.'

232

From the street Gisèle's house looked small with just an entrance door and a window next to it. As usual her front door had been left unlocked. They entered the cool of her house which opened up into a wide living space with four French windows to the old presbytery terrace surrounded by ancient terracotta balustrades. On the path the white gravel sparkled in the fierce light. She stepped into the shade of the giant fig tree. It was going to be a hot day.

Gisèle emerged from the dark interior of the house and put down a tray with strong coffee and a croissant for each of them.

'You have the best panorama in the village.' Léa helped Gisèle to unload the tray. 'It's like Tuscany.'

'Remember what I told you the other day, about memory? I'll show you something.' Gisèle picked up something from the tray and held out her hand. A small, dark object lay in her palm. 'Do you recognise what this is?' She handed it to Léa but remained standing, watching over the thing. The object was made of leather but it was hard as stone. It was the sole of a child's shoe. Tiny nails ran around the edge and the heel was worn down.

'This belonged to one of my ancestors, a girl. Her father was a miller. In 1794, during the Robespierre's Great Terror, he was arrested on the path to the flour mill. The mill sat in the deepest part of the gorge. The girl was nearly six and her brother was eight. They were on their way down to take some bread and cheese to their father because the men quite often had to work night shifts. As they got near to the mill they saw their father being dragged along by some men. The boy scrambled up onto the rocks on the left. He climbed into a cedar tree and hid in the branches. The tree is still there. The girl was on the wrong side of the track. She climbed down into the ravine. There wasn't time for him to pull her over to his side. He told the story later. He had to watch as she inched further and further down so she wouldn't be seen as the men approached. It's an almost sheer descent there with nothing but dry, sandy soil, sharp rocks and huge cacti sticking out. Her foot became wedged between two rocks. Her brother saw her sliding sideways until she was hanging upside down with her foot still stuck.

'They were dragging her father past on the path and she didn't make a sound. Then her shoe finally gave and she fell. It was getting dark. The whole village went to search for her. Their burning torches lit up the gorge. They found her down-river, all mangled under the waterwheel of the next mill of Sainte Colombe. The cacti had ripped her flesh. Next day they went down on ropes where she had fallen. The sole of her little shoe was still trapped between the two rocks. She was a tiny child.'

Gisèle wiped a tear from the corner of her eyes. 'She'd been chosen to keep the secret of the tombs if she reached the age of eighteen,' she continued, 'as it was, it passed to her cousin, my grandmother's great grandmother.'

Léa's hand began to shake. The small object suddenly felt hot and heavy in her hand, as if the girl's body was still attached to it in some way. She instinctively enclosed the tiny shoe sole between her palms. Something compelled her to close her eyes. She could see the girl, feel that her fear of the men on the path was greater than the fear of the dangerous but familiar ravine that she passed every day. Léa felt the girl slip away, down into the ravine, the scraping of

234

the dry earth, then the fall. There was a sudden vacuum and everything stopped. 'It was very quick,' she murmured.

She felt her friend's hand on her shoulder.

'Good,' Gisèle sighed, 'good. I'm glad about that. They said her skull was broken on a rock. She would not have felt the rest.'

'What was her name?'

'Séraphine.'

This was not the kind of history Léa had been taught in school. It was not about dates and battles and treaties. This was real, it was what people and their lives were made of.

'We are our past,' said Gisèle quietly, 'we can feel everything that's gone before, if only we let it.'

*

Away, away

32

Noirlac Village Café, May 9th

Armand rigged up his old wooden ladder. It wobbled precariously as he climbed, paint pot and brush in hand. After days of reflection and a good number of drinks to help along the thinking process, he would attempt the restoration of his sign in situ rather than run up the expense of a new one. He'd come to terms with the prospect that old Augusto would probably never settle his bill, let alone pay for a new sign.

Paul sauntered across the road. His dog rubbed a wiry flank against the bottom of the ladder, sending up a shudder.

'Arrête, stop. For God's sake, Paul,' Armand clung to the top of the ladder, 'stop that dog and hold the damned ladder.' The paint pot swung in his hand. Red paint spilt out, flecking the dog's ginger fur. 'Do you want another corpse on your hands?'

'Why? Who has died?' Paul wedged the metal toe cap of his boot against the foot of the ladder. 'Paint your sign, not the rest of us.'

The dog dashed to safety under the nearest café table. With an unsteady hand Armand began to redraw the damaged letters.

'Who knows what's happened.' Paul glanced over his shoulder towards the chateau, 'it's as silent as a grave over there.'

'I haven't seen the women since those damned removal people came.' Armand applied himself. His heart sank. His sign writing would not bear close inspection.

Paul stood patiently, now and then letting go of the ladder with one hand to take a puff on his loosely rolled cigarette smouldering between his craggy fingers. He tried to remember exactly what he had seen - on the day they loaded the furniture the old man had come charging through the village all the way to the big house, then he'd left, driving away like possessed. A few days later he was back again. At night a car had left the chateau, then a taxi had gone up the chateau lane. Since then, nothing, except for the visiting couple on the 1st of May. They had confirmed that Augusto was still there, apparently alone.

'It's a full time job to keep track of all the comings and goings,' Paul mumbled to himself. He took another puff from his cigarette which was fast disintegrating.

There was the soft crunch of tyres behind him. A car emerged from the chateau lane. A woman sat at the wheel. She peered at the two men, undecided about which way to turn. After a few seconds, she drew up by the café. Armand stopped painting and wiped his hands on the back of his trousers. The two men watched as a svelte woman in her late thirties emerged from the car. One hand tugged at her skirt, the other ran through her blond hair as she walked towards them.

'Excusez moi,' she began with an unmistakable English accent. She indicated the chateau. 'Could you tell me where I might find Madame?'

She stopped, embarrassed. 'I am Tania Spencer, Madame's sister.' This was going to be difficult. Telling the villagers what had happened at the chateau would be humiliating, but these two had a ring-side seat; they were her best bet. She tried to smile.

Armand climbed down, set down the paint pot and held out a stained hand in greeting.

'Enchanté.' He nodded. 'Yes, you look a lot like Madame.'

'I am looking for my sister. Have you seen her at all?'

Armand stood with his feet apart, ready for the next piece of information. He wondered why she was asking him instead of the old man back at the chateau.

'Ah, ça,' he lifted both his hands in a gesture of innocence and shifted from one foot to another, hoping for Paul's assistance. His neighbour stared at the ground and stubbed out his cigarette end with the toe of his crusty boot.

Tania bit her lip to stop it from quivering.

'The truth is,' Armand broke the awkward silence, 'we haven't seen Madame for a little while, ever since the furniture left.'

He blinked into the sun to escape the woman's puzzled gaze.

Tania fingered the buttons of her shirt. Diamonds glinted on her fingers. Her hands were long and fine and looked impossibly white on her blood red shirt. Paul cleared his smoky throat.

'Monsieur is still there, though.'

'Yes,' Tania tugged at her pearl necklace, 'but … he refused to let me in. Has anyone at all been to the chateau … lately?' Her hand grabbed her shirt a little harder, her frown deepened and she seemed to be fighting back tears.

Armand gestured towards the interior of the café. He couldn't bear to see a woman cry.

'A couple came some days ago. Something to do with Monsieur Augusto's books. The husband was English, but you'd never know. Speaks French better than we do,' he laughed. 'But they said they live nearby, in a village just the other side of that mountain. Come inside, I'll see if I can find them for you.'

Armand led Tania into the dark interior of his café, Paul's dog followed close behind, nuzzling the woman's expensive handbag.

'Now where is that telephone book?'

Tania was glad of the freshness of the interior. She discreetly wiped her eyes and sat at the bar. Paul clambered onto the next stool and sat beside her like a child.

'A Ricard or a glass of wine, Madame?' Armand slapped the telephone directory onto the counter with the flourish of the knight saving the damsel.

'Wine, please. Your Ricard is really too strong for me,' she smiled.

Armand poured a glass of red wine and the usual for Paul and himself.

'They lived at Sainte Colombe, didn't they?'

Paul nodded. 'Near the Abbey of Morterive.' He slurped his drink through the gap where his front teeth had once been. 'Beautiful place, the abbey, if Madame has time to visit it. People come from the world over to stay there. Never had the time myself,' he added dreamily.

Armand flicked through the book. 'What was their name again, Popol?'

'It was an English name,' Paul offered, 'there can't be many in Sainte Colombe. It's a very small village.'

Armand tugged at his moustache. 'Same name as that American President.'

'Not Clinton or Reagan . . . before that, les cacaouettes,' Paul volunteered, 'you know, the peanut man.'

'That's it,' Armand ran his finger down the list.

'There, Carter S. and L.' Armand turned the book to show Tania the entry. 'I'll write their number and address down for you.'

The wine hit Tania's empty stomach; she realised she hadn't eaten since leaving London.

'You can use my telephone, Madame, it's no trouble,' Armand reached under his counter.'

'That's very kind, thank you so much,' Tania declined. She had no idea what she was going to say when she made the call, but whatever it was, she didn't want to do it in public. 'I'll call them from my hotel.' She folded the paper and put the precious information into her wallet. She suddenly felt ungrateful. 'Do you think I could have something to eat,' she smiled, 'if I don't I might not get back in one piece.'

She sat by the window, looking out onto the dusty café terrace. From under one of the cheap plastic chairs a ginger dog with red spots on his fur emerged and came to stand in the café entrance as if to ask permission to enter.

The small quiche Armand brought her was more than she could manage. She ate slowly; it would have been ungracious not to finish it.

Armand and Paul gave a smile as they sauntered past to go back outside. They took up position in front of the café and stood, arms folded as they inspected Armand's attempt at sign writing.

'What's that, on Montferrus?' Paul shielded his eyes. 'There was a flash. It came from the plateau, right at the top.' He was too short-sighted to see that far.

'I've got my binoculars under the counter.' Armand dashed back into the café, giving Tania an apologetic nod as he raced out again.

'Give them to me.' Paul grabbed the binoculars. 'It came from up there, between the trees, on the edge. I still can't really see.'

Armand took the antiquated instrument from him and fiddled with it. 'The focus is a bit wonky. They were my father's.' He put the binoculars to his eyes and scanned the edge of the plateau.

'Ça, alors,' he exclaimed. There was a second flash and this time its source was unmistakeable. 'There, have a look.' He passed the binoculars back to Paul, 'between the two trees on the left. Tell me what you see.'

'It's a man.'

'I know. Recognise him?'

'It's Vilmorin. He's got some binoculars. That's what caught the sun. He's watching the chateau.'

The door of her hotel room shut with a discreet thud. Tania opened the tall window. It gave onto the garden terrace. She sat in the upholstered window seat and took a deep breath. Beyond the thick wall framing the terrace on three sides the vineyards were turning to gold in the sunset. Here and there long, black shadows underlined each and every shrub and tree. She closed her eyes. She would give it an hour before making the call to the couple in Sainte Colombe.

She had been on vacation in Italy and had found her sister's disconcerting message on her return to London. There was a great deal of background noise on the tape and her sister's agitated voice over it: 'Tania, I know you're away. I left messages on your mobile but you didn't call back. I have to leave here, now. It's too complicated to explain. I will. . .' There was a crackle; at that point the tape was full. Tania was alarmed. Her sister was not usually that impulsive. Something was very wrong. No matter how often she let the tape run over again she could not identify the noises in the background. She had booked the next flight to Toulouse, hired a car at the airport and driven straight to see Augusto only to be refused entry.

The hot shower soothed her a little. Wrapped in one of the luxurious towels she sat on the bed and dialled the number on Armand's note.

*

Yet I have something in me dangerous

33

Chateau de Noirlac, same evening

did not know how long he had been sitting, staring into the stillness of the garden. After a while he noticed that the sun had moved to the far right.

He rose, gathering all his strength. Again he stood in the hall in front of the library door. To his left the portrait of himself as a small boy hung in the dim light. The painting had a glow. Augusto stepped in front of the picture, squaring up to it. The boy's intense gaze seemed innocent enough, almost angelic at first glance. But as Augusto tried to stare his former self down he saw a triumphant mocking in the painted eyes. There it was then, the angel with the black heart. He thought of Léa as she had stood on the same spot, enthralled by the painting.

'You've finally found an admirer,' Augusto whispered. He reached and unhooked the picture from the wall, entered the library and closed the door.

*

Silver leaves, collected in her hair like stars

34

Sainte Colombe, May 9th, evening

'Léa, get the phone, I'm in the bathroom.'

'Hello,' said an English voice, 'Mrs Carter?'

'Speaking.' Léa gave a slight frown.

'I'm so sorry to disturb you. I got your number from the café at Noirlac,' said the woman. 'I am Tania Spencer. My sister....' She paused. 'I believe you met Augusto, my sister's husband recently.'

'Yes, we did, briefly,' Léa wandered into the bathroom and sat on the edge of the bath. Sam was rubbing his hair dry with a towel. Léa covered the mouthpiece. 'It's Augusto's sister in-law,' she whispered.

Sam frowned. 'Has something happened to him?'

Léa shrugged.

'I'm told you went to the chateau, not long ago,' continued the woman.

'Yes, we did.'

'I'm really sorry to ask you these questions,' Tania apologised, 'but I am trying to find my sister.' Her voice choked.

'No, that's okay, really,' Léa tried to sound reassuring. 'What did you want to know?'

'Did you go into the house? I mean, did Augusto take you inside?'

'We went to see him because he wanted to sell some of his books.' Léa heard Tania take a sudden breath which seemed to stick in her throat.

'It's just that . . . oh dear, I'd better start at the beginning.'

Léa looked at Sam. 'Would you not rather come over? We're less than fifteen minutes from the chateau.'

'That's very kind. I'm staying at the Hôtel de Citeaux. It would be best if I saw you. I'm so worried about my sister. I flew in from London today.' The woman's anxiety was palpable through the telephone line.

'I think you'd better come right away and I'll make us something to eat. Sam will explain to you how to get here.'

Sam rolled his eyes. Léa firmly thrust the receiver into his hand. He would have to put up with having his privacy invaded. She went down to the kitchen to see what she could rustle up in under thirty minutes.

Sam came down into the kitchen. 'Sounds like trouble to me.'

Léa was washing lettuce in a large blue and white bowl she had lugged back on the plane from Lisbon two years earlier. She had filled a small sack with minute coffee spoons, tiny ladles and other old fashioned cooking utensils

246

which she had found in a wooden-floored hardware shop, all but forgotten in the fashionable city centre. Tourists and the 'Beautiful People' of Lisbon bypassed the dark antiquated shop stacked to the ceilings with all manner of equipment for the catering trade. 'Real stuff, no tourist ever goes in there.' It was important to her to bring back genuine items from each place she travelled to. It prolonged her feeling of having been a part of it for a while.

She had smuggled home a fragment of a cast iron acanthus leaf from a Venetian fountain in the little Piazza just across the bridge from their apartment. It had broken off. It lay a few steps away from the fountain as she passed it several times on her way home. It would be swept up like so much rubbish by the street cleaners who did their rounds each Tuesday morning. Now the mere touch of the iron shard gave her a sensation of reaching into the past, like a door that opened, allowing her to become part of the time when the world was very different, when she would perhaps have been someone else altogether.

'You have vandalised our world heritage,' Sam had scolded her when she produced the piece of cast iron when they unpacked their car boot. 'They should arrest people for that sort of thing.'

'They were going to throw it away, so I saved it. Venice is falling to bits every day.'

'That's your slant on the story. I'm blaming you for contributing to its destruction. You should have handed it in to the authorities,' Sam said. 'things in Venice have got much worse ever since they let the big ships come into the Grand Canal. Their big waves erode the walls. That's why no one can live on the ground level any longer. And all the monuments are beginning to crack.'

The swirling cast iron shard had pride of place on the kitchen dresser and her eyes came to rest on it as she washed the lettuce.

'The woman sounds desperate,' Léa shook the moisture from the lettuce leaves. 'There's something very wrong here. It seems we are the only people Augusto saw since the furniture and the wife left.'

Sam remained silent for a moment. 'And the maid. Don't forget her.'

'I'm not forgetting her. We saw her in the car in front of the hotel that day, but Ophelia? We don't even know what she looks like. I can somehow imagine her, you know, being … somewhere now. People like her have options, connections, friends. But the maid, I just can't visualise her at all, out there in the world. There seems to be nothing to hold on to, do you know what I mean?' Perhaps her imagination was simply failing her.

'All I know is that somehow this whole thing with Augusto has totally got under your skin and you can't shake it off,' said Sam, 'it's all you talk about these days.'

'I know, but then he didn't get that close to you. I don't know whether it was him or what happened in that house that made my flesh creep. Anyway, dice me a few tomatoes. Tandoori prawn pasta is the best I can muster.'

The door bell rang.

'I'll go.' Léa wiped her hands. 'Watch the pasta doesn't boil over and chuck the tomatoes onto the prawns in the wok.'

A tall blond woman stood on the doorstep dressed in a cherry red linen blouse and skirt. A cream cashmere shawl covered her shoulders against the evening chill.

'You found us. Good. I'm Léa. Let's go into the kitchen, it's cosier in there.' No doubt the woman, like most English people, had arrived under-dressed for April, with no more than a thin shirt. This was the Southwest France, not Nice or Monte Carlo. Here the wind swept in not just from Africa, but from all directions, bringing cold air from the mountains, humidity from the south or rain from the Atlantic. When the Marin wind blew from the south it was so warm and humid that the washing hung dripping for days and after sun-set the air sank down from the Pyrenees and cooled everything down for the night. When the ferocious Cers wind hurled itself through the narrow village streets it rattled the plants so hard that they eventually broke at ground level.

The simplicity of the kitchen was always good to reduce stress. It felt more like home and conversations lacked the stiffness of a more formal room.

Sam stood in a cloud of steam from the draining pasta.

'This is Tania, Sam, Augusto's sister-in-law.'
He gave a friendly hello, but was glad to appear very busy. Léa pulled out one of the bentwood kitchen chairs. She noted the woman's pallor. Tania's fidgeting hands brushed her skirt nervously.

'Safety belts are all very well, but they do make such a mess of your clothes.'

Léa went to the wine rack and took out a bottle of Muscat.

'Have a glass of this, it'll straightened you out as if by magic. It's made by a young woman nearby who took over from her father three years ago. She now makes just twenty bottles of Muscat a year and it's divine. Gets better every year.'

Tania nodded gratefully as Léa filled three small glasses with the golden liquid.

'Food will be ready soon.' She threw a glance at Sam who was busying himself at the stove, mixing the pasta into the sauce with unusual concentration. How typically English, Léa smiled to herself. Emotions had to be kept down at all cost, talking about them was like giving something precious away, and talking about them with a strange woman was even worse. It was so different from the French who loved to discuss and debate anything from politics to why one should or should not feed the birds in winter. In France strongly held opinions on simply everything under the sun were the order of the day.

'What can we tell you?' Léa sat down.

'I'm so grateful to you,' Tania began, 'you are the only contact I have.' She put her hand to her throat trying to prevent a sob from rising. 'Ophelia left me a message, half a message really, on my answering machine while I was in Italy. The tape was full. If only I hadn't lost my mobile in Florence somewhere, I might have got her message sooner. She sounded very upset, in a dreadful rush. I haven't heard from her since, I have no idea where she could be or what has happened to her. It's so unlike her. She is not a rash person. It takes a lot before she cries for help.' She took another tiny sip of Muscat. Her hand trembled and she quickly set the glass back onto the table.

250

Léa put a hand on Tania's pale arm.

'One shouldn't jump to conclusions. If something had happened to her you would have heard by now.'

'You're probably right. But today I went to the chateau and … Augusto would not let me in and I ….' Tears welled up in her eyes.

Sam pulled out a chair and sat down. 'I'm not really surprised.'

'Why?'

'Your sister had removed every single item of furniture from the house. At least that's what he told us.'

'Why?' she asked again. The very idea of it seemed utterly incomprehensible to her.

Léa shifted on her chair. She suddenly felt embarrassed, as if they had somehow played a part in the sudden break-up of Ophelia's marriage.

'Augusto sold us some of his books,' said Sam. 'That's all that was left in the house. The books, a few carpets and some family portraits.'

'And that tapestry,' Léa added.

'Ophelia did that?' Tania murmured almost to herself, staring down at the table. She slowly shook her head. 'That doesn't sound like my sister at all. Not at all. She has such a sense of fair play, of justice.'

Sam did not meet her gaze. 'Perhaps it was a form of justice. Augusto did not claim that he had not deserved it.'

'I just can't imagine the house, emptied of life like that. I've been there so many times …. What else did you see?'

Léa glanced at Sam. It would have been cruel to tell Tania about the frogs in the pool.

'He took us upstairs,' Léa began and her eyes stayed on Sam.

'The rooms were all empty. The only one we didn't see was the one opposite the ballroom.'

'That's Zoffia's bedroom. Did you meet her?'

Sam's eyes gave a flicker. 'No. Augusto said the two women left on the same day.'

Again Tania looked puzzled. 'What would Ophelia do with her maid in tow?'

'Let's eat,' Léa broke into the conversation.

Tania bit her lip. 'You're the only people he let in.'

Léa turned her back to the table as she added some fresh chopped mint to the pasta. She set the bowls down on the table and served the food.

'This smells just like home.' Tania closed her eyes for a moment, inhaling the aroma of the spicy sauce.

Léa put a fresh candle into each of the candlesticks on the table and struck a match. The flame from it danced, like the flicker of the red hair of the running figure in the chateau grounds that day. Léa's eyes met Tania's.

'What is it?' She seized Léa by the wrist, 'please, tell me.'

Léa glanced over to Sam who appeared to be counting the prawns on his plate.

'It's probably not important,' Léa said lightly. 'Who lived at the chateau, apart from your sister and Augusto and the maid?

'It was just the three of them after the children left a few years ago. Ariana married and went to live in Madrid, Paplo studied at Harvard and lives in New York. Why?'

252

'A few days before we went for the books, we were passing by the chateau, quite by chance. We caught a glimpse of two women in the garden. At this time of the year the hedges at the perimeter are still quite bare, you can see into the grounds from the road.'

'What were they doing?' Tania's grip tightened.

'They were in the garden … running. One behind the other.'

'When was this?'

Sam put his glass down. 'We drove into the village and a removal truck nearly crushed us when the driver tried to exit from the chateau lane. It must have been a few days before we went to look at the books. Augusto said it was his birthday when we arrived.'

'The first of May,' Tania reached for her bag and consulted a small calendar. 'April twenty fourth, or twenty fifth?'

'It was a Tuesday,' Sam glanced at the calendar hanging on the kitchen wall, 'the twenty fourth.'

'So why hasn't she called me?'

'Perhaps she doesn't want to be found for the moment, by anyone.' Sam helped himself to more pasta. He tried to lighten his tone. 'No one disappears for good with that much furniture.'

Tania gave a deep sigh. 'I'm sure you're right. Perhaps she phoned London again and couldn't leave a message and I'm running around in circles here. There must be a reason why she doesn't want to be found,' she fiddled with the buttons of her shirt, 'don't you think there must be a reason?'

Léa and Sam exchanged glances. 'I'm sure you'll find out soon,' Sam reassured her.

'I've got to get back to London,' Tania shook her head, 'right away.'

'First we finish eating, Sam raised his hand, 'then I'll call the airport to get you on a flight.'

Sam closed the door and pushed the old iron bolt shut. His hand stayed on the cold metal for a moment, as if to make sure the world was securely banished to the other side of the heavy oak door. He rested his forehead against the wood and listened for Tania's engine to start up.

In the kitchen Léa was wiping the last of the bread crumbs off the table, slowly, deliberately, without lifting her eyes. Sam stood in the door; she did not look up. Each one was trying to gauge the other's thoughts in the silence.

'I need to go to bed,' Sam said after a while.

'Hum.' Léa avoided his gaze. 'So do I.'

Léa disappeared into bathroom. A long hot bath was her way of erasing troubling thoughts from her mind before the night's sleep. She would be a while.

The noise of the running water was soothing. She sank into the hot liquid and exhaled, sending the steam to curl away against the light of the candles she had lit at the corners of the tub. She wriggled her toes. They were sticking out of the water at the end of the bath. The water's surface reflected them with perfect symmetry, as if they were not attached to her body at all. Her shoulders ached. Whether it was from the anxiety about what had happened at Auch library or the fumes in the archive a few days ago, she couldn't say, but her whole body seemed filled with poison.

Breathe and calm down. She closed her eyes. She had learnt so much and discovered so much in the library. She should have felt some satisfaction. Instead she'd become embroiled in something which seemed always just out of reach.

When Léa opened her eyes again her chin had sunk into the water. Her hands floated beside her. They appeared to have grown, with deep ridges on the finger pads. Her toes had turned into white prunes. They looked quite dead.

Sam lay in the dim light of the bedside lamp. Visions of the old man in the empty chateau drifted into his mind's eye, slow and eel-like they coiled and slithered under his closed lids. He felt hinself roaming the chateau, touching the walls as he went from room to room. Objects which had seemed insignificant on the day of their visit suddenly loomed large. He began seeing books and more books, in all the rooms and their number grew wherever he turned. They towered high up to the ceiling in precarious piles. On each pile sat a grotesque brown toad looking down at him, watching with yellow bulging eyes. They jutted over the edges like medieval gargoyles from a church tower. It seemed to Sam that each pile represented the acquired wisdom of the toad enthroned upon it.

As he made his way through the maze the book towers grew denser, as trees do in a jungle, until it was almost dark at ground level. A melancholy sound reached him from somewhere and Sam tried to follow it. He could not feel his feet touch the ground and looked down at his shoes. The Persian carpet was a ripple of colours with spiralling swirls that snaked and twisted around the base of the book columns. Ever growing rings formed, as if a pebble had been dropped into a lake, all in slow motion. He realised that he was standing in water. The heavy sighs came from high up now and floated just under what appeared to be a ceiling. Then suddenly there was shimmering water above too and he seemed to be looking up from the bottom of a pool. The watery ceiling flickered, touched by a bright light that skipped over the ripples, a rhythmic dance of sunbeams forming, dissolving to form again. The weight of the water bore down on him. He tried to raise his arms. His movement set the book towers into motion and they began to sway. He shivered; the cold water was crushing his rib cage.

In his dream he closed his eyes. The books too were pressing down on him and he felt the towers collapsing all around him. Faintly, from the bottom of the pool, he heard Léa moving somewhere near to him and yet he remained under the silvery, rippling surface of his dream, a dream which he knew to be a dream, but from which he could not emerge of his own free will. He felt a strong touch now and he knew it was Léa's hand on his chest, freeing him from the books, dragging him out of the deep, out of his dream.

*

At night we'll feast together

35

Chateau de Noirlac, sunset, May 10th

The sun was low beyond the tall poplars at the far end of the grounds. Corridors of light cut in between them. Augusto walked along the cypress-flanked path leading to the pool. He was surprised to feel some warmth still from the evening sun and tried to shrug off the cold he had felt inside the house.

He carried a spade and stood peering into the frog-filled pool for a while, opening his nostrils wide, as if trying to identify some mysterious scent. He turned to the left and took the path past the mimosas down to the lake.

By the small bay that flattened out at one end the mud was deeply gouged; the dog had been digging again. In the shallow water lay a mound of twigs and branches.

Augusto began working at the sides, digging the muddy ground, heaping it into a long dyke to separate the bay from the main lake where the water was deep. The wet soil squelched; it was heavy to lift. The sun had turned into a quivering pumpkin. It squatted on the horizon, as if some great weight was pushing it down, out of the light into a dark, evil underworld. Augusto had never thought about it like that. It seemed strange that the crimson mass didn't rumble and roar and hiss like the mouth of a monstrous furnace, spewing liquid fireballs across the land.

He settled into a slow, regular rhythm as he dug. The moon rose, large and blood orange at first, then silver, turning shrubs and trees into black silhouettes. Slowly he straightened his aching back and rested his arm on the spade. He let his head drop back to take in a wider angle of the glass clear sky. Early evening stars appeared, one by one. He tried not to focus on any one of them in order to see them better, as he had done when he was a child.

He and his brother Carlos would escape their beds, climb through the window onto the old fig tree which offered its tangle of smooth branches to let them slide to the ground. Under the Argentinean night skies they lay gazing in wonder, competing to count the stars. But reason was set upon them by their education among boys of the English ruling classes. After a few years at Eton his brother became a musician; soon Augusto found himself at Harvard studying medicine.

The mystery of what happened to the melting sun in the evenings was forgotten. Questions about distant stars, about the existence of other planets, somewhere in an infinite universe, where two other boys might lie in the dark, remained unanswered. And now, what of the stars, of other worlds? Did they matter, did his joys, his grief, his emotions matter now or where all of them of no significance?

The moonlight cast a metallic sheen on the glistening mud barrier which now separated the small bay from the lake. Augusto laid the spade down. With his hunting knife he cut branches from the nearby reeds and willows and stacked them onto the mound of branches already in the shallow water.

He knelt down and pulled a sheet of folded paper from his trouser pocket and held it up, reading it in the moonlight before sliding it inside his white shirt. He took the knife in his right hand.

'Not long now', he muttered at the tousled pile of branches which lay before him, 'I'm here.'

Carefully, so as not to topple the heap, he crawled in between the layers of branches, like a beast into its laird, until the pile enclosed his entire body like a shell.

He waited until he had settled into a comfortable position. The time had come.

*

Come draw to an end with you

36

New York, May 16th,
the office of Augusto's son Pablo

His brand new office was a present to himself, the reward for a few hard years graft to make his reputation. Everything in the room oozed quality and confidence and reflected his success as a futures broker with clients from all continents. He was one of the youngest; his colleagues were envious of his talent and the many languages he spoke. He felt comfortable with almost anyone, with the exception only of his father.

He repositioned the silver framed photograph of his sister with her twins, his sister, dark and Spanish looking, her children fair haired for now with the same turquoise eyes they had all inherited from Augusto.

The ring tone of a Spanish guitar broke the silence. Pablo reached for his mobile and peered out into the depth of the city beneath, the yellow New York taxis weaving their way along the straight avenues, no larger than beetles. The city was slowly emerging from the morning mist.

'Ariana. Funny, I was just looking at your photo. You should see my new office. I'll email you some pictures. You and the kids have pride of place on my fabulous new desk. And Maman, of course. What's up? I've been so busy. I haven't had time to …'

He listened and put his hand over his eyes.

'When …?' He let himself fall onto his new leather chair and began swivelling around on it. The colour had drained from his olive skin.

'You stay where you are. I'll catch a plane in the morning.'

The door opened and Jo, his personal assistant peered into the room.

'Hi, there, ready for your breakfast, boss?'

'Yes. No. Just coffee, lots of it, please.'

'Trouble?'

'Family,' he sighed. 'Can you get me a flight for Toulouse, as soon as possible? Tomorrow?'

'Right on, boss.' Jo withdrew her head and closed the door.

*

With wisest sorrow think on it

37

Sainte Colombe, May 21st

'From Augusto's son.' Sam put the letter on the kitchen table. 'Augusto is dead.'

'Oh, no.' Léa stopped stirring the vegetable soup she had made and sat down. 'Why is his son writing to us?'

'Apparently Augusto has left us some books.'

'Can he do that? Under French law his son inherits everything. He's under no obligation to carry out Augusto's wishes.'

'I don't know, he doesn't say. He wants us to go to the chateau on Saturday. He's only here for a few days. After the reading of the will they're auctioning off some stuff.'

'I wonder whether they'll sell the house?'

Sam raised both hands. 'Léa. Stop your dreaming. We're definitely not staying for the house sale.'

They both sat at the kitchen table in silence. A small hissing sound came from the cooker.

'Christ,' Léa jumped up, 'my soup is burning.'

*

And all his golden words are spent

38

Chateau de Noirlac, Saturday morning, May 25th

The morning auction was poorly attended. It was clear that both the notary and the auctioneer knew that apart from the few threadbare carpets there was nothing much to be had.

The main doors of the house had been thrown open and Sam and Léa stopped in the doorway. A tall, olive-skinned man in his twenties spotted them. Stepping over a rolled up carpet he held out his hand to greet them.

'I'm Pablo, Augusto's son. Were you friends of my father's?'

They looked embarrassed. 'Not really,' Sam exchanged glances with Léa.

Pablo smiled. 'Sorry, you must be the Carters.'

'We are,' said Sam, 'but we only met your father twice. We bought some books from him recently.'

Léa bit her lip. She had not told Sam of her escape from Augusto's library when she had stopped off at the chateau on her drive back from Auch that night. Sam would have been furious at her stupidity.

'In that case you probably knew him better than I', Pablo said lightly. He ran a tanned hand over his jet black hair which stood in strange contrast to his turquoise eyes. 'To my father anyone who shared his interest in books was a saint. Come this way, please.'

He strode ahead towards the library. His jacket, trousers and shoes looked English, probably Saville Row, definitely tailor made.

'God, all those books,' whispered Léa at the sight of several large piles sitting on the parquet floor, 'where would we put them all?'

'Take what you want,' Pablo waved, 'but we'll do it later. Let's see how the auction is progressing.'

In the hall two men were dismantling a large brass bed.

'See. She was not completely heartless,' Sam muttered into Léa's ear. 'She left him a bed after all.'

'They're not ready.' Pablo watched the men for a moment. 'Most of the family portraits will be shipped to my sister in Madrid. Ariana left yesterday, after the funeral. We had a serv ice at the village church here, but my father will be buried in Madrid so that Ariana's children will have the grave of their grandfather near them. My sister is keen on family. She can't bear to part with the paintings, she wants her kids to know where they come from. I like to move around, not exactly practical with a dozen enormous paintings in tow. I'll take just one with me.'

He seemed relieved to have someone to talk to.

'Come, let's go up. I've been so busy with the lawyer and the will. I'm staying at the Hôtel de Cîteaux so I haven't had much time here. I want to have another look around. I haven't seen the house for a long time. Come with me, it'll stop me from getting sentimental.'

They climbed the wide marble stairs. Since their visit all the doors of the upper hall had been shut. Pablo opened one door after another, stepping into each room like a curious stranger. He stood in the bathroom door, hands in pockets. Over the sink a shelf remained. On it stood an old mustard glass with a tooth brush, next to it a half empty bottle of whisky.

'God.' Pablo spoke almost to himself. 'Didn't he have any toothpaste?'

He led the way through the double doors opening into the largest room and stood in the middle of it under the baroque ceiling-rose designed for the grandest of chandeliers.

'My parents used to hold parties in here when I was a child.' He did a couple of turns in the centre of the floor, 'totally extravagant, old fashioned balls really, some would have called them decadent.' He stopped, sizing up the volume of the room, perhaps trying to recapture a glimpse of the long gone festivities.

'Really loud music used to wake me up. To me it felt like the middle of the night. I came down in my pyjamas dragging my Teddy bear behind me. Sometimes I thought it was clever to make my entrance by sliding down the bannister. Most of the people I knew. They whisked me up in their arms and whirled me around. Some were English, others Argentinean or Spanish. I remember some Polish and

Russian friends of my parents. They babbled at me in languages I knew and others I didn't. It's the music I remember best of all. Ripping tangos and swirling waltzes. You got dizzy just listening to the orchestra.' He half closed his eyes and tilted his head, as if to hear something long forgotten.

'All of my father's friends could dance like dervishes, of course.' There was a touch of irony in his tone. 'The best I can do is … shake about a bit. Not that my father didn't try to teach me to tango, but all that hands-on stuff wasn't cool when I was fifteen.'

They left the room. Pablo closed the double doors, slowly with a strange deliberation, shutting away his childhood memories for a last time. Back in the wide hall they stood once again by the door that had remained closed on their first visit. Pablo stopped in front of it, rested his hand on the door handle.

'This is Zoffia's room.' He spoke in the present tense, as if he expected to find her sitting on a chair, combing her long red hair. He opened the door slowly. The room looked out over the garden and the pool and further down onto the lake half hidden by willows and reeds. In front of the shoulder-high fireplace, a light blue blanket was spread neatly on the floor. Around its edges, at measured distances, lay the heads of large white flowers, now wilted. A wooden hobby-horse in faded colours with a tattered mane and a broken rein was carefully positioned in the centre of the arrangement. Pablo bent down and picked up the toy.

'That's weird. I remember this. When we moved into the chateau, I found it in the barn. It must have been left by the boys of the previous owner. They had moved just across the vineyards when my father bought this house. I played with them in the barn in the beginning. There was something wrong with one of them; he was sent away. I was past the age of playing with hobby-horses. I don't remember it ever being in the house.' He fondled the sad looking mane. 'They had a prowler in the barn, quite recently. My mother told Ariana about it. She was very upset.' He let the toy drop back onto the blanket. 'So what is this doing here?' He shrugged and turned to take in the rest of the room. 'Old, old stories.'

Pablo went over to one of the windows.

'That's the lake on the left,'

'I know.' Léa followed him.

In the far corner by the second window a deep china wash bowl had been placed on a chair. A triangular chunk had broken from the rim. As Léa stepped nearer she saw that the bowl was full of water; in it floated a drowned pigeon, its wings spread wide and eyes half closed. Surrounding the chair dark water stains marked the parquet floor, a reminder of the pigeon's battle with death.

'Oh, no.'

Pablo came away from the window and bent over the bowl.

'Perhaps it got trapped in the room after the furniture went and no one heard it.'

Léa glanced over to Sam, about to speak, but Sam shook his head.

On the ground floor the Sainte Colombe notary had started the auction. Pablo paced up and down, from window to window, glancing out to the sunny forecourt, a far-away look in his eyes. The dishevelled head of a young man popped up outside of one of the windows. He was pressing muddy hands against the pane, trying to look in. Pablo stopped for an instant, gazing at the strange apparition, then continued his pacing. The figure outside dashed to the next window as Pablo passed it, and the next, gesticulating desperately.

'C'est moi, it's me, it's me,' came a muffled cry through the window from the contorted face. Pablo looked again. He turned his back to the windows to escape the wild stare.

'I don't know him,' he shrugged as he returned to stand next to Sam.

The young man outside was jumping up and down, mouthing inaudible words and stabbing his chest with his index finger.

Pablo shook his head. 'Probably the village idiot,' he whispered to Léa. 'Every village has one. We're the news, the big scandal here today.'

They went to sit in the hall with Pablo and listened to the notary race from item to item. The old kitchen went to an antiques dealer for a song. On the strength of the number of antiquated utensils it included he could probably open a kitchen museum. A threadbare carpet and odds and ends from Augusto's new kitchen were carried away by a gypsy and his companions. Sam went to the window and watched the two swarthy men bundle their booty into a battered van. They drove off with the rear doors held together with a pair of women's tights. A trail of black exhaust fumes swirled from the van as it disappeared down the lane.

Pablo had resumed his pacing, this time in the main hall and Sam and Léa joined him. All the paintings had vanished from the walls and the stairs. The sole trace of their existence was a series of rectangular shapes where for two decades the light had not bleached the Italianate wallpaper which now could only be found in the archives of the finest of Lyon's design house.

The only picture that remained was the small portrait of the boy; it was no longer tucked into the hall corner like on their first visit. It hung conspicuously, slightly askew, from a large nail crudely driven into the wall. It sat very low, almost touching the dado rail. What a strange place for it to hang, Sam thought. He couldn't imagine that the auctioneer or anyone else for that matter had given instructions to move it from its original place. Now the boys head in the picture sat at the height of an eight year-old child. It struck Sam that the picture's positioning was not random, but staged somehow. He remembered Augusto putting the ear from the broken marble bust on the mantelpiece, telling it to listen. This felt as if the boy in the painting was spying on the business in progress.

Léa gazed at the painting for a long while. The artist's bold brush strokes rendered it alive and fresh, as if the boy had got up and walked off after being painted only moments earlier.

'Will that be sold too?' Sam asked Pablo.

'I don't know what to do with it,' Pablo sighed. He got up and looked at Sam. 'I'm glad you came,' he said suddenly. 'It's a painting of my father, as a boy.' He came to stand next to Léa.

'I know.' She could smell an expensive after-shave on him.

'I hadn't seen him since that business with Zoffia started. My mother didn't know. I really should have told her, but there was never a right moment. We didn't know where she had gone to for nearly two weeks. My aunt Tania found her in a London hotel. All the furniture is still in a depot in Dover. I suppose by leaving my father like that she actually saved most of their possessions.'

Even though he seemed to have taken his mother's side, he had the same directness as Augusto. Another son who despises his father but turns out exactly like him, Léa realised.

'I hate that picture,' Pablo said slowly. 'My mother made me stand in front of it when I had tantrums. "Look at your father," she used to say, "and let him be your example. Now *he* was never a bad boy!"'

He paused and glared at the picture. 'Can you believe that? I mean, look at those eyes.' He paced up and down to calm his agitation. The grief and loathing he felt for his father were battling within him.

'With my mother there were only saints and devils and nothing in between. It left no room for disappointment, or forgiving. To her my father was perfect in every way, until she put Zoffia into his path.'

'What happened to Zoffia?'

'My father said her things were here when he returned from Paris but the rest of the house was almost entirely empty; not that Zoffia had much, just a few clothes, but they're not here now. Perhaps she came back or he gave them away.' Pablo shook his head. 'Who knows what went on here in the last few weeks?'

Again he stopped in front of the painting, his turquoise eyes fixed onto it. 'So who can I believe?' he asked the picture; he didn't expect an answer. He sat down on one of the plastic chairs standing against the wall.

'Anyway, it's all water under the bridge.'

'How did your father die?' The question had burned on Léa's tongue since they had arrived.

'He killed himself, cut his wrists, on the lake. I mean...,' he made a gesture of disbelief.

Léa felt a cold shiver run down her back.

'We had some magic times on that lake,' Pablo's hand brushed over his eyes, as if to wipe away the vacant, staring sadness, 'but he's desecrated it. It's nothing more than a tomb now.' His father's final act had robbed him of his childhood memories.

'Louis, the postman, raised the alarm. He looked through the letter box and saw the pile of mail. Apparently he spent ages banging on windows and doors and shouting through the letter box. Louis was very fond of my father despite their occasional spats about junk mail when they'd both had one glass of Ricard too many. They couldn't find my father in the house or the garden but his car was here. At first they thought he'd wandered off, you know, as some confused old people do.'

'He didn't seem confused to us,' Sam said.

'No,' Pablo sighed, 'he was not confused at all. As always with him, it was all planned, to make sure it would work to the last detail, like a stage play.'

Pablo got up again and paced up and down, hands in his trouser pockets. Léa could see he was clenching and unclenching his fists.

'No one had seen him. It took a few days before they unpicked what they thought was a pile of dead branches at the shallow end of the lake.'

The monk in the library in Auch suddenly surfaced in Léa's mind. She felt faint and turned away.

'What about the house, are you going to keep it?' she heard Sam ask.

'If it hadn't been for this business I would have been tempted, turn it into a hotel, maybe a conference centre or a school, or something. It's too big for a holiday home, but not now. Ariana, my mother and I agreed to sell the chateau, give it away, we don't care which, and be done with it. Perhaps some Englishman crazy enough will want to buy it. Doesn't simply *everyone* dream of owning a chateau?'

There was surprise on Sam's face. 'Those were your father's exact words.'

'I bet.'

'Do you know why he did it?' Léa asked quietly.

'Someone you've known all your life turns into a complete stranger overnight. Why he should pick on the lake is beyond me. I thought people either drown themselves or cut their wrists. What's the point of doing it in the shallow end of the lake where there is hardly any water? And that stuff with the branches, what is it supposed to mean?' He rolled his shoulders, a man trying to shed an oppressive load. 'He was above the water when he slashed his wrists, he couldn't possibly imagine that he would drown.'

Léa glanced over to Sam trying to make sense of what Pablo was saying, but Sam shook his head.

'They found this, inside his shirt.'

Pablo took a piece of paper from his pocket. 'It sounds familiar, but I just can't place it. My brain is rattled at the moment. You're into books, perhaps you know it.'

Léa trembled as she touched the paper that Augusto must have clasped in his dying moments.

It was a page torn from a note book. It was creased but the large writing sat clear and neat in the centre, like a poem.

Let the doors be shut upon him,
that he may play the fool
but in's own house.
Farewell

'It's from Hamlet,' said Sam. 'He is talking to Ophelia, before he says 'get thee to a nunnery.'

Léa handed the paper back to Pablo who showed no desire to take it.

'Perhaps Zoffia did just that,' Sam offered, 'she wouldn't need her things in a convent.'

Pablo nodded. 'She didn't go to London with my mother.' He seemed grateful to have found some way of making sense of the grotesque situation foisted on him.

'This is so typical of him. He always over-dramatised. It's like these people who jump into a grave when they lower a coffin at a funeral - theatrical.' He glanced back at the portrait with a disdainful look.

'Still, I love that painting,' Léa said softly. She wanted to appease Pablo's hatred of his father, lighten his pain.

Pablo reached, unhooked the picture from the wall. 'Here. Have it. Take it. Please.'

'I couldn't possibly.' Léa deliberately let her arms hang down by her side. 'I have no right.'

'It means nothing to you,' he insisted, 'to you it's just a beautiful work of art.' He turned his head away. 'I couldn't live with it.' He let go of the picture, forcing her to catch it before it hit the floor.

*

Outface me with your leaping in the grave

39

Chateau de Noirlac, later that morning

'You'd think that with so little to sell they would have finished by now,' Pablo sighed. He signalled for them to follow him to the library.

'Take what you want. My father was quite specific about that. He left instructions taped to the library door, 'All books to the Carters. Need to know where they go.' Pablo took a deep breath, exhaled as if he never intended to breathe in again. 'No one had any idea what he meant. Armand at the café remembered you and found your address for me. He is a good soul, clever too, wasted in that café.'

'Thank you.' Sam couldn't think of anything else to say.

Pablo waved his hand. 'Don't thank me. When it comes to the books, he knew I would have no use for them. He and I had such different interests.'

276

Sam and Léa began their search; perhaps they could use some of Augusto's books for their work. The library looked as though a wild boar had been let loose to forage in the room to its heart's content. Through the open door they could hear the auctioneer's monotonous drone. Pablo fingered the Latin American children's books and poetry volumes, opening and closing them one after another.

The jar on the window sill containing the yellow-eyed toad had gone. Someone had made an effort to wipe away traces of Augusto's liking for the macabre. Perhaps he had done so himself. Léa could imagine him, with that liquid, gleeful look in his eyes, tipping the grimacing toad specimen into the swimming pool, laughing at the startled live frogs which had taken up residence there.

The only remaining object filling a whole corner of the room was a giant aspidistra in a bulbous, blue and green Majolica jardinière.

'Maybe we can buy the plant?' Léa whispered to Sam.

A few old volumes had been swept onto the floor where Augusto's small desk had once been. Now they lay amongst a handful of creased sheets of paper. A slim book with a bleached cover caught her eye. It was one of those hardback notebooks covered in marbled paper. Its corners were frayed; how many fingers had opened it, turned the pages? It was covered in old water-stains and scuffed and dirty as though it had been retrieved from a dusty attic. Léa bent down and picked it up. A puff of mould rose as she leafed through it.

A torn strip of paper marked a page. 28th of June 1789 was inscribed at the top of the page, the year when the French revolution was about to errupt, spelling danger for the nobility. The text was written in a stiff, unsophisticated hand. Was this someone's secret diary? Léa recalled that on the night she had fled from Augusto's library he had mentioned finding old documents relating to the chateau's history. Perhaps this was one of them. The writing was hard to read. The once black ink had turned to a reddish brown and faded to mere shadows in parts.

Pablo was showing Sam a number of small leather bound volumes.

'This is all I want. Take your time. The more you take the better.' He left the library to resume his pacing.

Léa waited until he was out of earshot.

'Sam, you must see this. It's incredible. Listen to this. In 1788 a daughter of the Vilmorin family was married off to a Marquis. It says here she was born in 1776. That makes her just twelve years old.'

'Not all that unusual,' Sam shrugged. 'Girls were promised to old men, or rich men, often at birth.'

'I know. But listen to this:

> *My name is Antonin. I have been head gardener of the chateau of Noyrlac for these thirty years and more.*
>
> *I swear this to be a true account.*
>
> *A terrible fate has befallen my master's daughter, Mademoiselle Milena. Now that my master has left and the house is quiet again I will record the events so that one day the people of Noirlac may know what happened.*

'Not so loud.' Sam shushed Léa and indicated the open door. Pablo was pacing just outside. Perhaps it would not be a good idea to stir up more unpleasant facts. He'd had enough to contend with.

Léa read on in silence:

> *Demoiselle Milena Léanore de Vilmorin, twelve years of age, only daughter of the Comte de Vilmorin, was married to Marquis de Pourtales on the 1st of May 1788. Three weeks after the lavish wedding, in the night of the 21st of May, a very young woman was thrown out of carriage at our gates ....*

The next few lines were badly faded.

> *... found at dawn ... by the game keeper ...her face ... lacerated so badly, she was unrecognisable. All her hair had been cut to a stubble. Her arms were covered in bruises and welds. She was wearing neither coat nor dress, only underclothes such as a lady wears. She was carried to the room formerly occupied by Milena, the master's daughter.*
>
> *Only Monseigneur de Vilmorin and Lisette, a young chambermaid, were allowed to enter her room.*

'Sam, this is unbelievable,' Léa whispered. There was no mention of the girl's mother. She read on:

> *Before dawn the maid Madeline had been woken by Lisette's cries in the next room but found Lisette had been locked in. Lisette slipped her note under the door to tell Madeline of the night's events.*
>
> *At first light Madeline came running into the garden to show me Lisette's note. In it Lisette swore by the Holy Virgin Mary that she had attended to the injured girl until late into the night and brought her a draught to help her sleep. Lisette and Monseigneur de Vilmorin had tried to put the girl to bed, but she would not be moved from the gilded chair which had*

279

been Milena's favourite. She had clung to the armrests of the chair and it was impossible to loosen her grip. After Monseigneur de Vilmorin left the room the girl implored Lisette to put out the candles and to open the window, saying the night air cooled her wounds.

Lisette confessed that she had fallen asleep in the chair by the side of the girl. She was roughly woken before dawn by being seized by a strong man, whom she believed to be the coachman. Though she couldn't see his face she recognised his smell, seeing that he spent most of his life very near the rear end of the horses. The man pressed his hand to Lisette's mouth to stop her from screaming as he carried her to the maids' quarters in the attic where she was thrown onto her bed and locked in.

The writing got so small and crammed, Léa could barely decipher the next line.

Lisette was blamed for not watching over her charge.

Whispering through the door both servant girls agreed that the abused girl was in fact their mistress Milena. On reading Lisette's note Madeline rushed to Milena's room and found that both the girl and the gilded chair had vanished. Madeline informed the cook who went to investigate at dawn. She found Milena's chamber stripped bare - the bed, the rugs, wall hangings, mirrors and drapes – everything was gone. She told the kitchen maid, 'the room looked as if no one had ever lived in it.'

The stable boy reported that the coachman was patrolling the grounds with his shotgun and that none of the servants were allowed into the gardens or near the lake for a week, though normally carp and other fish for the master's table would have been caught there.

Lisette was kept locked in her room. Some days later we were told she had been dismissed.

Madeline saw Lisette being escorted by the coachman down to the rear gate through the orchards beyond the lake. Lisette intended to walk to her father's house in Sainte Colombe, the next village, but she never arrived.

One of the stable boys, Lisette's cousin, sent a message to her family. When her father heard of Lisette's incarceration he came to the chateau for an explanation. When he was given none he took up a daily vigil outside the gates, demanding to know where his fourteen year-old daughter was. After the coachman threatened him with a shotgun Lisette's father did not return.

Not long after revolutionaries in the region were stirring up hatred among the peasants who roamed the countryside, threatening the nobility. The Marquis de Pourtales and his family fled to their sugar plantations on the island of Martinique. The Vilmorin family maintained that Milena had accompanied the marquis. The servants knew otherwise. Neither Milena nor her favourite chair were ever seen again in the house.

Léa clutched the notebook. 'I'm not crazy after all. This is too horrible. Gisèle was right, there is something in this house.'

'I never said you were crazy.' Sam was nearly done with packing the books.

'They killed the girl, probably drowned her in the lake to save their honour.'

'Perhaps she died. If I were you, I would not show that to Pablo.'

Léa turned the battered note book in her hand. 'Maybe I should have it?'

Sam shook his head. He had finished packing the boxes. 'Better not. Haven't you had enough nightmares lately?'

'I already know what is in this book. Why should it haunt the new owners when the chateau is sold?'

Footsteps approached. She quickly slipped the little volume into the last of Sam's boxes.

'Found anything interesting?' Pablo looked in. 'They should be done soon.'

'Are you selling that too?' Léa indicated the sprawling aspidistra.

'Do you want it? I'll see about it with the auctioneers.' He went next door.

'I suppose you expect me to carry that home too,' Sam grumbled unconvincingly.

Pablo returned. 'Apparently it's not on the sale list. No one has expressed an interest in the plant. Take it. And take the plant pot too, no one will miss it.'

The midday sun beat down on them as they made their way to the car. Sam was hugging the huge jardinière. His face completely disappeared behind the jungle of broad leaves as Léa led him to their car like blind man.

'I wonder who will buy the house now?'

'I told you, we're not hanging around for the house auction this afternoon,' Sam mumbled from behind the foliage. 'I can't be sure you'll resist the temptation of putting your hand up and I'm definitely not buying you a chateau.'

'Even if they give it away?' Léa ventured. A grin flew across her face, 'only joking.'

She held the car door open. Perhaps it had been all wrong for someone like Augusto to dream of a normal life in this village with so much history. These big houses played a central role in the communities; they were the main, often the only employer for the farmers, their wive and children. Owners had responsibilities to look after the community. To be born in a village with a chateau was proof of a glorious past. Most great houses had been monasteries in the beginning, or they were built on former monastery sites. Augusto had lived here in splendid isolation. He had imported his friends and an alien life style; he had cut the village adrift.

Pablo strode across to them. 'Thank you for coming. Here is my card. If ever you're in New York, be sure to call me. I really mean that.' He shook their hands. 'Just wanted to say good bye. I'll be leaving shortly. I won't stay for the house sale.'

Sam watched Pablo disappear into the house. 'I don't blame him.'

By the gates an ambulance had stopped. A grey-haired man in a hunting jacket and a slim woman in a blue dress and apron were holding onto the young man who had been

283

shouting at Pablo through the windows earlier. He struggled as they bundled him into the ambulance. It slowly drove down the lane towards Armand's café.

The grey haired man had remained behind by the gates. He cast a long look at the chateau. Only someone standing very close to him could have detected the faint smile on his lips.

*

That one may smile and smile

40

Chateau de Noirlac, afternoon, same day

With its gilded corbels and ceiling rose what had once been a grand room looked faded and dusty in the afternoon light. The auctioneer walked in. Whispered gossip was snuffed out in mid-sentence. Chairs squeaked under the weight of shifting bodies to get a look at him; shoes scraped on the grit brought in from outside. He knew that they were all craning their necks to peer at him, a stranger from Narbonne.

In these villages, where everyone was related to everyone, people from the surrounding towns were *gavatches*, strangers; anyone coming from north of Lyon was doubly so. Foreigners, not being French, didn't count; Parisians were unmentionable, but all of them were viewed with suspicion. The sun, the wine, the cheap property were all they seemed to want; few gave anything back. The smiles and the friendly bonjour in the streets vanished as soon as the doors of the village houses closed.

The auctioneer inhaled, gingerly, testing the air without meeting the villagers' eyes, as dogs do when they assess an intruder. His nostrils twitched. Country auctions always had that biting smell of damp clothing dried in front of a smoking wood fire. The heady vapours of too many aperitifs lingered on the men's breath and on their moustaches; in the mountain villages their boots brought the earthy aroma of sheep dung into the auction rooms. Wafting over from the women was the sharp scent of supermarket perfumes, hastily sprayed on in quantity to mask the smell of cooking.

'Maître, bonjour.' The auctioneer greeted the Sainte Colombe notary who vacated his place for the change-over on the make-shift platform where a table and chair had been set up. The auctioneer had requested a cushion in anticipation of having to sit on a hard bench all afternoon as he had done in the previous week at the auction of the former boys' school in the neighbouring village.

'His buttocks are a tender as a young girl's,' the village men laughed scathingly, 'that's what happens when you sit in a plush office all day.'

They watched, smiling as the man was inspecting the cushion with an earnest frown, unaware that the joke going round about his posterior was sending the women into fits of suppressed giggles. He sat down and squared up the papers in front of him. It wasn't every day that he was asked to auction off a chateau. He had been called in by Sainte Colombe's notary who had dealt with the smaller stuff, the

286

family papers and the sale of the few remaining items earlier in the day.

'This afternoon,' he announced with gravitas, 'we are here for the sale of the Chateau de Noirlac.'

All eyes scanned the room to see who was present for the big event. The villagers had turned up in force. Curiosity drove them, as well as fear of change.

'Nothing good will come of this,' the older ones had warned when Guy Vilmorin had been forced to sell the chateau some twenty years earlier. 'It's a bad omen. You can't break the path of history just because your wife has run off,' Armand's father had wailed, 'now we'll all suffer the consequences.'

The link between the Vilmorin family and the village ran too deep. For the last week villagers had huddled in little groups at Armand's café. Over their aperitifs they mumbled and whispered and scratched their heads, trying to fathom what would come next. Rumours ran wild when the manner of Augusto's suicide emerged.

Armand watched and held his tongue. Talk and speculation would not help. Marie-Louise was exhausted. Her husband's pacing up and down until dawn had robbed her of sleep since the notary had told Armand that Augusto's son was selling up.

Now the whole village crowded into the room with three sets of French windows to either side of the ornate double door standing open onto to the forecourt. Many of the villagers had been in this room when they were children. Each and every year Guy's mother, Esmonde de Vilmorin, distributed tiny toys, much needed warm scarves and socks, precious coloured pencils or a picture book to the village children to welcome the New Year. When the chateau had been sold to Augusto Perez de Montsarrat there were no more New Year treats. Today they all wanted to be there, maybe for one last time, even though not one of them could raise their hand to bid for the great house.

'Some other dreamer from the North will ride into the village in a fancy car and buy it,' Paul grumbled. He was resigned to the fact that yet another foreigner with no understanding or respect for their close-knit community would be unleashed on them. The stranger would bring his foreign friends. They would marvel at the lives of these quaint little French villagers like himself with a look of bemusement tinged with pity, as if they were visiting the mentally retarded. Worse, a Parisian might take possession of the property. Southerners and the Occitans of this region in particular, harboured a visceral hatred of Parisians arrogance, a loathing which had not abated since the Middle Ages, if not before.

Armand took up position at the back of the packed room, arms crossed and sleeves rolled up. He had not taken off his apron. There was no need to show undue respect for the auctioneer from town who took on the manner of President de Gaulle, looking down his nose at the assembled crowd. Armand was a working man and not ashamed of it. The fingers of his right hand were drumming on his left arm. There was no point in opening the café until the auction was over. He was waiting.

A narrow faced, dark-haired youth in a yellow blazer was making his way to the auctioneer's table. Armand barely recognised his sister's son. So, Suzanne had somehow

288

succeeded in wedging her 'petit Francis' into the job as assistant to the Sainte Colombe notary.

Francis struggled through the crowd to reach the auctioneer's table. He stood, solemn as an altar boy in Sunday mass, with his hands folded in front of him. His coal black eyes were scrutinising the crowd facing him. He was proud to have been asked to assist today. He was born and bred in Sainte Colombe, not fifteen minutes away. Numbers were his strength in school and he dreamt of a career which involved money, lots and lots of it, if only on paper. Now he was junior assistant to the village notary. In the villages Monsieur Le Notaire liked to be called 'Maître'. Having studied law, a notary was only one small rung below the village priest who was as close to God as any man could be and to work in close proximity of such men, Francis was convinced, was to have a foot on the first rung of the ladder.

Today of all days it was important to look important. Francis hadn't slept a wink all night. To mark the occasion he'd had a haircut. Last night he had laid out his clothes – black shirt, black and yellow tie and his bright yellow blazer which his sister mockingly called 'your canary'. But Francis, elevated to his new post, knew that a well-dressed man could go far - a well-dressed man with the right strategy and a good head for figures, like himself, could even become village mayor one day.

He let his eyes glide from one face to another. Everyone from the village was here, bar the farm animals. And then it dawned on him. Everyone from the village was here, but no one else. He searched for strangers, but could find none. He looked to the auctioneer. This was all wrong. He had seen piles of leaflets and posters in the notary's office. What had happened to them? As it was, the sale of the chateau had been arranged in a great rush; the dead man's son had insisted on it. Blood rushed to Francis' head. The auctioneer had to be alerted, but his forbidding, haughty look, his expensive shirt and immaculate attire were intimidating. There was not one crease in his dark blue suit, as if he had travelled in his car from Narbonne standing up all the way. Francis would not have been surprised if he had waved as he passed through the villages.

Francis froze. What would his mother do now? His mother Suzanne was the notary's secretary, had been for years. When Francis left school she saw to it that no one but her son would be considered for the junior post in the notary's office. Only she and Francis knew how she had manipulated the application letters of other candidates, some much better qualified than her 'petit Francis'. Of course, there had been rumours, but they had not strayed beyond the village. Francis now blushed, but he was doing his best not to disappoint her. Suzanne would tire of her work one day; Francis burned with impatience to take over from her. He knew he could count on his mother to rub out any competition.

It was unusual to find a woman in her job. Francis could not imagine a girl as her successor. Girls were too keen to be liked, to please. As notary, or as his secretary, you had to command respect, even occasionally bully clients. His mother was the exception. She dominated people by her big voice, not to say her bodily attributes, which were tightly buttoned into her blouse. Men liked that sort of thing.

Even when he was in his teens, when his urges in that direction had manifested themselves in alarming and uncontrollable fashion, Francis could always tell when she was meeting a difficult client. She would wear her prim lace blouse, the sort that should be buttoned to the neck. But hers would be unbuttoned right down to the point where it threatened to let her God-given proportions spill out at the slightest movement. Once, when he had burst into her office with some news or other from school, Monsieur le Notaire had been sitting on the corner of his mother's desk and his hand, which had hovered very close over her cleavage, rapidly disappeared in his pocket and he dashed out of Suzanne's office. His mother had said something about her gold chain being snagged on the blouse buttons. Since that day, locked into the bathroom, Francis had compared the notary's nose, eyes and mouth to his own to see whether he could find any resemblance in his own features. So far his research had been inconclusive.

Suzanne always wore a gold pendant on a long chain that dropped heavily into her cleavage. One could almost see the steam rising from her breasts as she played with her jewellery during tricky negotiations. It seemed to work, but Francis had no such weaponry. He had to hone his skills in front of the mirror – the listening mode with a slight nod, the clasped hands for sympathy, showing that he would do his best but that his hands were tied, the grief-stricken expression when announcing a ridiculously low price achieved on a house sale. Francis could see his future laid out in a straight line, stretching to the horizon and beyond like a shining path. One day he would be somebody.

His mother Suzanne and Uncle Armand had not been close for years, not as brother and sister should be. Francis tried but could not recall when they had last spoken. Women. It was women who caused all the trouble. He would have to be more careful when it came to marriage. The whole village knew that Suzanne and Marie-Louise had always been rivals for Armand's attention. Suzanne had taken on airs when she began working for the Sainte Colombe notary all those years ago. But Marie-Louise got her man. Nevertheless, from the day of their wedding Armand's 'Marilou' felt looked down upon by her sister-in-law as she laboured in the café kitchen. If truth be told, everyone knew that even as children they'd had a fierce dislike of each other in the school playground. Marilou was the jealous kind. Perhaps that had spurned her on to lure Armand away from his domineering sister. After the wedding Armand had had no option but to side with his young wife.

Suzanne's work for the notary included placing adverts, sending out the posters and leaflets for auctions and house sales in the area. She had called in sick three days ago and Francis had not had time to drive to her cottage on the hill to see how she was.

'Let us begin,' the auctioneer intoned.

Paul grinned. 'Looks like he's been taking lessons from the archbishop of Narbonne,' he mumbled under his breath to his nearest neighbour. He balanced on a rickety chair in the last row near open the doors. The Villagers had crowded into the room, some stood on tiptoe, peering in from the courtyard. As there was no furniture left in the chateau most of the spectators had arrived with a chair or two on their backs. Paul's chair, which could hardly carry his weight, was bleached out and had stood in his garden for years. His ginger mongrel had parked itself between Paul's boots and settled down to a rattling snore which caused eyebrows to be raised.

'It's my dog,' Paul repeatedly pointed at Zozo, in case people thought he had smuggled a pig into the auction.

'700.000 Euros … or … un million de Francs,' the auctioneer translated with a superior smile, implying that the Euro was still not 'real' money to the unsophisticated village folk. There was total silence in the room. He shifted on his chair. They would play hard to get; it had to be expected.

'Alors?' He scanned the room. '350.000 Euros, let's start somewhere, …200.000 ….' His gaze was met with something akin to open defiance.

'Does no one in the room wish to register an interest? Anyone?'

A hand went up at the very back of the room. All the auctioneer could see was a hairy, muscular arm.

'50.000 Euro,' called a determined voice. Heads turned, necks stretched to see the man who had broken the stony silence. At least we're off, thought the auctioneer.

Francis' breath stopped. He knew what he should do but he couldn't do it. He should be pulling the auctioneer's sleeve, tap him on the arm, alert him that things weren't right, but he didn't know the man who had not even deigned to shake his hand. To nudge him would have been disrespectful. The leaflets, the posters, the adverts, what had his mother done with them? Francis was welded to the spot. His ears throbbed with the deafening pulse of his blood.

293

'Anyone for 180.000? 180.000 Euro … anyone?' The auctioneer ignored the ridiculous bid that had come from the back of the room. Surely it was a malicious joke. 'Come along, let's not play games. We're selling a chateau here, not a barn.'

Armand's stomach churned. He regretted downing a couple of Ricards on an empty stomach to steady his nerves.

There was not a sound in the room as the auctioneer looked from one side of the room to the other and back again, still hoping to start a belated bidding contest. No one stirred. He swallowed. Shabby though the chateau looked at first sight, it appeared to have no real structural problems; even the roof was still good. All that was needed was a fresh coat of paint, a good clearing of the garden, perhaps a few new gutters, though how anyone could persuade the frogs to stay away from the pool was another matter.

Pablo Perez de Montsarrat had refused to put a minimum reserve price on his father's house. Was it now to be sold for this paltry sum? The auctioneer could see his commission melting like butter on a hot-plate. Where were all the English with their dreams of owning a chateau? The restless feet shifting on the parquet floor grated on his already frayed nerves. He had to keep his cool. Pablo Perez de Montsarrat had left before his arrival. He would not have to face him with this disaster. The young man would probably be in New York by the time the sale papers had been processed. There could always be a convenient, exceptional delay, of course. So some old man's dream had collapsed, so what? Owning a chateau was hard work over generations, not a holiday. These foreigners really had no idea. They only had themselves to blame if it ended like this.

'50.000 Euros,' came the call from the back again.

The auctioneer shrugged. Absurd though the bid was, there was no other. Anything and everything was only worth was someone was willing to pay for it. Without a reserve he had no instructions to withdraw the house from the sale; the result of this auction could not be blamed on him. Reluctantly, he picked up his gavel.

Francis looked over the heads of the eager spectators to the back of the room. Armand stood, solid as a prize-fighter. Half hidden behind him Francis suddenly saw his mother Suzanne whispering into Armand's ear, then, smiling from ear to ear, she turned and fought her way through the crowd standing in the open doors.

'50.000 once, 50.000 twice ….' The auctioneer called in a strained tone; he was desperately hoping for a miracle, for another bidder to materialise. An eternity seemed to pass while everyone brazenly stared at him.

'50.000 Euro then, so be it. Sold.' The gavel went down as if in slow motion. A hail of applause exploded in the room. As if on a signal everyone turned their back on the auctioneer and rushed for the doors and out onto the forecourt to laugh and shake each other's hands. Only Armand remained. He stood, arms crossed, sweat running down his face. He could feel it catching in his moustache, the droplets hanging there before dripping down, one by one onto his chin and into his shirt.

The auctioneer stared at Armand in shock. The affront of the man, standing there, getting the chateau for pocket money, and parading his apron in an act of open provocation. The two men locked eyes and understood each other perfectly. Armand's eyes lit up. Take a good look at me, he murmured under his breath, me, the stupid villager and you, the big shot with the General's big nose. You've waved your flashy cufflinks at us long enough. Where is your patronising, plummy, pompous, preachy tone now? Armand could not think of any more words beginning with the letter P. There was something of a farce about the auctioneers's face. Marilou looks like that when her soufflé has collapsed, Armand mused.

At the back of the room a door opened and Guy de Vilmorin appeared, accompanied by a young man and two tiny boys who had barely learned to walk. Guy crossed the room and seized Armand's hand and wouldn't stop shaking it.

'Merci, merci, a thousand times, Armand.'

'It's nothing, Monsieur,' Armand glowed. At last it was safe to wipe the sweat off his brow. 'Occitan honour has no price,' he declared; he had never put it better.

Vilmorin turned to the young man by his side.

'Alain, do you remember Armand Arouet? Armand, you recognise my son Alain? He will be back here with us very soon. And these two, they are his sons, my grandsons.' Guy bent down and picked both boys up. 'They are twins. Boys, say bonjour to my friend Armand. I hope you'll thank him one day.' He took a deep breath. 'There is so much to do, Armand, for us and for them.'

Vilmorin's eyes were distracted by something over Armand's shoulder. Armand followed his gaze. By the open door two women were talking, laughing.

'It's Suzanne and Marilou,' Armand smiled wryly.

Guy de Vilmorin shook his head in disbelief. 'Today is truly a day of miracles.'

'Some things, Monsieur, are bigger than we are, that's all,' Armand nodded. He had done Guy's bidding. The solution had flashed into his brain at five in the morning. Alain was a young, successful surgeon in Paris with a brilliant future ahead of him. He was the ideal candidate for a bank loan. The local bank managers would be sympathetic to a son wanting to save his ancestral home on which many of the villagers' livelihood depended. The brand new hospital in nearby Carcassonne was in need of promising doctors. How could it not work?

Armand had run over to the Domaine de L'Espérou at dawn, knocked on the doors like a man possessed, trodden on Nanette's naked feet in his rush to see Guy de Vilmorin who was in his pyjamas and dressing gown. He, Armand had kicked the history of the village back into line, changed the future for its people. He was a hero. His café would be bursting with customers tonight and every night for a long, long time.

Armand put his hand on Guy's shoulder.

'I can get twenty or more men if you want to start work on the chateau tomorrow morning. But first I think I'll go over to L'Espérou and fetch Nanette. I think she would like to see what you look like when you smile.'

*

297

Adieu, adieu, remember me

41

Sainte Colombe, later that afternoon

'There, now you can sing 'I've got the Biggest Aspidistra in the World.'

'Like Gracie Field, you mean?'

'But please, not in that metallic voice!' Sam manoeuvred the massive plant into the hall. It looked twice as big as it had in Augusto's library.

Léa clasped her hands. 'It'll take up half the lower terrace, but it's perfect. It must be at least a hundred years old. It's got exactly one hundred and eleven leaves. I counted them in the car.' She pecked Sam on the cheek. 'The auctioneer looked a bit puzzled that you'd want to buy it. I can't imagine why it wasn't scheduled on the auction list, especially with that beast of a jardinière. It's a proper antique, worth quite a bit I should think. They were probably going to throw it out into the garden.'

298

Sam gave a mocking laugh. 'It's the only thing we could afford to bid for if it had come up for sale.'

'Never mind, thank you for my lovely present, even if Pablo really gave it to us.'

'That's the great thing about you. I could offer you a pebble and you'd be thrilled.'

'I'm a cheap woman, Mister Carter.'

Sam stacked the boxes filled with books against the back wall in the kitchen. There was nowhere else for them at the moment.

'Still, it makes you shudder to think that Pablo might throw the rest of the books away,' Léa sighed, 'they'll probably make a pile of them in the garden and burn them. I can't bear to think about it.'

'What would we do with hundreds of scientific books? And not even you can read Spanish poetry.'

'Those were so beautiful with their leather-tooled covers.'

Sam was straining to lift some of the boxes. 'I know what you mean though about burning books.' He stood back to see if the stack was secure, 'didn't someone say that wherever they burn books they'll be burning people next?'

'Please, don't. We're not in the Middle Ages.'

'Who said anything about the Middle Ages?'

'I've had enough of grim thoughts lately, so please don't add to them.' Léa examined her brown parcel on the table. She carefully unwrapped the painting.

'I can't believe he actually gave me this. I've never had anything like it, not one as good as this anyway. This is major twentieth century art. Where shall we hang it?' Her finger ran over the painted features of the boy. She suddenly shivered.

'I don't know,' she put the picture down. 'There is too much of everything in that family. They're so . . . excessive, even Pablo.'

Sam wiped his brow with a dusty hand. 'That's Latin passion for you.'

'No. There is a strange violence in that house, some sort of destructive energy flowing about, I don't know how or why, but I can feel it.'

'What makes you think that passion is always a positive thing?' Sam heaved the last two boxes into place. 'Tea time.' He took the picture from Léa's.

'Let me see. Does it have a hook or something?' He turned the painting over. 'It's painted on wood, probably an oak panel. Ouch!' He sucked the tip of his thumb. 'There's something sharp sticking out here.'

The brown tape which held the dark backing board in the frame was still in place on three sides, but at the bottom edge only a few paper shreds remained. There were scratch marks where the tape had been removed.

'It's this new pin in here. It's broken off. Some people....' Sam hated sloppy handy work. He went to fetch the small pincers from the tool drawer and levered the offending pin out. The board came up just a little where he had freed it. A light green edge showed between frame and board. He pulled. It was an envelope addressed to Augusto.

'Huh, a secret', Sam said conspiratorially, 'now why would someone hide something in this picture?'

Léa peered over Sam's shoulder.

'God. It's that letter. I remember the colour of the envelope.' Léa's hand went to her mouth. 'You remember, when we went to buy his books?'

The feeling of foreboding she had felt during their first visit rose in her stomach.

'Please, Sam. Don't. Just don't. It's none of our business.' She turned her back on him and crossed her arms over her chest.

'If he didn't want anyone to find it, he would have burnt it.' He extracted the pages from the envelope.

A sudden irrational, but absolute certainty overcame Léa. Augusto knew that his son would not want to keep the picture he had hated so much. His father had simply left them the books in order to lure them back to the chateau at the time when his son would be there, his son who would give the painting to Léa who had admired it, his son who could neither bring himself to sell, nor to destroy it.

*

You come most carefully upon your hour

42

Sam unfolded the pages and laid them out on the table. The date read 27th of April.

'Oh, God. It really is his wife's letter. Please, we have no right.' Léa sat down.

'I disagree. Perhaps it gives some explanation which would help Pablo to understand.' Sam began to read:

Augusto,
After what you did to me I can no longer address you as Dear.
You will get this letter on your birthday and this is your birthday gift. It is the only gift you deserve.

Léa pushed her chair back and began pacing the room. 'No, Sam, no.'

'There is a reason why he put it there. Pablo was right, the old man was more than a trifle theatrical. He wanted someone to find it. You're better at reading people's handwriting. Read it to me.'

Léa perched at the end of the kitchen table. The paper in her hand trembled as she read.

Living with you was heaven and in one single day it turned to hell - for me - and there is no reason why it should not be so for you. What I am about to tell you is the only consolation I have left.

The day I found you with Zoffia I realised that when people speak of a broken heart they do not know what they are talking about. I didn't, but I do now.

Standing in the door, watching you and Zoffia, I did not recognise her at first. In twelve years I had never seen her in the nude. Perhaps one simply doesn't look at the body of a maid. There was this beautiful body, moving with such grace. To see your wilted skin beside her was obscene. Everything changed in a split second. In an instant I saw you as the old man that you are, all bones, a husk. I don't know how it happened, all of a sudden you were a stranger. My heart was an explosion with nowhere to go; the pain choked me. I could not breathe and that is why it took so long before either of you noticed that I was there at all. It seemed I was invisible to the world, and to you, that I had ceased to exist altogether. There was such intimacy, such closeness, such complicity of movement between you and Zoffia. This was no sudden sexual aberration on a sultry afternoon while your wife was away. It was real, it was loving. You were not cheating on me, you had cast me out of your heart.

I made arrangements to leave on the day you left for Paris. Zoffia, who would normally have packed for me, was hiding in her room.

I wanted to be out before you returned. When the removal men began loading the furniture (you stripped me of my life - I only took your home) Zoffia stormed out of the kitchen, red hair tossing wildly. She started screaming and blocking the men's way.

As if I needed more proof of your disloyalty, when you left for Paris you gave her your contact number in case I should cause her any trouble.

'In France all property belongs to the man,' she shouted at me and the removal men.

'We are not French,' I replied, but she wouldn't have it. Perhaps she imagined that everything would be hers if I left one day, and I wondered if you had promised it to her. She had ripped off her apron and was wearing her long white Indian muslin dress. The embroidery on its hem was the only clue that here was not a mad woman who had just escaped from the Marjac asylum in her night gown.

I got one of the men to help me lock her in the garden salon to put an end to her screeching.

'That's where we picked up the books,' Léa whispered.

The firm had agreed not to reveal my destination to anyone. By mid-afternoon they had finished loading.

'And they nearly crushed us as they left and demolished half the café in the process.' Sam shook his head. 'What a way to go.'

304

I went into the garden salon. Zoffia was sitting on the empty floor crying. Her long hair was in a mess and hanging over her face. I told her to pack and leave.

'I have nowhere to go', she wailed, but to me her cries sounded like the howl of a hyena baying for blood.

When you suddenly appeared after she had called you, she thought she had won the battle. After you left again she went quite mad. She had expected that you would throw me out, discard me like some broken object.

'It's your fault. You brought me here,' she howled. 'I was just seventeen. I was still a child.'

'Then this is your chance to make a life of your own.' I tried hard to hold on to my dignity. I offered her six months' money until she could find another position.

'But this house is my life. It's your fault,' she screamed like a child in a temper. 'Augusto loves me.'

It was the first time in twelve years I heard her use your first name. Her familiarity shocked me.

'Ophelia is old. He said so, he said so.' She was beating her chest with her fists.' It...was... my... turn!'

The only thing I had wanted to keep close to me where the two little marble busts we had made of Pablo and Ariana. They stood on the mantelpiece. Zoffia rushed over, picked them up and smashed the bust of Ariana against the edge of the fireplace.

Léa put a hand to her forehead. 'The little marble ear, remember?'

I caught Pablo's bust in mid-air. I was screaming. I unlocked the French windows to the garden. She pushed me out from behind. She was so strong in her fury. I ran down

305

*towards the pool to get away and to try and regain my
composure, but she followed me, shouting that she was
better off dead than without you.*

'Oh, Sam,' Léa tried to control her voice, 'we saw that,
when we stopped that day to look over the wall.'

On the tiled kitchen floor Sam's chair screeched as he
pushed it back. He got up and looked out of the window.

*I was hugging Pablo's cold marble bust to stop the pain.
That's when the depth of your infatuation with Zoffia hit me.
Something inside of me burst. She was rushing up behind
me. I was sure she was going to push me into the pool. I
turned and hit her with the marble bust and she looked at me
and smiled and toppled past me into the pool and began
floating on her back and the reddest blood I've ever seen
was flowing out of her red hair which was spreading out
very slowly, like wings which seemed to be keeping the body
afloat.*

As Léa read her voice got fainter.

*I ran back to the salon. I realised I was alone in the
house. Then I saw that the removal men had not taken down
the tapestry. I had told them to leave the old Persian carpet
in that room. They probably thought that was one of them.*

*Suddenly everything fell into place. It was you - you had
loved Shakespeare's Ophelia and when we met my name
called out to you. You had Millais' painting made into a
tapestry for me, but it was really for yourself. To offer your
wife an image of a drowning woman as a birthday present
seemed strange to everyone but me, who had fallen in love
with Shakespeare's Ophelia and Millais' painting through
you. It was all so romantic. At that moment the tapestry*

showed me that I was just the instrument to find Zoffia for you. With all that red hair, she was your real Ophelia.

'We were there when it happened.' Léa looked at Sam in alarm. 'We're the only witnesses to a murder.'

'It depends who you can believe,' Sam said quietly. 'She felt threatened, so it could be construed as self-defence, manslaughter maybe.'

'We saw them … we actually saw them … seconds before Zoffia was killed.' Léa's voice cracked as she read on.

Everything began to happen automatically. I went back to the pool. She was drifting in the middle. Birch leaves had blown into the pool and were collecting in her hair like stars. I couldn't get into the water with all the blood floating in it. I couldn't reach her, so I let the water out. It took a long time. I sat by the side of the pool. It was getting dark. I found some old Wellington boots in the barn. When most of the water had drained I pulled her onto a tarpaulin I'd spread out. I managed to get her up the steps of the pool. I dragged the tarpaulin with the body to the lake and rolled her into the shallow water. Again she floated face up, like in Millais' picture. I couldn't understand it. I thought drowned people floated with their backs up.

Léa stopped.

'Do you remember when we went upstairs with Augusto and he blocked the door to Zoffia's room?' Sam nodded. 'I thought she was in the room, because there was that noise of water and china clinking.' Léa laid the letter in her lap. 'It was the drowning pigeon thrashing around in the china bowl.'

307

I went to the library and took your big leather-bound Shakespeares. I laid them on top of her to weigh the body down. In an absurd way it seemed apt, but it didn't work. Perhaps the lake was too shallow at that point and the body could not turn over. It occurred to me that the loss of all the blood might be the reason for her floating. There was a bright full moon;her eyes shimmered under the half closed lids. Her hair, which had stuck to the body, began to fan out again in the water and her face glistened, as if made of solid silver. And I stood and watched her dress, sodden but still floating where little air pockets had remained and I suddenly heard myself say:

‘Her clothes spread wide and mermaid like
awhile they bore her up…'

like in Shakespeare's text and I knew that this is how it was meant to be.

Again I went back to the library, looking for something heavier. Your historical atlas was the largest book on the shelves. I thought it ironic that the volume so precious to you finally, finally sank her. I gathered all the reeds and branches from the edge of the lake and laid them across her body and kept piling layer upon layer, until there was a mound and she had vanished under it. It looked like a pile of branches, collected up after the winter, ready for the burning. Here and there the white cloth bubbled up to the surface, the cold moon light turning the tiny spheres into gleaming silver beads. Coppery threads of hair got entangled in the twigs and now and then they trembled, cobweb-like on the water's surface.

Léa sank onto the nearest kitchen chair.

'I understand why he was so shaken when he got the letter,' Sam said, 'she didn't spare him any detail.'

'They haven't found her,' Léa gasped, 'Sam, they haven't found Zoffia. They thought it was just Augusto on the lake….they had no idea….' Her head was spinning, she wanted to wretch. 'What are we going to do, Sam?'

'I don't know,' Sam rubbed his forehead. 'I can't even work out who the real victim is in all this. Is there more?'

Léa nodded and cleared her throat.

I spent the night lying fully dressed on the old brass bed, not understanding how our blessed life together could end like this. At first light I got into the car. I packed the marble bust of Pablo with what shards of Ariana's I had been able to rescue into a box and put them on the passenger seat next to me. They would travel away with me, away from you, forever.

On this day, your birthday, this gift of my deed, this document of madness. For what little is left of your life, may you treasure Ophelia's bequest.

The letter dropped out of Léa's hand and onto the table. She rose and went to the window to stand next to Sam, to feel the warmth of his body. Her knees felt like cotton wool. Outside a patchwork of colours spread to the horizon under a deep azure sky. The land lay untouched by human emotions. Nature lived by a different clock, moved at a different rhythm, cared nothing about what people did to each other.

'Just look at that,' Léa whispered, 'beauty everywhere.'

Sam laid his arm around her shoulder. After a long while he turned and picked up the phone. Léa listened as he began dialling for the police. He handed her the receiver.

***

Acknowledgments

My thanks go to the Arts Council, England, for making the publication of this book possible, to Michael Hasted for his infinite patience, for putting up with my late nights, to Nashi Rahman for her invaluable proof reading, to Rosemary Hartley for reading the manuscript in the early stages and her useful comments, as well as all fellow writers and critics on the YouWriteOn.com website for their very knowledgeable and objective comments. Also to author Jane Bailey for offering contacts. I'm grateful for the unexpected comments from a number of agents who encouraged me to publish.

I am endetted to the library in Auch for giving me access to their wonderful archives.

SOME SIMPLE POISON

Book 2 of **THE LANGUEDOC TRILOGY**

by Ata Burchardt

will be published in the spring of 2016

Read the first three chapters overpage

SOME SIMPLE POISON

to be published in the spring of 2016

Read the first three chapters here

SEPTIMA

The milky haze of dawn showed on the horizon. He looked back at the village. There it was, high up, the last house, his mother's lair, brooding at the top of her terraced garden that cascaded to the old fortification wall high above the dark tossing waters. Perhaps she was sleeping, probably not. A ribbon of white mist began to snake in the depth of the gorge.

There were no street lights on the path to Mount Septimania. To his left a sunflower field hugged the curve of the path, impenetrable as a forest. There was something human about their proportions as they stood to attention, round heads ready to face the first light, their arching leaves reaching out to each other, an army on parade. On a bank to his right, beyond a dense layer of shrubs, the convent's cemetery. Here and there one of the small white crosses reflected a little light. At the sharp bend of the path he glanced back to the cemetery gate. Next to it, in a small shrine, a candle flickered, illuminating a waxen face. A nun was kneeling, hands folded in prayer. She must have heard him; her head turned and he saw half a face bathed in candlelight, peering into the darkness in his direction.

After the bend the path became steep; the stones underfoot grew coarser; it was hard to see where his boot would land. He set down his bags and felt for his mobile. The torch from it was enough to light his way up and around the back of the chapel where he had left the car, hidden among the dense broom.

***

1

June. Victoire was back in Sainte Colombe for the summer. Early holiday breaks were the privilege of university professors. The heat had become fierce. From mid-morning until late afternoon people sheltered from the sun in the deepest shade of fig trees with a grenadine or citron pressé. The buzzing of insects interrupted conversations; hands waved, irritated, hoping to protect food from a host of flies which had multiplied in the village since the heat had set in. Villagers retreated for a siesta, doors wide open and hung with curtains that wafted in a rare breath of air.

In the shadow of the church Marco made his way to the end of the winding street. To his left the school yard was deserted. Ahead lay the bridge leading to the convent. Minutes earlier a tidy line of primary school pupils had been ushered into the convent for their school lunch. Children who ate at home had drifted away.

On the thick stone wall of the bridge a lizard sat basking in the heat, feet anchored in the cracks. Marco leaned over the edge of the wall. The hot stone burnt his palms. The raging spring waters of the gorge had shrunk to a meek stream in the last couple of weeks. Silver rivulets of water snaked their way around boulders, lying squat like lazy toads, glistening in the sun. One side of the bank was already scorched by the heat, on the other grasses and wild flowers had sprung up, now safe from the rushing river.

Marco heard a sound, twigs snapping underfoot. He leaned over further and saw a girl in a blue flowered dress, bending down, picking buttercups. She straightened up and raised her head, aware that someone was looking down on her. Marco recognized the pudding basin haircut and the forget-me-not blue eyes.

'Bonjour, Annette. What pretty flowers, who are they for?'

'It's Maman's birthday.'

'Are you giving her a nice present?'

The girl shook her head; her golden hair caught the light.

'No. I don't have any money. I'll just give her the flowers.'

Marco felt in his pocket where a few coins had accumulated.

'Would you like to give her a present?'

The girl nodded.

'Perhaps I can help you?' his fingers were pressing the coins in his pocket. 'Wait, I'll come down.'

He walked to the other end of the bridge to a small gap where he could climb down to the water's edge. He stopped and checked in all directions. The descent down the foot-wide cut was as steep as a playground slide. Sweet wrappers and paper had blown off the bridge and were trapped in the coarse grasses. Marco's heart began to thump as if he was

317

climbing a mountain. He set foot onto the river bank. The light bounced off the wet boulders; it hurt his eyes.

'I'll help you pick lots more flowers, shall I? Your maman will have an enormous bunch for her birthday. Would you like that?'

The girl smiled and nodded. Annette was not a bright child. She was only nine but had already been held back in her primary school twice since the age of five. The trusting child with the bright blue eyes was teased by the school boys, but she never retaliated.

There's not a bad bone in that girl, the old women in the village said.

'Look,' Marco indicated, 'under the bridge. Those are much bigger.'

The girl skipped over some stones into the half-light under the stone arch. As she bent down her short dress rode up and Marco saw the white of her knickers. Deep inside of him something pulsed; something wild and urgent that he had kept cloistered in his room had escaped. No, he thought, but he was already following the girl and moved to stand behind her. He laid his arm around her. She turned abruptly and was staring at him with her blue, blue eyes, confused. He cupped a hand under her tiny chin. The sunlight reflecting off the water made her eyes look even brighter, here in the shadows.

'You do have very pretty, forget-me-not eyes,' he whispered, 'they deserve a bit of something extra, don't you think? I'll give you some money so you can buy a really nice present for your mother. Here,' he held out the coins from his pocket.

A shy smile played on her face as she reached for them. His hand pulled back.

'I had my birthday yesterday. I'm sixteen now, but I have no maman, no papa. I'm all alone.' He squatted down so his face came level with hers. 'But if I am nice to you, will you be nice to me?' With that he pulled his hand further back, waving the coins.

'What kind of nice?'

He noticed that she had a lisp.

'A secret kind. So? Is that a bargain then?'

Her eyes went to the hand holding the coins.

'Yes,' she nodded, 'I promise.'

He stood up. His hand rested on her shoulder. How bony it felt, like a bird. He slipped the coins into his trouser pocket.

'There is another place where I keep more money.'

The girl's eyes fixed on his face, puzzled by what kind of favour he was asking of her. With a sudden move his hand gripped the back of her neck, with the other hand he unzipped his trousers, pulled her head close, closer, until she was breathing hard and began to struggle. But he held her fast now and the explosion he had longed for came at last. For a moment he relaxed his hold and the girl began squealing.

A woman's voice came from above.

'Who is there?'

'Annette … Annette,' whimpered the girl. And Marco let her go.

He looked up. Victoire's head appeared over the bridge wall. Her neck strained like the gargoyles on the church. He pulled back into the shadow of the bridge and pressed his back against the damp stone wall. He stuffed his shirt into his trousers and tore the zip shut.

319

The girl was trying to scramble up the river bank, slipping on the dry soil. She fell, rolled down again, her head hit hard on a boulder at the water's edge.

Victoire came sliding down and rushed to kneel beside her.

Marco stood under the bridge, paralysed. The girl lay crumpled like a limp doll among the wet stones. Victoire knelt by her side and cradled her head in the crook of her arm. She waved at Marco with a blood-stained hand.

'Go, for God's sake, go. Don't let her see you,' she hissed as she tapped Annette's cheek, softly calling her name.

Marco stepped past them and watched as Victoire splashed the girl's face with some water.

'Annette, Annette, open your eyes. You fell, you've hurt your head.'

Annette tried to raise her head.

'He came down, the flowers, he …'

'You've hurt your head,' Victoire continued. She gave Marco an angry stare.

'He took me …,' Annette's limp hand indicated the bridge.

'Now, now. There is no one here Annette, you've had a shock.'

Annette whimpered. 'He did …'

'Quiet now, Annette. You were picking flowers, you fell on a stone and hurt yourself, that's all. There is nobody here.'

Victoire put her hand behind Annette's back and again waved Marco away.

'I'll take you to the doctor in a minute.' She pressed the edge of her skirt to Annette's bleeding gash. 'It's just a bit of blood.'

Marco waded upstream, reached the river bend and turned to look back. He watched, hidden by the branches that hung down to the water's edge. The girl was sitting up and Victoire was talking to her, examining her head.

After the next bend he struggled up from the gorge, grabbing the thorny bushes right and left of the steep overgrown track, finally heaving himself over Victoire's garden wall. His arms were scratched bloody from the climb. He sank to the ground, exhausted. He stayed there, staring up into the sky, the gravel pricking his sweating skin through the thin shirt.

The church bells struck two. The children would be back in school, sitting down for afternoon lessons this very minute. He didn't want to think about what had happened. What had driven him to seize Annette under the bridge? How could he explain this to Serge? His brother had always looked after him.

He was nine when meningitis had struck overnight and everything changed. The illness wiped part of his memory. He no longer understood what the teacher taught. Victoire's father was the village school teacher, the ogre strutting at the front of the class. Frustrated in life, he had poured his wrath over two dozen children between the ages of five to eleven before they could escape him by entering a lycée or an agricultural college, depending on their academic abilities. The man governed by fear. He inflicted punishments on the pupils that no one could comprehend, yet no one dared

321

intervene, no one dared question the authority of the school teacher, the sole educator in the village. He was only one removed from the mayor and the notary, both of whom barely took second place to Monsieur le Curé, the nearest a man could get to God, or so he never ceased to remind his ever dwindling flock.

After his illness Serge had sat with Marco, night after night, reading, helping him to draw numbers and the letters of the alphabet; reading, writing, additions, multiplications, everything had to be relearned. And Marco made up lost ground and more. In the school yard Serge had protected him. When their father lost patience with his frail son, Serge had defended him fiercely, taking the beatings in his place.
Never, never tell Serge about what happened under the bridge - the mere thought of it threatened to choke him. Victoire would sort it out. Educated people, they always knew what to do, what to say. Had she not told him to run for cover?

At this moment he had no other wish than to lie there and watch the swallows and swifts criss-crossing high against the blinding midday light. His breathing was slowing. He closed his eyes.

Foot steps. A shadow fell over him.
'Wake up. Marco. Get up,' Victoire commanded.
He sat up and clenched his arms around his knees.

'Listen to me,' Victoire's voice was a low hiss, 'no one, no one must know about this or you'll spend the rest of your life in jail. I'm not thinking of you. I'm doing this for your … family, for our village.'

'Thank you,' Marco said meekly. Was she doing this for Serge, his good and clever brother? Serge had had his sweet revenge when it came to Victoire's father. Now Serge was not only the village school master but also the school's director. Now patience and kindness, not terror and beatings, were the order of the day. Serge had also sat on the village council, something that had always been denied Victoire. Why would she be so keen to help him? It didn't make sense.

'You listen to me now - this is what happened. The girl had a fall,' Victoire continued, 'she bumped her head and has concussion. You were not there.' She stamped her foot. 'Look at me.'

It was hard to meet her eyes.

'Where were you? Marco? Answer me.'

'I was not under the bridge.'

'And what do you know about Annette?'

He had to think for a moment. What was it she wanted to hear?

'I don't know ….'

'Precisely. You know nothing,' Victoire interrupted, 'you heard she had an accident, by the bridge. From me, it was I who told you.'

He gave a faint nod.

'Annette had an accident, by the bridge. You told me.'

'And you were here, all day, working in my garden, you hear?' She made to walk away. 'Just so you know, I took her to the doctor's surgery. He says she is concussed. She didn't say a word to him about you or what happened by the river. She didn't see you walk away. Let's hope she doesn't remember.'

Marco's head sank down.

'Clément is taking the overnight train from Paris. He is bringing some important people. But you'll have to make up time now with the garden jobs.' She looked around and heaved a sigh. 'How could my grandmother let this garden run so wild. It's going to take years to get it into shape.' She indicated a raised bed to one side. 'Over there, all that needs trimming, and clearing away. I want to be able to see those roses, every single plant, and don't leave one weed around them, give them room so they can regrow.' She stood over him. 'That'll explain the scratches on your arms. It might be a good idea to show Clément how much work you did, don't you think, if questions are asked, just in case. However, you will have to go to confession.'

'I can't ... I can't tell the curé.'

'You'll have to or you'll rot in hell.' She started up towards the house. 'I don't care how you tell the priest, but you must confess your crime before God.'

'Yes,' was all Marco managed to say. He picked up the garden tools.

'Why are you doing this, covering up for me?' he called after her.

She stopped, glanced over her shoulder.

'Are you complaining? I have my reasons. Just watch that I don't change my mind.'

Marco's mind was racing. What was she planning for him? Whatever it was, in his heart he knew that from now on he would be her pawn, to do with as she pleased.

Through the lace curtain of her bedroom Victoire watched Marco struggle to dig out the wild plants that had invaded everything since her grandmother had died.

The boy was timid and slight for his age but strong enough to work the garden. He would be easy to manage after today's incident. He was sixteen but could pass for fourteen. There was no telling what he had done under the bridge; none of the girl's clothing had been interfered with. Admittedly, she had not actually seen anything, but the child-like guilt on Marco's face had spoken volumes about what he had done, or had intended to do. Perhaps today had been a blessing in disguise. Using him as permanent gardener would keep him off the village streets; he would work for little money to instruction while she and Clément were still teaching in Paris.

With every year the wait to return to her village, to the house she had inherited now, became more unbearable. Somehow, knowing that her father was just a village away, up there in the dark mountains, no longer troubled her as much as in earlier years. There was of course the constant anxiety of how to erase what he had done from the villagers' memories. But with him confined in the asylum, banished forever, she would turn her grandmother's house into a home filled with light, the overgrown garden into a small paradise, sitting atop the old fortifications with views to die for.

She had been to see her father, made her perfunctory early summer visit only to find herself sitting opposite him being glared at without a word. She had uttered a few banalities; there was no way of reaching into his world of deep, brooding anger. She had patiently sat across a table from him, counting the minutes, staying for a full hour to give the impression that she cared. Her mother, now living with her younger sister in a small fishing village near the Italian border refused to visit her husband at whose rages she had suffered for years. And yet, on the way home Victoire had suddenly pulled into a lay-by and an explosion of uncontrollable sobs and tears almost suffocated her. It took

325

her half an hour to compose herself before she felt safe to drive home. After all these years of life in Paris her father's disapproval, however deranged now, still wounded her to the quick. Would the shame of what had brought him to the asylum ever die down?

She was weary of city life. Clément's university colleagues, all eminent professors, and their Parisian wives were so demanding. Behind her back some whispered that 'Victoire has no conversation'. Though a professor of Spanish herself, she had never reached the academic heights of Clément and his colleagues. She had never gone beyond teaching the freshers each year. Around the dinner table she couldn't compete with the best brain of academia in their cerebral debates of all things philosophical. She contrived to invite them to dine in their own turn-of-the century apartment rather than go to their houses so she could busy herself with the food during their endless evenings. After dinner Clément would open the four French doors from the dining room to the roof terrace she had planted with trailing geraniums and climbing wisterias. While the guests marvelled at the view onto a leafy Parisian square below she could get away to clear up the kitchen with the help of her home help to prepare a tray with fine chocolates and tiny glasses of Calvados or Drambuie liqueur. Clément's friends were very fond of the 'digestif' ritual.

Victoire gazed across the overgrown garden. Marco was getting down to work. He would have to rebuild the terraces, make them sweep all the way down to the old fortification wall, and although expressly forbidden by successive mayoral decrees, build over the access to the old disused public path in order to extend her garden. Though forbidden, many villagers had done so and no one ever came to check. Right at the bottom, on what was to be the lowest of the terraces, the waist high remains of the old fortification wall would have to be consolidated. She could already see herself, sitting on it, having captured the best views the village had to offer. Here was something which would stir up the envy of the Parisians. The sooner she could turn her grandmother's house and garden into a beautiful home, the easier it would be to persuade Clément to give up Paris for a life in the sun. It might be another ten years before she and Clément could bow out from their highly paid university professorships.

For an instant she almost felt pity for Marco, orphaned so young with only a brother and an ageing aunt to protect him. That boy wouldn't hurt a fly, everyone in the village always said so; he would be pliable and do her bidding.

She went to stand in front of the armoire mirror, turning her head to the side to search her temples for greying hairs. My Latin blood, she reflected, we blossom earlier than the Northerners, but we ripen earlier too, until we drop off the tree, bruised and wrinkled from life in the scorching light of the South. The sunburnt cleavage was the first to wrinkle. She unbuttoned her dress, ran her hand over her breast bone. On other women she had thought the creased skin not unlike the rear of an elephant; soon it would be happening to her. She cupped her hands under her breasts and lifted them – there, that's how her cleavage would look in a few years.

Though her midriff had spread a little, there was still a good waist. An expanding waistline was the price she was paying for entertaining their Paris friends and colleagues. No, she would not allow herself to go the way of other women of her age. The solution was portion control. She

327

would sip her wine more slowly, eat more slowly, while filling the glasses and plates of others. The trick was never to be seen with an empty plate or an empty glass from now on.

Clément and his friends would be arriving in the morning. She heard the front door. Sabette was leaving. She had been polishing the floors and ironing sheets all day.

Night fell. Bats were swooping around the church tower. Marco had carried on working by torch light.

Avoiding the pools of orange haze cast by the street lamps he tiptoed down to his house, brewed himself a strong coffee. There was a hole in his stomach and it wasn't hunger. He didn't sleep.

As the church clock struck seven, Marco made his way to the boulangerie, as he did every day for his morning ficelle. To his left, across the monument square, Marcel, the old grocer was doing his yearly balancing act on an old ladder, repainting his sun-bleached sign. After a long summer and a short winter no more than the first four letters of the word EPICERIE were legible. One of these days Marcel would topple off the ladder, leaving the village with a shop simply called EPIC. Best not to wave to him, Marco thought, keep still, unnoticed for a while.

At the baker's Colette was wrapping two baguettes for old Antoine.

'Imagine, she fell down all the way to the river. Wanted to pick flowers. Victoire tells me she's quite confused, what with the concussion. She'll be off school until that nasty gash on her head heals.'

'Just the sort of thing Annette would do,' old Antoine remarked, 'not the brightest little light in our village, is she?'

'Ficelle, Marco?' Colette reached for the bread sticks in the big basket standing upright under a rack filled with rolls. 'I expect Victoire told you, about Annette?'

'She did. Poor thing,' Marco muttered. It would be the topic of the day. So Victoire had already put her version of the incident around the village. He should have felt relieved but somehow he didn't. 'I didn't get off my knees in her garden yesterday. She wanted the roses absolutely perfect before Clément and his friends arrive this morning.'

Marco laid his coins on the glass counter. He lifted his arms, showed the bloody scratches.

'This is what I got for my pains.'

The women in the queue tut-tutted.

'You know what she's like,' Marco said with a sigh.

'Mmm.' Colette pressed her lips together and rolled her eyes. She could not be seen to complain openly about her customers.

'I didn't get a chance to listen to the whole story,' Marco added as he left the bakery.

'Poor boy, only sixteen,' Colette said. 'His mother dead when he was small and who would have thought his father would die and leave Marco living alone in that big house. It was his sixteenth birthday two days ago; his brother had asked me to make a beautiful cake for him with a football on top of all things. He's really a child still. Victoire is working him much too hard.'

Marco crossed over the village square to the church. The early morning sun felt good on his face. He pushed the portal.

On the right, against the wall, just before the defunct baroque pulpit, the hollow confession cubicles, purple velvet

329

curtains drawn back, waited to trap their prey. To set foot into these coffin-shaped spaces would be like leaping into the void, a black void from which he would never return. Monsieur le Curé would not be waiting for sinners at this time of the morning. The village priest was probably still snoring in bed. Marco imagined the rotund figure on his back in washed-out underwear, his paunch pointing to the ceiling like a loaf of bread that had risen too quickly.

He wandered to the front of the church and faced the altar. It was quiet; the night had not yet left this vast space. Marco shivered at the thought that long ago, perhaps as far back as the Middle Ages, his ancestors had stood at the exact same spot, perhapsblike himself now, having a sin on their conscience that they could not bring themselves to confess.

For the first four hundred years the building had been a wealthy monastery before being turned into a church when the richest village women were buried under the altar of the Virgin. Even at the time of his great-grandfather around two thousand people had huddled close together, mostly in the squat, overcrowded artisan houses at the bottom of the village, many of which had become holiday homes for their descendants or simply been left to fall down. Monsieur Lagarde's grand house by the upper bridge and similar ones which surrounded the church were for the masters and the the mill owners. Ermine Perec's house had been part of the old chateau, now long gone.

Marco tried to conjure up the stream of pious villagers, looking old before their time from hard labour, pouring through the portal for Sunday mass after a week of back-breaking work in the mills powered by the gorge waters.

With its high vaulted nave and the richly decorated columns, the church's proportions were far too ostentatious for the five or six hundred remaining villagers of Sainte Colombe, most of whom had given up on going to church altogether except for funerals. Sunday mass, now broadcast on television in the French language, was more colourful than that of the village priest in his ash covered old suits and his battered beret which he often forgot to remove for his sermons. His mumbled sermon in Latin was followed by the usual reprimands of the villagers, as if they were ignorant children. Only those who offered gifts of food and other luxuries which he expected at Christmas, New Year and Easter could gain his approval.

Marco did not know what to do. His guilt weighed heavy on his shoulders, trapped his breath between his ribs.

Why did Maman die? he asked in a hushed voice, and now Papa. With Aunt Amaline's help he had somehow got used to growing up without a mother, but his father's death just six months ago had turned his life into a seering loneliness. He was alone in the house and a silence louder than the gorge waters after a storm.

In the semi-darkness, on the left of the altar, stood the life-size statue of Saint Peter. Its face of fine marble painted in delicate colours was smooth as wax; the life-like eyes gazed intently at Marco. The red Caunes marble with its fine veining made his long, gold-edged robe flow almost like velvet. A lion, carved in white marble, leaned its flank against the saint's leg. The beast had a savage grin; its teeth had been cut into sharp points; long claws protruded from the powerful paws. The saint's left hand rested on the lion's head as though it were a tame dog.

Marco reached and stroked the hand. It moved. He stumbled backwards as if he'd touched a live wire. Was this a sign, and what of? He approached the statue again, tested

331

the marble fingers. The hand shifted; it was loose. Someone must have broken it, slipped it back under the edge of the sleeve, hoping it would not be discovered. He looked around. He was alone. He gently eased the cold hand out. It sent a shiver through him. This is a holy object, he thought, as holy as the rest of the church. Long ago someone had sculpted a rough piece of stone into this exquisite shape with the most perfect fingers. The hand would have to be stuck back on, but who would do it? On a sudden impulse, he slipped it into the inside pocket of his jacket. In churches people prayed to relics, fragments of bones, trapped in tiny glass boxes, said to belong to one saint or another, didn't they? Saint Peter's hand would be his very own relic; he would bring it back, some day.

He made for the church portal, holding the marble hand inside his jacket pocket. As he reached the heavy door there was a faint whimper coming from beneath the defunct pulpit, now cordoned off. As he approached the dark corner he spotted a cardboard box bound with string. Something inside the box was moving. There was the noise again, no more than a small whine. Gently Marco knelt down and lifted the lid a fraction. From inside a pair of dark brown eyes looked out. Someone had abandoned a puppy. Sunday mass was four days away. There was no way the young animal could survive until then. Its brown fur looked unkempt but on seeing Marco a tiny tail began drumming in the small space.

*

2

Ten years later

'Marco.' Victoire's voice coming from the house was sharp. Marco knew the tone.

'I know, I know,' Marco mumbled under his breath, 'let me know who pays my wages.' He had been forced to offer his services to others in secret. A few days earlier the rumour that he had been seen gardening for Monsieur Lagarde had infuriated Victoire. The largest village house by the upper bridge, with Louis XIV architectural ornaments and a splendid formal garden falling in terraces down into the gorge, was a thorn in her side. A *gavatch*, an outsider from the North, she had called Lagarde.

'Traitor, Marco, you are no better than a traitor,' she had spat on her way down from the upper terrace to come to a stop on the level just above him.

'These people, they come here and lord it over … you.'

Her point was not lost on Marco. They would never dare look down on her, but on him, a simple villager who had left school at fifteen and was now no more than a manual labourer in her eyes. The argument had left him drained.

'Madame Victoire,' he had tried to reason with her, 'it's impossible to live with the salary you pay me. I have to light and heat my house in winter seven days a week, just like you. I don't get cheaper electricity because I only work four days a week, and I have to eat and keep my car running, somehow.'

'Your father's house is too big. You don't need all those rooms,' she had interrupted harshly. 'Get a smaller house, you're not married, not likely to be so now. Which girl would want you as a husband if she finds out what I know, wouldn't you say?'

She would never let him forget. How often did she taunted him, threatened to expose him over the years?

'The house is all I've got in the world. It's a beautiful building. I could never move. How could I? My father would turn in his grave if I were to sell it.'

In his mind's eye he could still see the look in Victoire's eyes at the word 'sell'.

'Have you never thought,' she suddenly said almost sweetly, 'about how much easier life would be in one of those little pink bungalows up there on the hill outside the village, with all the comfort of central heating, no more carrying coal or chopping wood for the winter?'

Always on the hunt for houses for her friends, Marco thought. He had heard her telling them, 'Just imagine, you'd sit on the terrace with a glass of wine.' That was the dream she was dangling in front of the Parisians.

Of course his home would be a prize catch. The house looked out on the leafy church square; the high rooms with their covings and opulent ceiling roses were airy and filled with light all morning. The entrance hall had a fine vaulted ceiling. From the wide terrace at the back of the house there was a breath-taking view over the garrigue and the Pyrenees beyond. It would be enough to seduce even the most unromantic of Victoire's friends.

Marco's great-grandfather had been mayor of the village when the water wheels of all the mills along the gorge were still churning day and night. He had remodelled the family home, turned it from a plain village house into a *maison bourgeoise*, a building fit for a mayor. The date on the triangular pediment above the main door said 1908. The window and door surrounds, adorned with scrolls and corbels, were a testament to the family's importance. Below and to the left of the rear terrace mediterranean oaks reached for the waters in the gorge; they had been planted nearly two hundred years ago by his family. On the other side a fig tree spread its broad leaves to give much needed shade during the summer months. When the figs hung heavy and soft Marco carried trays of the purple fruit to Mélanie's grocery shop for a little extra income. Autumn brought the mushrooms. Winters were not so kind, sending him to search the communal woods near Marjac for wood he could dry out under the terrace to sell as kindling at the Christmas market. It was a hand-to-mouth existence but no amount of money would make him sell the house.

'Well? Think about it. You'd get a good price for your house, if I sell it for you you won't even have to pay agency fees.' Victoire stood above him, arms crossed, expecting an answer. He gave none. With a dismissive shrug she returned to the upper terrace. She let herself fall into one of the garden loungers and lit one of her black Russian cigarettes. It occasionally dawned on her that the people of her native village were no easier to control than the Parisian intellectuals. Here she would have to find new ways to get what she wanted.

Marco glanced around the garden. The raised beds for flowers, the potager filled with herbs and vegetables, the paths laid with pale Provence stone, the steps that swept up in a graceful curve from one level to the next, all this was ten years of his work. She had paid him a minimum hourly rate on the pretext that villagers have to stick together, to render each other services for the sake of their century-old traditions and loyalties. What if he had been master of this house?

'You'll see,' Mélanie warned from behind her shop counter, 'when our old village houses have all become second homes for her friends, they'll choose Sainte Colombe as their primary residence to avoid paying the high Paris taxes. Then they'll have the vote in our village elections. Victoire won't need any of us anymore.' Mélanie had recently taken over her father's ailing grocery shop and had invested her savings to refit the shop.

'And I for one will have no shop, because they'll drive to the supermarkets.' A hand gesture as if she was tossing something overboard said it all. 'And then, 'ploof,' she whispered, 'no cheese, no wine, no fruit or anything else for the rest of the village.'

Mélanie indicated the small square outside her shop where nearby residents parked their cars by the Monument to the Fallen.

'I can see them now when they're here for their holidays. They come back from the supermarkets in town, trying to hide their shopping from me.'

'Marco. I haven't got all day.' Victoire stood in the open terrace door leading to her dining room.

He reached the upper terrace.

'You took your time.'

'I've had to turn over the soil of the bottom rose beds. It's heavy work for my back.'

'Never mind your back.' Victoire waved her hand as if he was a tiresome insect to be brushed away. 'You to cut a new path, along the left side of the terraces, all the way down, just wide enough to squeeze through. Someone, one of the gavatches, the new people, has made trouble at the mayor's offices about not having access to the river in the gorge,' she huffed, 'I wouldn't be surprised if it was that woman. She'll probably come knocking, demanding access, just to make the point.'

She was referring to the English woman who had bought the defunct mill just beyond the ruin of the village gate.

'Tressa you mean?'

Victoire's had taken an instant dislike to the bucksome woman.

'Why would she?' Marco suppressed a grin, 'she's got her own garden and her meadow is in the nicest part of the gorge.'

'She meddles with everything, thinks she's got a right to change the way we've always done things.'

'It won't be the first complaint about access to the path,' Marco said, 'they'll soon calm down when they see how the bramble has invaded everything. When I go fishing down there I have to wade up-river from the old flour mill.'

'Well, don't tell anyone about that or else we'll have them all crawling around at the bottom of my garden, spying on us. You know perfectly well that we have all built our gardens over the communal path along the gorge. Everyone knew it was illegal.'

'The path is still accessible under my terrace, Serge makes sure of that.'

'Oh, your clever, clever brother. Perhaps I'll come round to your house tomorrow to try it out. We're all as guilty as each other, so no one can point the finger at the other one,' Victoire retorted. 'For the moment, just cut it to a foot's width, no more, trim the shrubs a bit so they don't poke anyone's eyes out, in case somebody comes knocking and wants to get down to the water, that's if anyone wants to break their neck on that over-grown descent.'She turned back into the house. 'At least this way we can claim we provide a right of way,' she grumbled.

Marco nodded. Victoire didn't want to be caught out.

'I'll do it this afternoon,' he waved. 'Have you thought about the rail on the wall?' he called after her. She did not reply. He returned to his work on the lowest level of the garden. It was the most beautiful of them all. It had been built right out to the medieval fortification perimeter. No more than a knee high wall now stood between the gravelled semi-circle of the last terrace and a sheer drop, straight down into the gorge and the wild water strewn with jagged boulders. He had long argued with Victoire that the wall was too low, that he should install a safety rail.

'You'll just have to be careful not to fall down.' She now called. 'Besides, I like sitting on that wall. No one has ever fallen into the gorge from here. My grandfather sat there, so did my father.'

A sudden memory shot through her mind. The day her father found out that he would be sent to the asylum he had climbed onto the low wall and strutted up and down on it, arms stretched wide and head thrown back, staring up into the sun, singing Ave Maria. The entire family had run screaming into the garden. Her grandmother had collapsed and was never the same again. The next morning the men in white coats came and dragged him away and it felt as though the light had returned to the house.

'Anyway,' Victoire had insisted the last time Marco had reminded her, 'now this is all mine. I won't let you spoil the view. The best painter could not have imagined such a panorama. But people like you …what do you know about art?'

Was this garden he had made for her not a work of art?

Victoire had cried when her father had died, out of sight of the villagers, up there, in that home in the mountains, where they put those whose mind no longer grasped the consequences of their actions. The asylum had not alerted her that he lay dying. Perhaps those taking care of him had judged that a family that rarely visited would feel relief when such a burdensome relative died. The morning after his death, when they had called, she drove up the winding roads alone to the remote village of Marjac. He had always hated the way the dark mountains folded themselves around the villages up there. He had grown up in the last house of Sainte Colombe, high above the gorge with the rolling vineyards to the East and the high Pyrenees to the South.

When she had arrived in the Marjac asylum the building smelled of old people and stale food. The blue speckled lino running along the corridor had recently been mopped; the disinfectant used was no match for the odour of urine the closer she got to the room where they had laid out his body. The nurse made a move to enter the room with her. She found herself unable to make a sound but signalled that she wanted to be alone.

Many had been frightened of her fathe, even before insanity struck its final blow. His moods could change from peaceable to raging in seconds for no apparent reason. When she was not yet in school he would bounce her on his knee and indulge her, but as she grew he began to inflict the raw, unpredictable punishments on her that he dished out to the other school children. A strawberry eaten between meals was a crime. More than once she had been made to sit at the dinner table with her hands tied behind her back for a whole day, forced to watch the family eat their meals. Something deep inside her still churned at the thought of it.

By the time she was seven years old fear had made her wary. In the afternoons she would have to calculate when it was safe to cross his path. Before dinner was a bad time, unless he had been to the café for his aperitif. By the way he would shut the door on his return she could tell whether he'd had one of his increasingly frequent arguments with someone over a drink and she would contrive to enter the dining room at the very moment when the soup was ready to be served. After dinner, when he sank into a digestive stupor she was safe, unless he had picked a quarrel with his wife at table, scolding her for putting too much or too little salt into the dishes.

After her father had grabbed a boy by his jacket and dangled him out of the first floor window of the tall school house Victoire's mother had removed her daughter from the Sainte Colombe school. From then on Victoire endured her father's vitriolic reproach for not coming first in all subjects in her new school. There was a constant implication that she would never attain the position of school teacher as he had.

Throughout her childhood and adolescence she felt that whatever she did her father would never think her good enough. It was this that drove her on in her university years at which point he missed no opportunity to imply that the only reason she had been accepted was because of her physical attributes, that no doubt every course director and professor hoped to seduce her once she was his student. In her father's eyes she had not merited the place on the strength of her intelligence and hard work. Why, she wondered, when he had been such a difficult, violent man, did any mention of him send her into a rage?

*

3

Aunt Amaline had heard Marco's car puttering up the road by the village cemetery. Her house sat high on the hill, surrounded by a cluster of tall umbrella pines populated by her flock of peacocks. Her scarf fluttered in the breeze as she waved from the edge of her lawn. Marco waved back through the open car window.

It was to his aunt that he came for warmth and love after his mother had died; there wasn't a thing in the world that Marco could not talk about with his aunt, with the exception of the one event that had bound him to Victoire these last ten years.

Victoire's richest friends would give their eye-teeth for Aunt Amaline's house, Marco mused as he turned off the steep main road onto the stony path leading to his aunts property, though whether they would be able to shift her peacocks was another matter altogether. They were territorial birds, they chose their habitat and there wasn't a finer place for them for miles; Marco's aunt had inherited them with the house.

His car whirled up the dust on the way up until he stopped under the pines. Before he had time to open the car door two peacocks flew down and jostled for space on his bonnet. Their beady eyes and cold stare had frightened him when he was a boy; giving way or retreating was not in their nature. Whenever he had tried to shoo them out of his way their sharp peck on his bare legs would send him running.

He got out of the car. There was a commotion in the trees above him and a male and a female landed at his feet. The male strutted back and forth as if to show off his female.

'Alors, César, got yourself a girlfriend, have you?'
Amaline crossed over from the house and embraced Marco. As she did so another half dozen birds rushed towards them.

'They've been so excited in the last few days.' She looked around. 'I don't know what it is. The day before yesterday Titus chased a viper into the undergrowth and killed it. Then he ate it. César got into a terrible fight with him this morning.' She indicated the strutting male. 'He should know better, he's nearly thirty years old. The two of them were leaping high into the air. I had to separate them with my garden rake. In the end Titus beat a retreat; he flew to the top of the pines and screamed his head off as though someone had stabbed him. I'm sure he could be heard in Spain,' Amaline chuckled.

'There, and now he wants to make up with me.' She gently stroked the shimmering plumage of the male. 'People never think of peacocks as flying birds, but with a couple of wing beats they are up on the highest tree. Their wings are so strong they could knock you down if you get in their way.'

'Perhaps it's the weather or are they all in love?'

'Look how he fusses over his girl, you'd think he was a soppy teenager.' Amaline laughed, 'for once I have lots of females to go round but if this carries on I'll have to find a way of keeping the boys apart or sell one of them.' She

343

wagged her finger at the two warring males. 'Just watch it. Come on, Marco, let's have a glass of Muscat.'

Marco and his aunt sauntered over to the house, followed by a procession of the birds.

'They're after their treats. All they do is eat, eat, eat. If I don't give them anything for an hour they all try and get onto my window sill and make such a racket I can't get any peace. When the weather is so nice all my windows are open. I've got a job to stop them from jumping into the salon at the moment.'

Amaline's salon looked out onto the pines. The tall window was wide open and as they entered the room they were greeted by half a dozen peacocks gathering, looking in from outside, eager to be fed. From a box next to the window Amaline picked a handful of dried fruit and seeds.

'No fighting, take your turn.'
She fed each one a morsel of fruit, starting with the largest male and finishing with the small females.

'Hierarchy, that's what they understand. That's why I named the boys after Roman emperors.'

Amaline turned to Marco. 'You're very quiet, is something the matter?'

At her words Marco suddenly burst into tears. He sank onto Amaline's divan and buried his head in his hands. Amaline went to sit beside him and put her arm around his shoulders.

'Tell me, I'm sure we can put it right.'
'I can't explain,' Marco wept.
'So? If you weren't going to tell me why did you come?'
Marco gathered himself, wiped his face with his sleeve.

344

'It's Victoire.' It would have felt so good to be able to tell his aunt why Victoire had such a hold on him.

'The elections for mayor and the village council are still a whole year away and she's already all worked up.'

'Huh. Léon Pennac, the old dog. He may be getting on in years but he still has plenty of fire in his belly,' Amaline chuckled, 'and not only when he sits behind his big mayor's desk.'

'I heard, I heard,' Marco wiped tears from his eyes, 'his wife is the only one who doesn't seem to know why he's always popping up to Liliane's house to check on council business, or so he says.'

'I'm surprised Victoire hasn't tried her charms on him.'

Marco shook his head. 'I don't think she could bring herself to seduce that man, he's too old, but she intends to destroy him all the same. She's definitely gearing up to undermine her rivals in good time.'

Warnings about dire consequences if Marco should talk about what went on in her house now rained down on him daily. As the weeks went by Victoire was pulling the noose around his neck ever tighter.

Amaline gave a deep sigh.

'That woman, since the day she was born her father fed her nothing but hatred and now she has a belly full of it.'

She leaned over to look into Marco's eyes. 'Look at me. Why do you still work for her? God knows her father was cruel enough to you when he was your school teacher and she doesn't seem much better.'

He could tell neither his brother Serge nor Aunt Amaline what he had done to little Annette under the bridge ten years ago. He stared at the floor.

'She knows something about me … I haven't even told Serge. It could cost him his job.'

'Everyone does something stupid or something they regret or are ashamed of, especially when they're young, but that is no reason to become someone's slave.'

'She won't let go of me, accusing me all the time of gossiping about what goes on with her husband, why he's constantly disappearing to Paris … and all the trouble with Didier. That boy is totally out of control. Because she wants to run for mayor again she's frantic. It took me a long time to see her game. She digs around for people's secrets just to get a hold over them. I heard her whispering with Clément about sending Didier away, somewhere, anywhere, but he won't go. He's blackmailing her with something, and she's … blackmailing me.'

Amaline rose, went over to the window and gently stroked one of the little peahens.

'God help us all if she ever gets to be mayor.'

'How can you stop her?' Marco sounded utterly defeated.

'Don't forget my Euric was mayor, twice. There wasn't a more honourable man than your uncle. We were the envy of the surrounding villages.' She came back to perch beside him on the divan. 'Don't worry, there are ways and means, and I know what they are. Now, let's have that Muscat and then I'll cook us a nice lunch.'

Amaline went into the kitchen. 'Could you bring in some wood?' she called. 'I'll fire up the range and make us a soufflé and braised butter leeks or would you prefer roasted vegetables and lamb?'

Marco jumped up from the divan. Just talking to someone had made him feel better.

346

He ran over to the shed. He had to brush the peacocks aside as he loaded up the small wheelbarrow and started to push it towards Amaline's side door.

On the path a car came to a sharp halt, causing the birds to flutter into the lower branches of the pines. It was Victoire. She was wearing a florid figure-hugging, low-cut dress and a heavy necklace. She struggled out of her car and stood in her high heels for a few moments as if waiting for someone to hurl a coat to the ground to let her step onto it to preserve her shoes.

'Victoire? Are you looking for me?' Marco set down the wheelbarrow. She strutted towards him. From her stance it was clear that she was on the war path. His heart pounded against his ribcage.

'Marco! There you are! I've been searching the village for you. And what are you doing? Working for other people again.'

'Madame Victoire, this is my aunt … I just….'

'You just, you're always just … doing this or that when I want you.'

Amaline came towards them.

'Victoire, leave my nephew alone. If he helps me that's nothing to do with you. He's here for lunch.'

'Having logs for lunch, are you? Roast or stewed? Give me the recipe sometime.'

'Calm down, Victoire, you're as excited as my birds. What is the matter with everyone?' Amaline shook her head. 'What right do you have to ….'

Victoire's face turned red.

'It's not for Marco to gallivant about, spreading gossip about what I do. He's my gardener and no one else's. Besides, why don't you ask him why that is?'

347

Marco flinched. Was she going to bring up the story about Annette now or was she just fishing to see if his aunt knew about it?

'Honestly, Victoire, I was just taking some logs in so we can cook. If you need me I'll be straight down after lunch.'

'Excuses, nothing but excuses. Will you never learn?'

Her agitated tone had attracted a number of peacocks; they surrounded her, fixing her with steely curiosity. The hens huddled together behind the males like dutiful wives seeing their men off to battle.

Victoire took a couple of steps back.

'Call off your ... vultures.'

'They've not been known to eat people, yet.' Amaline gently pushed the birds aside.

Victoire shifted on her high heels.

'They always look so ... outraged, so suspicious.'

In your case, Amaline mused, they might have good reason.

'Come inside. Let's have a glass of Muscat. I don't know what upsets you so. Has something happened about the election?'

It wasn't the first time that Amaline had witnessed Victoire's frantic efforts to get elected. The thing today was to pacify her, to persuade her to leave Marco alone.

Amaline took Victoire by the elbow and guided her towards the house. The peacocks followed. She showed Victoire into the salon; the birds were jostling to peer into the room through the open window.

'They're always hungry. Here, Victoire, give them some pumpkin seeds, you'll see, they won't harm you, as long as you feed the big male there first. If he behaves they all follow his lead.'

348

She handed Victoire a handful of the seeds from a box next to the window. Victoire scattered them on the outside window sill and quickly withdrew to the centre of the room.

Marco poured the golden Muscat into three glasses and handed one to Victoire. Their eyes met. She's still fuming, he realized; she's just pretending to be polite. He went to sit in his uncle's old leather armchair. Years had gone by since Uncle Euric's death but the scent of his cigars still oozed from the armrests polished to a shine by his uncle's old bony hands.

'Sit down, Victoire.' Amaline indicated the divan.

Marco bit his lip. What on earth could they talk about?

'On second thought, Aunt Amaline,' Marco rose, 'I think I won't stay for lunch.' He emptied his glass.

'I promised to post a parcel for Serge as soon as the Post Office opens at two o'clock.' He glanced at Victoire. 'I'll be at your house straight after that.'

He kissed his aunt, nodded at Victoire and left the house. He crossed to the pines and glanced over his shoulder. Through the open window he saw Victoire on the divan, sitting up so straight one would have thought she'd swallowed a broom. Without switching on the engine he let his car cruise down the path; three peacocks swooped from the pines and escorted him to the main road.

Amaline settled in the armchair Marco had vacated.

'I want you to stop harassing my nephew. God knows he's had enough misfortune in his life with his illness and his mother dying when he was so young.'

'I expect some … loyalty from him.'

'He is loyal, to you more than to anyone. The way you treat him I often wonder why.'

'I also expect gratitude.'

Amaline was aghast. 'For what? Just because you let him work for you for a pittance?'

'Huh. Have you never asked yourself what he's done to deserve that?'

'And you,' Amaline interrupted sharply, 'what is it that you have done? You're a bully. All I hear is that you're digging around for the dirt on your rivals. For heaven's sake, the elections aren't until next year and you're already running around bad-mouthing everyone.' She picked up the newspaper and waved it at Victoire.

'Your letters to *L'Occitan* newspaper about Léon Pennac and the village council are pathetic. I'd be the first to say he's not the best mayor we've ever had, that was my Euric, but even so. A child can see through your shenanigans. You can fool a lot of people, but not me. In all the villages around here people are starting to call you a mad woman … they say you're going the same way as your father.'

'Your nephew …'

'My nephew,' Amaline interrupted. She rose and went over to the window and held out some seeds to a young peahen, 'whatever small sins Marco may have committed, I'm sure they're nothing compared to yours.'

'Your nephew,' Victoire hissed, 'I caught him under the convent bridge, ten years ago, with little Annette.'

Amaline turned and fixed her gaze on Victoire. 'And? Two children? Is that something worth gossiping about?'

'He was … in the middle of … abusing her,' Victoire took a deep breath, 'or at least going to,' she added, triumphant.

'Huh,' Amaline exclaimed, 'you would have put the Grand Inquisitor to shame.'

There was total silence; even the peacocks at the window seemed to have frozen.

'Ten years ago Marco was barely sixteen, still a child, and an orphan. His father had just died. If you think,' Amaline continued, 'that you can enslave him for life because of something you didn't even see with your own eyes you are mistaken. My Euric grew up with your father. I read my husband's diaries. And before you think of it, no, you won't find them in this house. My sons took them when they moved to Argentina to set up their vineyards, but I can have access to them anytime I need to. Isn't email wonderful these days?'

'How dare you bring my father into this?'

'Oh,' Amaline almost chuckled, 'your father has *everything* to do with this. You obviously don't know what he got up to with the little girls in the village, and the young boys. It didn't seem to matter which to him. And it all started again after he was removed from his post as school teacher, the year before your mother had him locked up in the asylum. There would be plenty of people in this village to give evidence, in case ....' Amaline turned her back on Victoire and continued to feed the greedy birds. 'The thought of you sitting in the same chair as my Euric and misusing the mayor's office for your own purposes turns my stomach. Never, *never* ever. I will see to it ... and if you do, it will be over my dead body.'

Victoire slowly rose from the divan and pulled herself up to her full height. Her eyes fell on the Muscat bottle on the coffee table. The peacocks' heads shifted; they watched as she reached for it. Three silent steps on the Persian rug and she stood behind Amaline. The bottle swung down on the back of the Amaline's head. For a moment, the old lady

351

swayed a little. Her head turned; eyes full of astonishment met Victoire's, then her legs gave way and she slumped to the floor.

Victoire was surprised how calm she suddenly felt; a great obstacle had vanished in seconds. What now? she wondered. The peacocks were staring into the room, eyes fixed on their owner lying motionless on the floor.

She dragged the limp woman over to the divan and heaved her onto it. There was not much blood. She turned Amaline's head to face the backrest of the divan. The peacocks began to shriek their piercing cries into the room. The largest male leapt onto the window sill; his voluminous tail flicked back and forth; another bird followed.

Slowly Victoire moved over to the feed box. Peacocks eat anything, she recalled, grains, snails, snakes … flesh?

'You want some food?' she said quietly and held out some rings of dried apple. The birds greedily snatched at them. She pulled her hand back. The large male hopped into the room, his tail sweeping the parquet floor and the rug behind him. This was the way. Victoire picked up the feed box and held it out to the other birds. One by one, they jumped, first onto the window sill, then into the room. She laid a trail with the dried fruit and seeds towards the centre of the room. She could imagine the scene now, peacocks perching on the gilded Louis XVI furniture, screaming to be fed. The thought almost made her smile. By the divan there was a silk rug; she scattered a handful of the feed onto it. A sprinkling of it fell onto Amaline's back; the large male stretched to peck at the seeds nestling in the wool of the woman's cardigan. Why not? Victoire emptied the box over Amaline's body.

'There you are,' she whispered, 'you'll eat all that up in no time.'

She rushed over to the window, pushed the two panes together until there was only a small gap. She snagged one of the lace curtains over the handles to prevent the window opening more than a crack, certainly too narrow for even the slimmest of the birds to escape.

She straightened the carpet and searched for bloodstains; there were none. She grabbed the bottle; there might be traces of blood and hair on it.

Outside the house all was quiet. She pulled the front door shut behind her. Amaline would wake up in a room full of her darlings driven mad by hunger; that would teach her a lesson.

Victoire got into her car. Nearing the main road she hurled the bottle into the deep overgrown ditch at the corner. I'm not even shaking, she thought. As she drove over the bridge with the sun in her eyes a shadow passed overhead, then another and another, too swift for her to see what had cast them.

End of chapter 3

SOME SIMPLE POISON the second book in the Languedoc trilogy will be published in the spring of 2016
The book was written in the memory of Christine Detrez and Nenou Puel

Author biography

Ata Burchardt was born into a refugee family and was brought up in Vienna, Germany, Luxembourg and educated in France. After her exams she came to London to learn English and studied art in London. Working freelance she translated close to 400 films for the British Film Institute and became art editor for Time Out Magazine. Moving back to France she worked in advertising and for Paris and German fashion magazines. In the Languedoc region she created a book and design business, taught at a book museum and edited *Writers' Voice, France,* a short fiction publication for established English and American East Coast writers. She returned to England to write features for magazines, review theatre and book festival events. She has written plays for radio and the stage. *The Fool's House* is the first book in a trilogy set in the Languedoc. For the moment she lives in Gloucestershire with her husband, Michael Hasted, a writer and theatre critic.

SEPTIMA

For more about the author's work, interviews, plays, reviews and journalism go to the website:
A.N.Burchardt, writer and translator

Lightning Source UK Ltd.
Milton Keynes UK
UKOW04f1836280717
306268UK00001B/167/P